*A Choice of Crimes*

## As Elizabeth Linington:

CONSEQUENCE OF CRIME
NO VILLAIN NEED BE
PERCHANCE OF DEATH
THE PROUD MAN
THE LONG WATCH
MONSIEUR JANVIER
THE KINGBREAKER
POLICEMAN'S LOT
ELIZABETH I (*Ency. Brit.*)
GREENMASK!
NO EVIL ANGEL
DATE WITH DEATH
SOMETHING WRONG
PRACTISE TO DECEIVE
CRIME BY CHANCE

## As Egan O'Neill:

THE ANGLOPHILE

## As Lesley Egan:

A CHOICE OF CRIMES
MOTIVE IN SHADOW
THE HUNTERS AND THE HUNTED
LOOK BACK ON DEATH
A DREAM APART
THE BLIND SEARCH
SCENES OF CRIME
A CASE FOR APPEAL
THE BORROWED ALIBI
AGAINST THE EVIDENCE
RUN TO EVIL
MY NAME IS DEATH
DETECTIVE'S DUE
SOME AVENGER, ARISE
THE NAMELESS ONES
A SERIOUS INVESTIGATION

THE WINE OF VIOLENCE
IN THE DEATH OF A MAN
MALICIOUS MISCHIEF
PAPER CHASE

## As Dell Shannon:

CASE PENDING
THE ACE OF SPADES
EXTRA KILL
KNAVE OF HEARTS
DEATH OF A BUSYBODY
DOUBLE BLUFF
ROOT OF ALL EVIL
MARK OF MURDER
THE DEATH-BRINGERS
DEATH BY INCHES
COFFIN CORNER
WITH A VENGEANCE
CHANCE TO KILL
RAIN WITH VIOLENCE
KILL WITH KINDNESS
SCHOOLED TO KILL
CRIME ON THEIR HANDS
UNEXPECTED DEATH
WHIM TO KILL
THE RINGER
MURDER WITH LOVE
WITH INTENT TO KILL
NO HOLIDAY FOR CRIME
SPRING OF VIOLENCE
CRIME FILE
DEUCES WILD
STREETS OF DEATH
APPEARANCES OF DEATH
COLD TRAIL
FELONY AT RANDOM
FELONY FILE

# A Choice of Crimes

LESLEY EGAN

DOUBLEDAY & COMPANY, INC.
GARDEN CITY, NEW YORK

All of the characters in this book
are fictitious, and any resemblance
to actual persons, living or dead,
is purely coincidental.

*This one is for*
*Miriam and David in memory of Glendale*

Why comes temptation but for man to meet
And master and make crouch beneath his feet,
And so be pedastl'd in triumph?
White shall not neutralize the black, nor good
Compensate bad in man, absolve him so:
Life's business being just the terrible choice.

—Robert Browning,
*The Ring and the Book*

*A Choice of Crimes*

# ONE

In the last six weeks, there had been three motels held up in the downtown area of Glendale. The MO showed a pattern; it was probably the same pair on all the jobs. The latest one had been last night, and the night desk clerk had just been in to make a statement. Varallo and their female detective Delia Riordan had listened to him, and Delia typed the statement, and he had signed it and left three minutes ago.

Now Varallo laid it down on his desk and said, "The same pair all right. Mexican, Cuban, broken English, early twenties, one about five-ten, one shorter, the tall one with a moustache. Nobody tells us what the gun might be—just, a gun." He sighed. It was the kind of random thing they so often got, and few places to look. "I suppose the first thing we do is hunt up Raimondo Reynaldo and ask for an alibi."

Delia was silent, staring at her typewriter. The first place to look, of course, had been in Records, for any names which attached to similar descriptions and charges; and Reynaldo had shown up right away. He was twenty-six, he matched one of the vague descriptions, and he had spent eighteen months in Susanville for armed robbery. Aside from that there was no evidence on him at all. "You daydreaming?" said Varallo. "I said, Reynaldo."

"I heard you," said Delia. "Yes, obviously. And probably a waste of time." She sat up and lit a cigarette.

The big communal detective office on the second floor of Glendale Police Headquarters was empty except for themselves and John Poor typing a report at his desk across the room. It was Friday, so Katz was off. O'Connor and Forbes were out talking to a rape victim; where Burt and Thomsen were Varallo didn't know. Probably out processing the latest burglary scene; and the latest additions to the strength, Leo Boswell and Jim Harvey, were out somewhere on that hit-run felony from Wednesday night. The crime rate was up in Glendale, as the population rose, and the chief had argued some money out of the city fathers; eventually the department was supposed to get at least three more plainclothesmen and twenty or thirty uniformed men, but just when was something else. Boswell and Harvey were just out of uniform and somewhat younger than the rest of the detectives, but they both seemed to be fairly intelligent and congenial, and would shake down all right with time and experience.

"I suppose," said Delia, "we ought to hear what he has to say." Neither of them made an immediate move to get up. Whatever Reynaldo said, nothing was going to come of it.

Varallo regarded her lazily, his mind only ticking over halfway. It was the middle of May, and as usual they were having a little heat wave: it was close to ninety on the street. In here the air-conditioning was on, thankfully. O'Connor had been annoyed at having to take on a female detective, of all things, but she had been with them for eight months now and he had to admit that she was a good girl. Nearly six years a Los Angeles Police Department policewoman, and a very good record, and about the highest score possible to get on the detective exam: a smart girl. And, it appeared just recently, fluent in Spanish, which was always helpful to a cop in California. And no arts and graces about Delia: she looked like a plain Jane at first glance, but she was quite good-looking at a second, fine small features, a straight little nose, blue eyes, and dark brown hair in a short severe cut. But she didn't do anything about the looks: a very minimum of makeup, plain dark dresses or pantsuits, no jewelry but a plain seal ring.

And they knew more about her now: her father something of a legend in the LAPD, and Delia his one ewe lamb—that was why she was in this job, had bucked for rank so young. Rather a funny ambition for a girl, but not unprecedented. And she was good.

He glanced through the statement again and said, "Nothing much in this at all. We can guess what Reynaldo will say. Hell. More legwork for nothing, but I suppose we'd better get on it." He stood up, and the phone shrilled on his desk; he picked it up.

"Varallo . . . oh, hell. What is it? Well, give me the address. . . . So we get sidetracked."

"On what?"

"Duff wasn't too clear. The squad called in a child abandonment, but there seem to be ramifications."

Delia grimaced, getting up and reaching for her handbag. "People."

"What we have to deal with. We'd better take your car." He drove one of the compacts, a Gremlin, no use for transporting witnesses.

Delia's ancient Mercedes had been totaled at the end of that case last March; she was driving a new Chevy sedan. Outside, the bright sun was glaringly reflected from the cement of the parking lot; the heat struck them like a physical blow as they came out of the air-conditioning. It was par for the course in southern California; June usually brought a little respite before the summer really started with at least three months of the relentless heat. Climbing in beside her, Varallo gave her the address as she switched on the air-conditioning and the engine simultaneously.

It was one of the oldest streets south in the city. The city had grown north toward the foothills, and if it possessed anything like a slum area it was south of Chevy Chase, east of Glendale Avenue. This street was shabby and narrow, lined with a mixture of old single houses, duplexes, and a couple of four-unit apartments. There were two squads sitting outside one of those, with patrolmen Tracy and Harper standing on the sidewalk talking with a civilian. An ambulance was parked ahead of the squad cars. The two uniformed men looked up as Varallo and Delia joined them. "So what have we got?" asked Varallo.

Tracy just said, "Christ." He looked at Delia. "No sight for a female."

"Or anybody," said Harper.

The civilian was a thin man about forty, conventionally dressed in a gray suit; he looked pale and shaken. "All I can tell you, their name is Contreras. They were always late with the rent, and we'd just got an eviction notice—as I was telling these other officers—that's why I'm here—and they're gone. I just went

in to see the state they'd left the place—oh, my God—" He put a
hand to his mouth, looking sick.

"It's the right-hand upstairs apartment," said Harper.

Varallo and Delia went in. There was a tiny square entrance
hall, a door to either side: the name-slot beside the left one was
empty, the other bore a smeared handwritten slip that said *Gonzales*. The stair was precipitous and uncarpeted. This place
would be about sixty years old, and over the years various tenants had used it hard, a minimum of maintenance been given to
it. The walls were stained, the stairs shook under Varallo's
weight. At the top there was a tiny square landing and two more
doors; the one to the right was open. Past it they came into a
square living room completely bare of furniture and very dirty.
The two white-clad ambulance attendants were standing there
smoking.

"They said there'd be some front-office boys coming," said the
bigger one. They looked at Delia curiously. "I don't know what
for. Jesus, what a thing. Jesus. I've seen this and that on this
damned job, but never nothing like that. I suppose we got to
take it somewhere, but you tell us where."

"In there," said the other one, nodding at an inner door. "The
guy who came with the eviction paper found it. God."

Varallo pushed that door farther open; they went in and
looked. Delia made a strangled sound, and involuntarily he said,
"*Dio!*"

The creature lying in the doorway of a narrow slot of a closet
across the little bare room was at first unidentifiable as human,
or sexed; it was just a grotesque malformation, something that
shouldn't be. About the size of a small child, it had a huge mis-
shapen head, arms that ended in stumps, malformed legs bent
crookedly inward. It was making a low bleating noise and moving feebly. It was filthy with its own excrement and long in-
grained dirt.

They looked at it for one minute that was too long, and
Varallo steered Delia downstairs again. After the stale and
newer smells in that room, the hot dusty street was welcome.

"Yeah," said the first ambulance attendant, eyeing them.
"What a thing. I looked long enough to say it's female. And no

wonder somebody wanted to be rid of it. But what do we do with it?"

Abandoned children, of course, were automatically sent to Juvenile Hall; Varallo decided to pass the buck to the logical place. He used the radio in the squad to call in to the desk; Sergeant Duff consulted with Juvenile Hall and came back with the expectable direction to dispatch it to the General Hospital. Somewhat reluctantly the ambulance attendants carried a stretcher upstairs.

The civilian was Rodney Marsh, one of the partners in the realty company which owned the building. "All I can tell you," he repeated, "is the name. Contreras. Alfredo Contreras. They'd rented the place for five months. Always late with the rent. These low-rent places are a damned headache the last few years, we're going to unload them. Used to be good bread-and-butter income, but since we've had this influx of Cubans from the East, and the blacks drifting in from L.A.—hell's fire, I'm not prejudiced against anybody on account of their names or color, it's the kind of people they are, damn it, and God knows a lot of white riff-raff coming in too. And you can't screen people now, they yell prejudice and equal rights—I don't know anything about these people, and I don't think Bob does—my partner."

The patrolmen went back on tour, and Marsh drove thankfully away; the ambulance departed. Varallo and Delia went back upstairs to the filthy apartment and looked for anything of significance the Contrerases might have left behind, but there wasn't anything except a few pieces of moldy cheese and a quart of sour milk in the dirty, ancient refrigerator. They tried the door across the landing, and a middle-aged woman opened it a crack and said, "No Inglees," to the badge. Like so many of her kind, she could probably get around in English adequately, but it was a convenient plea to avoid talking to cops. Delia switched to her fluent Spanish and was scowled at. They got a reluctant name, Rosario. She knew nothing about the Contrerases, not so much as how many there were. People came and went, one did not pay notice. Children, she knew nothing of any children. They were gone; well, she had not seen them go. She had never spoken to them.

Downstairs, they got no answer at one door; at the other, a fat

Mrs. Gonzales was amiable but entirely unhelpful. Both she and her husband worked all day, the only reason she was at home today was that she had to see the dentist, and he had made such torture for her she stayed home with his little pills. She did not know the upstairs people at all, perhaps she had seen them come and go a few times, that was all. A man and his wife, perhaps one or two children, big.

"Big?" asked Delia.

"Oh, grown almost—fifteen, sixteen, like that." And that was all.

They sat in the Chevy's air-conditioning and lit cigarettes.

"Ordinarily, just a misdemeanor," said Varallo. "But here, I'd say child abuse too. See if he paid the realty firm by check. And it's twelve-thirty, do you feel like lunch before writing the report?"

"Not much," said Delia. "I'll pick up a sandwich later on." She dropped him in the parking lot at headquarters to pick up his own car, and went upstairs, stopping for a cup of coffee from the machine down the hall.

O'Connor was sitting back in his desk chair talking with Jeff Forbes, who had one hip perched on a corner of O'Connor's desk. There was a 510 form rolled into the typewriter but O'Connor wasn't doing anything about it yet. As usual he looked the complete tough, his curly black hair tousled, jaw stained with a blue shadow; he had hung his jacket on the chair, and the shoulder holster bulged under his left armpit with the weight of the .357 magnum. "And just what the hell," he was saying bitterly to Forbes, "are we expected to do with that? It was so dark she never really saw him, to see what he looked like—no idea what clothes he had on—oh, she couldn't say what size he was, just awfully strong—she didn't see where he came from, just all of a sudden he was there, just as she got to the car— Women!"

"Well, after all, Charles," said Forbes reasonably, "she was pretty shocked and upset—she'd just got raped. She's only about twenty-three, and the doctor said she'd been knocked around some."

"I'll say amen to that," said Delia dryly, sitting down at her desk. "This is the nurse at the Memorial Hospital? Even nurses aren't so tough to take a rape all so calmly, Lieutenant."

"All right, I expect too much," said O'Connor resignedly. "All she does give us is that he speaks broken English. The little he said to her when he jumped her."

"Last night?" asked Delia.

"She's on the three-to-eleven shift. She was late leaving for some reason. And that staff parking lot behind the hospital must be damned dark, and there are bushes along one side. He could have been lying in wait there for a while—"

"Or just walking up the side street when he happened to notice her come out and got the urge," said Forbes. He hoisted his lank length off O'Connor's desk. "Are you going to write a report on it at all?"

"I'll get to it, I'll get to it," said O'Connor, who hated the typewriter. "It's time for lunch, damn it. What were you out on?" he asked Delia.

She told him, and he just hunched a big shoulder in comment. Leaving the virgin form in the typewriter, he got up and put his jacket on, resettled his tie that was crooked as usual, and was on his way out when Leo Boswell came in with a big black fellow. Boswell was looking pleased; he was a stocky, sandy young fellow with a perpetually cheerful expression which rather annoyed O'Connor. "Something accomplished, something done," he said. "This is Pete Henderson, Lieutenant. You like to sit in and hear what he has to say?"

They had been looking for Henderson ever since his prints had shown up at the scene of a burglary on Glenwood Road last week. "Where'd you come across him?" asked Forbes.

"At his sister's place in Hollywood. After we put the A.P.B. out on that hit-run car, I just went over to ask her if the family'd heard from him, and there he was having a beer in front of the TV."

"So you and Jeff can talk to him," said O'Connor. "I'm going to have lunch."

Boswell marched Henderson toward one of the interrogation rooms down the hall, Forbes ambling after. Delia finished her coffee and rolled triplicate forms into the typewriter, began to type the initial report on the abandonment, call it that for the time being. The job, of course, was anything but glamorous, and there was a surprising amount of paperwork to it.

She had just finished the report and separated the copies, readied them for dispatch to the usual places, when Varallo called in. "Contreras paid the rent with checks on the Bank of America. I'm just going down there to see if they know anything useful, such as where he works or whatever. Anything new down?"

"No, it's being a nice quiet day," said Delia.

"Good. I'll be in sometime."

She put the phone down and lit a cigarette. A nice quiet day—for the average police headquarters and the average police detective. Belatedly, she realized that she could welcome a little lunch too, and got her handbag and went out to the place half a block down Wilson, for a sandwich and another cup of coffee. She wondered if Boswell and Forbes were getting anything out of Henderson; of course the prints definitely tied him to the burglary, and it was academic whether he talked or not. She wondered if they would ever catch up to the Contreras family: and about that miserable horror they had left behind. Sometime the hospital had better be contacted.

And it slid into her mind involuntarily—*Some vessel of a more ungainly Make: "They sneer at me for leaning all awry: What, did the Hand then of the Potter shake?"* She set her cup down with a little rattle, annoyed at herself. Ever since that night last week when she couldn't sleep and had picked up a book at random to pass the time, finding it was the *Rubaiyat* only after she'd got back into bed, bits and pieces of old Omar had been coming back to her unbidden. Adolescent second-rate stuff—some of it—wasn't it, or was it?

She got back to the office at two-thirty and called the General Hospital. That was a big place and she talked to a number of people before she got hold of an intern who knew anything.

"Oh, God," he said. "Only if there was a God, He wouldn't let things like that happen, you know. Of course the thing is a mindless vegetable—just a spark of life there. Something of a miracle it is still alive, I'd say it had been starving and unattended for several days at least. Toss-up if it'll live. Be a blessing if it doesn't. If it does, it'll have to be institutionalized, of course. What? Well, it's almost anybody's guess, but I don't think it can be over a couple of years old. Somebody's taken some care of it, or of course it'd have died soon after birth—that is, up to a few days ago."

That was, expectably, all the hospital could say. Delia thanked him, and had just put the phone down when O'Connor came back, flung off his jacket, scowled at the form in the typewriter, sat down and attacked it. There was nobody else in the office. Of course there were three heist jobs to work, apart from the motel heisters, and as usual several burglaries.

Into the big office from the landing came a nice-looking, gray-haired old lady. She hesitated in the doorway, and Delia got up. "Can I help you?"

"Well, I don't know. Maybe I'm a fool for coming here, but I don't think so." She looked doubtfully at O'Connor, who certainly looked the part of the big, tough cop without many brains; she looked at Delia. "Are you one of the detectives? The sergeant downstairs said I should talk to one of the detectives up here."

"Yes, that's right, I'm Detective Riordan. Won't you sit down? What's it about, Mrs.—"

"Mrs. Potter. Frances Potter." She was probably in her seventies; there didn't seem to be any happy medium, old ladies were either fat or thin, and she was thin—a spare, rather tall old lady with nicely waved silver-gray hair and bright blue eyes. She had a round, still pretty face. And she sounded like a very forthright, down-to-earth old lady. She was rather dowdily dressed in a bright blue cotton dress, the usual old-lady oxfords with cuban heels. She sat down in the chair beside Delia's desk and looked at her appraisingly, clasping her big white handbag in her lap.

"I'm just as glad to talk to another woman," she said, "because it's all kind of a rigmarole and a man might not follow it—I mean, a man who didn't know the people. Fred understood it all right—my husband, I mean—and he thinks there's something funny about it too. He couldn't leave the stock, of course, but he said my mind 'd never be at rest until I found out more, and he brought me down yesterday in the pickup. My lord alive, it's been six years since I was in Glendale, and I wouldn't have known the town—how it's changed."

"Yes, it has. Brought you from where?"

"Greenacres, up in Kern County—I don't suppose you've ever

heard of it. We've got a ranch outside of town, cattle mostly, but Fred puts in a few crops most years. I just don't know where to begin to tell you—" She looked thoughtfully at her handbag, and went on. "Well! I expect I'd just better start at the beginning, is all. It's about Marion Austen. Mrs. I'm sorry if I seem to ramble on, but you've got to know all the background to make head or tail of it. I was born and raised in Glendale—graduated from Glendale High I wouldn't like to say how many years ago." She smiled slightly. "And naturally I had some girl friends here, and my closest friend was Marion—Marion Peterson she was then—and Sylvia Lloyd, she's Sylvia Bates now. Well, my brother Bill went up to the college at San Luis Obispo, and he met Fred there—that's how Fred and I got together, he was just taking a couple of agriculture courses, didn't graduate. After we were married and up there—he was working for his father then but we got our own place a couple of years later—Marion and Sylvia and I kept in touch, of course. I'd get back to Glendale once in a while, not often when the children were small, of course—but we wrote back and forth pretty regular. Sylvia got married to Don Bates, he was in real estate and did pretty well, he's been dead four years, no, five, and she's living with her son and his family over in Phoenix."

"Yes." Delia wasn't taking any notes; she didn't know there was anything here to take notes about, and Mrs. Potter seemed to be satisfied just talking and being listened to.

"Marion married a fellow named George Austen, and they lived here ever since. They never had any children—Marion would have liked a family, but he wouldn't agree to adopt any, you see, and she couldn't have any. He was an accountant at some brokerage place in L.A., they never had much but enough. And looking to when he was retired, they started to buy an apartment house here, got it paid for, and that's where Marion 'd been living since George died nearly seven years ago—he was a good few years older than Marion. When he died, she said she'd just rattle around in that house by herself—it was a nice three-bedroom place on Sonora—and she sold it and moved into one of the apartments. It was easier for her too—she collected the rents and so on herself, and it's the kind of place where tenants stay, a good solid middle-class place—it's on East Dryden. Well, I don't seem to be getting on. The way I say, even though I had family still here, I didn't get back to Glendale just so often—Fred and I had three children, the two boys and a girl—and my brother and his wife were raising their four down here, but they always liked to come up to the ranch, so it was that way mostly when we got together. But I got down once in a while. Naturally I came down for Mother's funeral, that was nearly twenty years ago, and later on for Dad's. But now the children are all grown and gone— neither of the boys wanted to stay in the country, Freddy's a lawyer in Santa Barbara and Bob's in electronics, works at that JPL place here, they live in Burbank. Amy's married to Dick Page up home, he'll come in for his dad's spread, of course. Now I've got to tell you about the tapes."

"The tapes?"

"The tape recorders. It was Bob got us into it. I'm just as spry as I ever was, or nearly," and she smiled at Delia, "but I do have a little arthritis in my hands. Marion learned typing in school and she always typed her letters, and so did Sylvia until she sprained her shoulder a few years back, it bothered her after that. And Bob and his family were up visiting when he heard me complaining what a chore it was to write letters, and he said we ought to come into the twentieth century and make tapes to each other. He got me my first tape recorder, and I can't tell you how we all enjoyed it, you know. It's been a real blessing. Now I'm alone in the house most of the day—Fred'll be out all day mostly —my lord, how annoyed I was at that man when he was laid up with a broken ankle four years back! You can't sit and talk to a tape machine with anybody around. But it's been the best way ever to communicate—you know, I felt as if the clock was turned back and we were girls together again. Of course, I got to making tapes to Bob and Ann too, and Freddy and Gay, but oftener to Marion and Sylvia, and my sister Charlene in San Diego. And they all got recorders and made tapes to me. I'm sorry to ramble on," said Mrs. Potter, "it's just, you ought to know that we tell each other every little thing—it's so much easier when you're just talking, sitting in a comfortable chair—you know? When we started the tapes, five or six years back, we began using thirty- minute ones, but these days we all use ninety-minute ones and sometimes at that we'll go on to a second one. Just every little thing that'd been happening since we last heard from each other."

"Yes, I see."

"Now, I had a tape from Marion—" Mrs. Potter opened her handbag and brought out a cheap notebook. "We all kept schedules, when we got tapes and sent them. So I could think, did I tell Marion about that heifer calf, or what Fred said about the well pump, and I'd look and see I made her a tape the day after, so I'd know I did tell her. And I had a tape from her on the first of May. She'd made it April twenty-eighth, it used to be it'd only take a day reaching me but the mail service is getting worse and worse." Now she was all business, grave-faced. "I made her a tape the same day and mailed it on the second, and on the fifth"—she took something else out of her bag and laid it on the desk—"I got it back. Like that." The little parcel was a padded envelope, addressed to Mrs. Marion Austen at the Dryden Street address. It was postmarked Bakersfield, and below the address was scrawled the one careless word *Deceased*. "I never had such a shock in my life! Deceased! I didn't believe it. I tried to call her on the phone, but it just rang. So I called Clyde Burriss. I never knew them at all, I'd only met them a couple of times when I was here, but Marion and George and the Burrisses were close friends a long time, and though they didn't go out socially any more—shows and things so expensive, and Marion never was one for gadding much, and poor Mrs. Burriss had a stroke last year and is in a wheelchair—I knew they'd know about Marion. I got the number from Information and talked to Mr. Burriss. And he said it was so, she'd died very suddenly on April twenty-ninth, and the funeral was on May second. He said it was heart trouble. And that's what's wrong about it," said Mrs. Potter flatly.

"Why?" asked Delia.

"Because her heart was sound as a bell, that's why—the doctor had told her so. Marion was seventy-four, the same age as me—and Sylvia for that matter. But she was well as could be, still driving and doing her shopping and anything else she wanted to do. She always used to say, it's the lean horse wins the race—she'd stayed thin and lively like me. And she wasn't one to go to doctors much—now and then anyone has to, and they'd gone to the same GP for years, until he retired last year. I can tell you

exactly when it was," said Mrs. Potter. "It'd have been about the
first of December, she said there was so much flu going around
she was going to have a flu shot just to be on the safe side, and
that was when she found out Dr. Harvey was going to retire. But
it was that day he went all over her, and she said he told her she
had a remarkably sound heart, that she was in wonderful shape
for her age. She was pleased about it."
"Oh, I see. But—"
"And to go all of a sudden like that—I know a lot of people
die unexpectedly of heart attacks," said Mrs. Potter, "but it usually turns out that they had some heart trouble and didn't know
it, doesn't it? It just seemed very queer to me, when the doctor
had told her how strong her heart was. Well, I called the lawyer
—Mr. Burriss told me his name. Adler. Hugo Adler, he's got an
office in one of these new high-rise buildings up on Brand. Me
the country cousin, I don't like elevators. I went to see him this
morning, and that was a waste of time. Anyway, I'd called him
on the phone last week." This, of course, was Friday the thir-
teenth; that would have been a day or two after the funeral. "I
didn't get anything out of him—he was nice and polite, very
sorry I'd heard about it so sudden and so on, but she'd died of
heart disease and that was that, the doctor said so."
"Well, I don't know, I suppose an attack could come without
warning," said Delia, not sure of it herself. "If a doctor—"
"How do we know? Or what doctor? I don't know a thing
about that lawyer," said Mrs. Potter. "Marion and George went
to him years ago to make their wills, and then Marion made another one after George died, that's all they had to do with him.
Anyway, I didn't feel right about it. And Fred thought there was
something funny about it too. And I called Sylvia on the phone
to tell her, and she remembers what Dr. Harvey said too, and I
don't care, Miss Riordan, it *is* funny. Queer. And I wanted to
come down and—and look around on the spot, so Fred brought
me and I'm staying with Bob and Ann over in Burbank. I saw
the lawyer this morning, and what he did tell me, now I think
it's even queerer. He said one of the tenants found her, noticed
there weren't any lights in her apartment and went in and found
her, the door was unlocked—and of course there weren't any relatives to call but the tenant—it was Mrs. Fowler lives in the op-

posite apartment and she and Marion had been friendly—knew about the Burrisses and called him, and he couldn't leave his wife, poor man, so he told them the lawyer's name, and he took care of everything. The way he put it. Miss Riordan—" Mrs. Potter bent forward earnestly and for the first time she looked her age; her eyes brimmed with sudden tears. "As far as I can make out, she was just bundled off to the mortician's and a notice put in the *News-Press* and that was that—it wasn't decent, it wasn't right! I don't know if you think there's any reason for the police to look into it—I mean, it just doesn't seem possible that an ordinary respectable woman like Marion was *murdered*—but there's something queer about it!"

It was an odd, rambling little tale, but Delia rather thought so too: something just a little queer. She said so. "I don't know if the lieutenant will think it's worth the time, but I'll put it to him. We'll see. It won't do any harm to ask some official questions."

Mrs. Potter was grateful, and said so. "If I'm just imagining things, I'd be as glad to know it. I was of two minds about coming here—Bob said you wouldn't listen, but Ann said go and try. And if there's anything else you want to know, any help I can give you, I'm staying on for a while—I'll give you the address, it's Sunset Canyon Drive in Burbank." She got up, a brisk and spunky old lady, and nodded at Delia grimly. "I hope maybe you can prove I'm wrong, but I don't really think you will. I've just got a feeling about it."

Delia put it to O'Connor, who had finished fighting the typewriter. O'Connor might look like the brainless tough cop, but he hadn't made rank on this good force without reason. He rubbed a hand over his blue-stained jaw and said there might be something funny about it at that. "It might be worth just a quick look, Delia."

Varallo came in a minute later and said he'd found out that Alfredo Contreras had worked for a local construction company but had quit his job two days ago. He was overdrawn on his account at the local Bank of America. He was said, via a couple of the men who'd worked in the same crew, to have hinted that he could supply any dope any of them might want. Nobody had

been interested. He had further confided to one man that his
brother was in with the syndicate.

"Oh, for God's sake," said O'Connor.

"Well, it may give us another place to look for him," said
Varallo mildly. He was north Italian, Vic Varallo, with a crest of
tawny gold hair: a handsome big man, six inches over O'Connor's dark stockiness. And in the last couple of months Delia had
got to know his wife; Laura's car had gone on the fritz and she'd
stopped by a couple of times, near end of shift, for a ride home,
and been friendly to Delia. They'd gone out to lunch together
once, on Delia's day off. Varallo was older than the other detectives; Delia had heard some story about his holding rank on a
force upstate, starting in again down here. He was an easy-going
man, Varallo, a good detective. He smiled at O'Connor and said,
"Tomorrow's another day, Charles. There's always the legwork."
He drifted out; it was getting toward end of shift.

Boswell and Forbes had got a confession out of Henderson,
and he'd been booked in for the burglary. There would be the
usual routine to do on the rape; Forbes and O'Connor had probably started on that, looking in Records for likely suspects. Now,
go and find them and lean on them, hope that one of them
would come apart and admit it. And somebody ought to hunt up
Raimondo Reynaldo and ask him some questions about the
motel heists.

And, with the crime rate up, even in quiet Glendale, it was
very likely that something would come along for the night
watch, Bob Rhys and Dick Hunter, to make more work tomorrow.

Varallo went home to the house on Hillcroft Road, where his
roses—an unlikely hobby for a cop—were basking contentedly in
the heat, and kissed Laura while three-year-old Ginevra came
squealing to be picked up. Seven-month-old Johnny was peacefully asleep, with the gray tiger Gideon Algernon Cadwallader
assiduously on guard on top of the nursery dresser.

O'Connor went home, to the house on Virginia Avenue, inevitably to be assaulted on the other side of the driveway gate by
the effusive outsize blue Afghan Maisie. "Down, damn it!" he
said to her, but Maisie was impervious to curse or correction; she

bounded ahead of him into the kitchen, where Katharine told him he had time for a drink before dinner. He surveyed her dark, slim person fondly—his Katy was always nice to come home to—and said he needed one. He went down the hall to shed his jacket, and peered in at seven-month-old Vincent Charles, peacefully asleep. The job was a thankless job, never ending, and frequently very boring; the class of human nature they were dealing with was usually so stupid. But at least there were other things in a man's life than the job.

Delia made the light at Riverside and Los Feliz, and a couple of blocks on turned left onto Waverly Place; half a block up she turned into the drive of the old two-story Spanish house with the red tile roof.

She came in the back door. There were three crystal shrimp servers waiting on the kitchen counter, which told her about dinner: an expectable dinner for a hot day. Shrimp salad, and plenty of buttered toast with a mound of potato salad and another bowl of tossed salad, and possibly cheese crepes, and something like fresh strawberries for dessert. She went down the hall to the living room. The air-conditioning was humming along nicely. They were sitting there watching TV; they looked up and Steve said, "You're early."

"I made all the lights."

"So you go and get comfortable, we'll have dinner," said Alex. "Anything interesting go down?"

"Not much. One rather messy thing."

He grinned at her fondly, handsome old Alex with his silver hair. Alex Riordan, losing his first wife after twenty years of childless marriage, had married a girl half his age only to lose her in childbirth a year later. They had managed somehow, he and Delia, with a succession of housekeepers, until the year he was sixty-five and Delia was thirteen. He'd been full of plans for her first time of entering the junior target-pistol competition—he'd started her with a gun on her seventh birthday. Then, just two days before his official retirement, he'd gone out on his last call—Captain Alex Riordan, Robbery-Homicide, LAPD—and taken the bank robber's bullet in the spine. That had been a bad time, for a while, and then they'd found Steve—ex-Sergeant

Steve McAllister, LAPD, just short of twenty-five years' service when he lost a leg in an accident: a widower with a married daughter in Denver. The three of them had been together for fourteen years now; the new leg didn't hamper Steve from manipulating Alex's wheelchair, and Alex had always liked to cook. Of course, of course, it had had to be this job for Alex: she was all he'd ever had.

She went upstairs to her bedroom, and the first thing she saw were the two envelopes on the dressing table. She seldom got any personal mail; junk catalogs would be left on the hall table downstairs. Steve would have brought these up here; she picked up the top one and knew why.

Her heart didn't turn over as it would have once; it just gave a sickening lurch at the return address. Mrs. Adam Mayrant, Santa Monica.

And suddenly, surprisingly, she was thinking about Mrs. Frances Potter. They had kept in touch, she and her old school friends. *Wrote back and forth pretty regular.* Back in high school, Delia and Isobel Fordyce had been best friends, inseparable. And of course you couldn't think about Isobel without thinking about Neil, which was all past and done with and settled and forget about it— And she knew what this would be: she slit the envelope with her thumbnail quickly . . . announcing arrival of Neil Douglas Mayrant, May seventh, eight pounds . . . the boy Isobel wanted, after two girls, and they had named him for—

Present to buy. And of course Alex wouldn't have seen the address without thinking of Neil too, Neil he had hated like poison, and Steve would have smuggled this up— She ripped open the other envelope and looked at the contents and said, "Damn."

She had been feeling unsettled and, well, queer, for a while. And it was, of course, for no very cogent reason, that birthday present that had started it. Her birthday was on April twenty-seventh, and Alex and Steve had proudly presented her with an expensive target pistol, that S. and W. Masterpiece. "Time you got back to serious practice," Alex had said. A target pistol. Well, she was a cop, wasn't she?

Her twenty-eighth birthday. And in the second envelope was

the announcement of the tenth reunion of her graduating class
from Hollywood High School—come and meet old friends—

She hadn't seen Isobel for eight months. Talked on the phone
a couple of times. There just wasn't time—there never had been
time, after those three years out of high school when they'd both
gone to Los Angeles City College—because after she joined the
force, she'd been on swing shift so long—and always the extra
study, bucking for rank—she had to make rank on the job, for
Alex. All the courses, the Spanish, police science, fingerprinting,
photography, anything that might be useful on the job—

Those women, with young families to raise, busy lives, had
kept in touch.

But Isobel meant Neil—and how Alex had hated Neil, another
strong character of course—

A nephew for Neil. And time, time moving on so inexorably—
*The Worldly Hope men set their hearts upon Turns ashes—or it
prospers: and anon, like Snow upon the desert's dusty Face,
lighting a little hour or two—is gone.*

Old Omar be damned. Time—ambition. These days it was
Dr. Neil Fordyce of the archaeology college of Arizona University, and two years ago, which was the last she'd heard—Isobel
firmly nonpartisan—he'd been on a dig in Peru somewhere—

She wouldn't bother about the reunion dinner. No point.

"You coming down to dinner?" called Steve.

"I'm coming," said Delia. "Just a minute."

# TWO

On Saturday morning the only thing the night watch had left them was another burglary, discovered about eleven-thirty when the householders came home: a single residence on Spencer Street. They still had, of course, three burglaries to work from last week and the three heist jobs aside from the motels. The pharmacist who'd been held up on Thursday night was coming in to look at some mug shots. It was Jim Harvey's day off, but Sergeant Joe Katz was back; he'd hang around to take the pharmacist down to Records.

Varallo went looking for Raimondo Reynaldo. The latest address from Records was in Montrose. Delia had already gone out somewhere, and everybody else was on other jobs.

Just after he'd taken off, the latest bereaved householder came in with a list of missing items; his name was James Mortimer, and he was annoyed. "Damn it," he said, "we were just up the block playing bridge with neighbors." The list wasn't long: a few pieces of good jewelry, a transistor radio, a tape recorder. Rhys's report said that there were good deadbolt locks on back and front doors, but several of the screens were flimsy; the burglar had broken in the screen on a back bedroom window without much trouble. On the face of it, it looked like amateurs, juveniles, or both.

"Did you leave any lights on, sir?" asked Katz.

"No, of course not."

"Well, it's a kind of elementary precaution, Mr. Mortimer—give the impression that the house is occupied."

"Listen, for God's sake," said Mortimer, "don't you know about the electricity rates? The damned bill was over a hundred last month and we're groping around like in a fog with twenty-five-watt bulbs all over—who can afford to leave lights on? I don't suppose we'll ever see any of this stuff again, damn it."

Katz didn't think so either, but he didn't say so.

At the address in Montrose, which was an elderly frame house in need of paint, a rather slatternly looking young woman in shorts and a halter opened the door to Varallo and looked at the badge. "Him!" she said. "That Raimondo. Yeah, he's my husband's brother. No, he isn't here, and he's not gonna be again, I have anything to say about it and I do. No-good bum, that one, lazy as a cat and a cop record too. I told Joe, you kick him out or I will, see? Held a lousy two-bit job while he was on parole, and then quit—laying around the house alla time—"

"Do you know where he went? When did he leave?"

"Last week. Finally." That still put him on the spot for the motel heists. "I don't know but I could guess. He can always run to his mama. The old fool, she'd take him and figure everybody else mean to him. Well, she lives in Fresno."

"You have the address?"

"Who writes letters? I couldn't say. Well, it's Mrs. Rose Reynaldo. All I'm interested in, he's out of our hair."

Varallo went back to the office and put in a call to Fresno police headquarters. On this job you had to be thorough, picayune as it sometimes looked. The sergeant he talked to was cheerfully cooperative; somebody would look up Rose Reynaldo and talk to Raimondo if he was there.

There were several other possible suspects for the motel heists; heading the list were Danny Lopez and his brother Pedro, and one Manuel Perez. Katz was down in Records with the pharmacist, and everybody else out on something; Varallo found Boswell idly chatting with one of the desk sergeants downstairs, and they went out looking for those men. It was a tedious way to go at it, but about the only way. As they started out, O'Connor and Forbes were coming in with, probably, one of the possibles on the rape, a beetle-browed lout in dirty clothes, looking sullen.

And there were other things left over from a couple of weeks back and last week: and indictments coming up next week, for a pair of heisters, a burglar, and a juvenile on an involuntary manslaughter charge.

O'Connor and Forbes got nothing out of the possible suspect on the rape; it was all up in the air. No evidence at the scene, and the only reason to pick this one up—his name was Tim Reyes —was his record of attempted rape. He hadn't any alibi, and there was nothing to tie him in either, and it appeared he was fluent enough in English when he wanted to be. Eventually they let him go.

"Though the broken English," said Forbes thoughtfully, "could be put on, Charles. They're usually pretty stupid, but it could be."

"One like this, that's crediting him with too much imagination and forethought," said O'Connor. There were still several names out of Records to go looking for, but as they sat there for a few minutes, reluctant to leave the air-conditioning, Patrolman Tracy brought in a man they had been wanting to see. Richard Bland. There had been an A.P.B. out on his car since Thursday morning.

"I spotted it in a public parking lot up on Glendale Avenue," said Tracy. "I was just about to call it in when he came walking up to it."

"And isn't that nice," said O'Connor. He gave Bland his most sharklike grin. "We're very glad to see him."

Bland was about twenty-eight, a little too paunchy and already going bald; he sat and glowered at O'Connor and Forbes and answered questions reluctantly. Well, yeah, he'd moved from the address that was still on his license, he just hadn't got around to changing it with the DMV. He didn't know the cops wanted to talk to him, why should he, and anyway he hadn't done nothing.

"Leaving the scene of an accident, Mr. Bland, adds up this time to a felony hit-run, you know," O'Connor told him. "That woman, Mrs. Ruby Wynn, was hurt pretty severely when you slammed into her in the crosswalk—she'll be in the hospital awhile."

"Well, for God's sake, I didn't realize I hit a—person, I thought maybe it was a dog, is all. Listen, I couldn't afford another driving ticket, I already got two this year, it'd cost me my license, see, and I got to get to work. It was damned dark along there, I never saw anybody—"

"It's light enough that the woman's husband spotted your

plate. Of course it's an easy one to remember, isn't it—vanity plate, RICHY B. Had you been drinking?" As he admitted, he already had two moving-violation tickets dating to eight months ago, and on one there'd been some suspicion of driving under the influence.

"No, no," said Bland hurriedly. "Well, I might've had one drink, that's all. Listen, I was late for work, see. I was in a hurry—" He was, it appeared, a waiter at Pike's Verdugo Oaks, one of the classier restaurants in town. "Listen," he said, "I never meant to hurt anybody—I'm awful sorry about that—I never did nothing like this before—"

"Oh, take him away and book him in," said O'Connor to Forbes disgustedly. He did get tired of the dumb louts. They already had the warrant, since they had identified him through the plate number.

Varallo and Boswell drew blank on the hunt for more suspects, except for Danny Lopez; he was where he was supposed to be, at his job in a garage down on Central, and he denied hotly being mixed up in any heist since he'd been out.

"You can ask the priest," he told them fiercely, "ask anybody knows me—I don't want t' see inside the joint ever again, I'm keepin' clean, an' that's straight. I swear on a Bible. Joe too. I swear it—we're both clean." The garage owner couldn't give him an alibi, but for what it was worth said he'd turned out a good enough worker.

"I thought about it some, take on a guy on parole, but he's worked out OK, all I can tell you."

Joe was off parole now and working as a box boy at a market. Unexpectedly he came up with an alibi for the first motel heist; he and Danny had been playing poker with some guys around then. One of the other men supplied the date, because it happened to be his birthday.

Manuel Perez had disappeared from his last known address in Burbank and nobody knew where he'd gone. Well, that was the way the job went.

They landed back at the office at noon to find a new call just down; they didn't get beyond the lobby, or time for lunch. "Assault of some kind," said Duff at the switchboard. "It's Louise Street." He passed over the slip with the address.

It was one of the oldish apartment buildings on that old street, close in downtown: a dingy red brick place. The squad was just pulling away as Varallo parked the Gremlin in a red-painted zone down from the front walk.

There was a stout middle-aged woman waiting for them inside an open door labeled MANAGERESS. "Not that it's any good asking me questions," she told them, "because I don't know any answers. What? Oh, I'm Mrs. Colquhoun—Nora Colquhoun. She only moved in here a couple of months ago, and if it was up to me I'd be asking her to move out, but I don't own the place. I've got a good idea that fellow's been living with her, and I don't like that sort of thing, though these days it seems nobody thinks that's a reason to kick a tenant out, when there's no complaint besides, and I'm bound to say she was quiet, no loud parties or anything. Anyway, the reason I came to find her, Miss Redding up in Twelve had complained about her Venetian blind, and I was going up to look at it when I come past Ten and heard these awful moans and groans. Door was open so I went in and there she was, all bloody and naked. Been beat up good, I'd say. What? Well, her name's Gloria Carson, or that's what she said. I got no idea who the man is—I've just seen him half a dozen times, come in with her, but not to describe him good—just a young fellow, kind of long dark hair, scruffy sort of clothes."

"You're sure it was the same man each time?" asked Varallo. She looked taken aback. "Well, I thought so. I couldn't swear to it. Tell you the truth, that never crossed my mind. You don't think—"

"We don't know," said Boswell cheerfully. "I take it the ambulance has been here."

"Took her off about twenty minutes ago. She did look awful," said Mrs. Colquhoun with relish. She couldn't tell them anything about the girl's possible relatives; all she knew was that she worked at Peggy's dress shop over on Brand, and yes, she had a beat-up old car, a Falcon.

The car was in the carport assigned to her apartment. The apartment was typical of its vintage: shabby and furnished with a collection of odds and ends, but except for a few traces of a fight, clean and neat enough. The table beside the double bed had been knocked over, and in the living room the rug was kicked back at one side. There was a smear of blood on the glass top of the coffee table.

"Let the lab loose and see what shows," said Varallo. He called in from downstairs, and Gene Thomsen came over in a mobile lab truck. Varallo and Boswell went down to the Memorial Hospital, which housed Emergency, and after a wait talked to one of the interns. He shrugged at them and said, "She'll live. Somebody beat her up—she's got a couple of cracked ribs, slight concussion, bruises all over. You can probably talk to her tonight or tomorrow—right now she's under sedation."

"Damn it," said Varallo in the Gremlin, "I got sidetracked off that Contreras. If he wasn't just telling a tale about a brother in the dope business—have a look for the name in Records, anyway."

"What's that about?" asked Boswell, and Varallo started to tell him, switching on the ignition.

Hugo Adler, attorney-at-law, had an airy and well-furnished office on the tenth floor of one of the newer high-rise buildings on North Brand Boulevard. He hadn't kept Delia waiting; the smartly dressed middle-aged secretary hadn't left her two minutes before he came out to the anteroom, stared at her badge with astonished curiosity, and showed her courteously into the inner office.

"What on earth can I do for the police?" He looked at her with lively interest. "You're a detective? Well, for heaven's sake. What's this all about?" He was a man in his fifties, with thinning sandy hair, a sharp-nosed thin face, shrewd pale blue eyes; he was rather foppishly dressed, with a flamboyant tie.

"Mrs. Marion Austen," said Delia. "Mrs. Frances Potter came to see us—"

"Oh, for heaven's sake," he said again, this time crossly. "That. But there's no reason—I quite understood that she was shocked and upset, of course Mrs. Austen died very suddenly, but I can't make out why this Mrs. Potter seems to think there was anything wrong, for heaven's sake. The police don't think there was anything wrong? That's crazy."

"Well, we don't know," said Delia. "If you'd just tell me all the details, just what happened, from your viewpoint—"

He sighed, fiddling with the pen on his desk. "Of course it was awkward," he said. "It always is—a sudden death—any death, when there's no family. I didn't know Mrs. Austen well—had known her for, oh, twenty years—but I'd only actually seen her a few times. I'd drawn wills for her and her husband, that was all. Later, for her. But I suppose people always think of a lawyer when there's trouble. That was the reason they called me."

"Who?"

"The people who found her dead. One of the tenants at the apartment, I don't recall the woman's name, she found her first, I think, and then the maid turned up—the maid that works there. It was awkward, of course. It was two weeks ago last night—my wife and I were just sitting down to dinner. I went over, of course—the least I could do—and very fortunately one of them knew the name of her doctor, so I got hold of his answering service. When I explained the circumstances—that is, when he finally called back—he suggested calling a mortician at once, said he'd take care of the death certificate and so on. Well, of course I am Mrs. Austen's executor—there wasn't anyone else to make arrangements. It was," said Adler morosely, "damned awkward. That time of night. I called Kiefer and Eyrick, explained the position, and they sent someone for the body."

"What time was that exactly? That same night?"

"Well, certainly. We could hardly just leave her there, after all," said Adler. "And she was certainly dead, there wasn't any point in calling an ambulance. Well, I must have got there about seven forty-five, and I did the phoning from this other woman's apartment—Pigeon, Byrd, I don't recall the name—it was at least nine-thirty when the doctor called back, and after ten when the men from Kiefer and Eyrick came."

"And there wasn't any difficulty," asked Delia, "about the doctor issuing a death certificate?"

"Oh, no, of course not. As it happened, the doctor had seen her only a few days before and was familiar with her condition. It's quite outrageous to suggest that—well, really, I don't know what you or Mrs. Potter think you are suggesting! It was all unfortunate, the way it happened, but people do die suddenly after all, and not everyone has relatives."

"When was the last time you'd seen her before that?"

He thought. "It was sometime in March, I could look it up. She came in to make a few changes in her will. She was a very sensible old lady, of course. Knew her own mind."

Delia considered him: a very conventional type of lawyer, he struck her, and he'd probably dig his heels in at being asked about the will. Leave that until this whole thing fizzled out, as it probably would, or began to look more important. It was likely, in any case, that she'd left most of her possessions to the two old friends. "Did you make the funeral arrangements?"

"Yes, the next day. As I say, I'm her executor. Kiefer and Eyrick are always reliable, and she'd put in the will what she wanted done. She already owned a plot in Forest Lawn—she and her husband had bought a double lot there some years ago. It was a very simple service—she hadn't been a church-goer, and Kiefer and Eyrick supplied a minister. Of course there'd been a notice in the paper, but there weren't too many people showed up—she'd never been a woman to socialize much, I gathered."

"I see," said Delia. "Well, thank you very much. Do you remember the doctor's name?"

"Certainly. Dr. Cushing—Andrew Cushing, it's a medical clinic on Glendale Avenue. Really what the police interest is—"

"I don't know that we have one," said Delia. "Just—being thorough." He got up politely as she rose. And he had been more bewildered than annoyed, she thought, riding down in the elevator. Mrs. Potter's dark suspicions of the lawyer were probably unfounded.

What about the doctor?

The medical clinic on Glendale Avenue was quite new and handsome, with its own parking lot. The brass plate on the front listed four doctors, all general practitioners. Inside, a cramped room held seven people awaiting appointments. A brisk receptionist eyed Delia and said efficiently, "New patient—if you'll come through here, please, and fill out our standard form." Delia followed her into a tiny cubicle with a weighing machine to escape the crowd in the waiting room, before she brought out the badge. The receptionist was astounded, annoyed, and coldly furious at her refusal to say what it was about; the doctor was extremely busy, he'd never had anything to do with the police, he couldn't be expected to take time off from office hours. . . . Delia went on patiently asking, and in a fury the receptionist stalked out. A minute later she got the doctor. He looked at the badge coolly, at her impersonally, and took her into an office about seven by ten with a desk and two chairs cramped together. He asked, "What's this all about?" He didn't look as if he was worried about keeping patients waiting another ten minutes or two hours.

"Mrs. Marion Austen," said Delia.

"Should I know her?" Dr. Andrew Cushing didn't look over thirty; he couldn't have been in practice long. He was a very good-looking young man, with curly auburn hair, a handsome straight nose, a firm mouth; his expression was just a trifle arrogant, a little smug: a young man very confident of himself.

"She was your patient," said Delia. "She died suddenly two weeks ago last night, and—"

"Oh," he said. "Oh. That one. What about her?"

"You were quite certain of the cause of her death?"

"What the hell?" he said. But he looked simply surprised. "Naturally. You don't mean to say the police think there was anything wrong about it? That's ridiculous. The woman could have dropped dead any minute. What interest have the police got in this?"

"One of her friends has suggested that it was a very sudden and unexpected death."

"Well, if you haven't anything better to do than follow up idle gossip, I have," said Dr. Cushing curtly. He stepped to the door and spoke to another white-clad minion. "Have the record in a second—of course it'll get destroyed at the end of the month, so you're lucky. Like to know what this friend of hers might know about medicine. Oh, thanks, Ella." He took the manila folder and pushed it across the desk. "Show it to any physician you like. Of course there's just a bare record there, blood pressure and pulse and so on—she was to have come in for the works, electrocardiogram and X-rays and so on, the following week. But I didn't need any test results to tell me what was there. I didn't have to guess. There was pronounced arrhythmia—irregular heartbeat—

the heart was undoubtedly a good deal enlarged. Emphysema, of course—all the signs you'd expect, swelling of the extremities, elevated blood pressure—the systolic pressure was way up—I knew what the tests would say."

"But you never gave them to her."

He shrugged, opened the folder. "I saw her on April twenty-sixth. She had an appointment for May third, for the tests I wanted to run. It would have been that next Friday night she died, yes. I remember. I checked the answering service about the middle of the evening because I had an obstetric patient getting ready to deliver, and somebody had called about the death, left a number. I told the man—I don't think it was a relative—I wasn't surprised. Got the name of the funeral director they were going to use."

"And the next day you made out the death certificate, after you'd seen the body?"

"I never saw the body," said Dr. Cushing. "Why? I'd seen her four days before, and I knew the condition she was in. I dropped it off at the funeral home—it was a pure formality, they have to have a certificate to bury a body is all."

"And suppose"—Delia looked at him thoughtfully—"somebody should tell you that another doctor who saw Mrs. Austen last December had told her her heart was absolutely sound. Because one did."

"Then he was going senile," said Cushing promptly. He pushed the folder at her again. "Any doctor would know what the condition was, just by this record here—go and ask one. I didn't know the police went nosing around after silly rumors." He was looking annoyed now.

And really, thought Delia, putting the folder in the glove compartment, what did Mrs. Potter know about the other doctor? Harvey. Just that Marion Austen had been going to him for years, and that he had retired. Possibly he had been going senile —didn't know his business any more.

There had been a new phone book out in March, of course; he wouldn't be listed as an M.D. any longer. But possibly someone at the apartment would remember his first name.

Remembering Mrs. Potter's description of it, she had to agree when she saw it: not a smart modern apartment building, but

solidly built and well maintained, a modest ten- or twelve-unit
place on a quiet street. It was two-storied, built in a line at one
side of the lot with a grass-bordered walk leading down the
front, and just a glimpse of a line of garages at the back, where
there must be an alley leading to the side street. It was white-
painted stucco; the grass was neatly trimmed. She found a parking slot up the street and walked back.

The apartments were two-storied: front doors only on the
ground floor. The name slot beside the door nearest the street
still bore the typed name AUSTEN. The next one down was labeled FOWLER. She pressed the bell.

"—Just terrible, to die all alone like that—" Mrs. Bernice
Fowler was a natural talker, didn't need questions to start her
off. She didn't seem startled or concerned that a police officer
was asking questions, possibly took it as some necessary legal re-
quirement, something to do with the will; she was a good-
natured, amiable woman, probably not very intelligent. "Just terrible! She was such a nice woman, and she hadn't been sick at all.
We've lived here about ten years, you know, we knew her pretty
well." Mrs. Fowler was a buxom blonde in her middle forties.
"Started buying a house over on Palm, but neither Bert or me
likes yard work, we got fed up with all the work to it, and taxes
going up, and seeing we haven't any kids, an apartment's easier
all round. I'll never forget that day. Why, I'd seen her just that
morning when I gave her the rent check, she looked fine, I don't
suppose she knew there was anything wrong with her heart. It
was along after dinner I had a craving for some ice cream, the
heat wave 'd just got started, you know, and I went up to the
market—it was when I came back I noticed her kitchen light
wasn't on. Our two back doors side by side, you see, and I came
in the back—and usually about then she'd have been cleaning up
in the kitchen after dinner. So I just stepped out my front door,
and there wasn't a light in her living room either—and she never
went out evenings—and I felt just a little uneasy, and I tried the
door and it was unlocked and she always kept it locked after
dark—and I was just going to get Bert when Rena came up—"
"Rena."
"Rena Perry, she does housework for some of the tenants here,

the Costellos in Twelve are both crippled with arthritis and the Robertsons both work—she just used to do the heavy work for Mrs. Austen, floors and windows and so on. She's a nice girl, well, young woman. And maybe Mrs. Austen did suspect there was something wrong, because she'd asked Rena to come and stay that night, said she'd been having dizzy spells and was afraid of falling. And of course it was then we all three went in and found her—oh, it was awful—not that there was anything *horrible*, the poor thing looked quite peaceful, just like she was asleep there on the bed—but to think of her dying like that all alone—"

She did remember the doctor's name; she remembered that Marion Austen had been vexed about his retiring, she'd gone to him so long, but of course she hadn't been one to run to doctors. The first name she didn't remember at all.

Delia stopped at the place on Wilson for a belated lunch, and ran into Varallo and Boswell. They told her about Gloria Carson, and Varallo said, "You can go and ask some questions at Peggy's dress shop. Does anybody there know who the boyfriend is and so on. Gene's going over the apartment, but if there are any shortcuts it'd be useful. There are still a dozen names out of Records to look for on all the other jobs. And it might not do any harm to talk to that nurse again—Sandra Maxwell. Maybe now she's calmed down she'll remember something more about the rapist."

Of course one of the annoyances of the job was having to switch from one thing to another. Still thinking about Marion Austen, Delia drove back to Brand, found a parking place, and walked down the block to Peggy's dress shop.

It was a small place specializing in large and half sizes. It didn't look too prosperous; since the Galleria had been open, shopping on Brand had fallen off. There wasn't a customer in the place, only the owner, Mrs. Harling, a tall busty woman with white hair. She was shocked and shaken to hear about Gloria. "All these criminals around, you're not safe in your own home any more! When she didn't come in this morning I tried to call her, Gloria's always here on time or if she was sick she'd call me, but nobody answered the phone—"

Gloria Carson had worked there for nearly a year, had had a reference from another women's store in Hollywood. She'd been quite satisfactory and efficient, a nice girl, said Mrs. Harling. Oh, yes, she had mentioned a steady boyfriend, was hoping he'd ask her to marry him—she knew his first name was Bruce, but couldn't recall a last name, she'd only heard it once or twice. "It was an ordinary name, something like Woods or Wiley, something like that." And there was a sister who lived somewhere around here, she couldn't say where.

From there Delia went to talk to the Maxwell girl, who hadn't gone back to work yet. She lived with her parents at an apartment on West Glenoaks, and she couldn't add anything to what she'd told the other detectives yesterday. She was a pretty blonde, not an RN but one of the LVNs, and she had worked at the Memorial Hospital ever since she'd graduated from that course two years ago. "I never thought anything about going out to the parking lot at night, but of course there are usually a crowd of us together, coming off shift—I was a little late leaving on Thursday because, well, I'd been talking to one of the interns—" All she could do was repeat the story, he'd grabbed her all of a sudden from behind, he'd been awfully strong, and spoke broken English. "He just said, 'You no scream, I keel with knife,' as far as I can remember—he knocked me down so fast, I never got a glimpse of his face—"

And while it was the first place to look, the rapist—or the heist men, any of them—might not be in Records. Yet. The lab hadn't turned any evidence in the motels, and one of the clerks had said those men wore gloves.

By then it was three-thirty. And ordinarily Delia was a conscientious city employee; but she'd only taken half an hour off for lunch, and she wanted to get this done today. She drove over to the Galleria, that handsome big shopping mall with its excellent choice of shops, and went into Buffum's department store. Up in the nursery section, after rumination, she decided on a hand-knitted fluffy white shawl; it wore a rather shocking price tag, but Isobel would love it. She found a card, and unexpectedly had difficulty drafting a brief few words of congratulation. "Yes, gift wrapped please, and will you send it for me."

While she waited for her change, her mind turned idly to

those old ladies chatting with each other on their tape recorders. Ninety-minute tapes . . . It would be lovely to have the time for a long, long talk with Isobel, even on the phone, the way they had used to do, God, how many years ago? On swing shift her first three and a half years on the force, that played hell with any social life, not that she had had time then for that—all the courses, all the homework crammed in, because face the facts of life, a woman bucking for status in what was usually a man's job had to be just that much better, have that much more to offer, to get there. And she'd got there—just eight months back. Qualified as Detective nearly a year before she had a chance to apply for this job—promotion slow in the LAPD—on this much smaller but efficient force.

Time, the ruthless. It had taken time. No time for the long talks on the phone, lunch dates, with Isobel or anybody.

She liked Laura Varallo. Laura was older, of course, but companionable and—nice. Maybe on her day off next week—

She looked ruefully at the little change from thirty-five dollars and went out to the parking lot. They charged a fee for mailing, of course, but she couldn't very well have taken it home and wrapped it herself, Alex always so curious, asking questions—because Isobel meant Neil Fordyce—how Alex had hated him, because he'd been afraid of him, of course—

She bent to unlock the car door, and she thought, if Alex had known the bitter fights they'd had, the savage feeling between them—but of course you didn't have savage feelings about anyone not important to you—

For one second, she was reliving one time, real as when it happened—fumbling blindly with the lock and the key—

Summer evening six, seven years ago, when? Just the feel of the warm night, the reality of the moment sharp in her mind. In Neil's car parked outside the house on Waverly Place.

"You're just a Goddamned stubborn little fool, hellbent on wasting your life on account of that bullheaded old tyrant—"

"That's stupid, it's stupid, Neil, it's not Alex, it's what I want—"

"You don't know what the hell you want, he's dominated you all your life but you'll have to get away from him sooner or later, my girl—"

"I don't want to get away, don't you see, I'm all he has—can't you see—"

"My God, you've got your own life to live—you can't live his over again, Delia! Damn it, I know you better than you know yourself, and I know we love each other." He was holding her too tight, and his mouth was insistent. "I know we can't get married until I've got my degree and a job—but if you'll just say it'll be all right then—you put in a little time on your damned stupid police force, satisfy him, and in a couple of years—"

"I can't, I can't do it halfway, can't you see that—why can't you understand—it's no good, it'd be deserting—" Evading his hard grasp, wrenching the door open— The little vignette sharp and clear as the moment it happened, the roof light on as the door opened, and Neil there twisted around under the wheel reaching for her, lean wide-shouldered Neil, his thin, not quite handsome face with its heavy eyebrows and mobile mouth drawn to bitter tightness— She slammed the door on it and ran up the front walk, praying blindly that she could get upstairs before she began to cry.

Varallo landed back at the office at four-thirty, empty-handed. O'Connor and Katz were there, having just let another possible rapist go. "Handful of nothing, damn it," said O'Connor. "There's just nowhere to go on it."

"So we put it in Pending and forget it," said Katz philosophically. "What can't be cured."

"I've got some of the same," said Varallo. "Has Fresno called me?"

"I don't know, we've been busy."

Their female detective came in, and Varallo glanced at her, looked back, and asked, "You feeling all right?"

"Perfectly all right, why?" she asked a little sharply.

"Just thought you might be feeling the heat. Where've you been?"

"Talking to the rape victim. She gives us nothing new. And not much from the dress shop on the Carson girl—the boyfriend is Bruce something."

"Helpful," said Varallo. "Oh, well, hopefully she can tell us eventually who beat her up." The phone rang on his desk and he picked it up. "Detective Varallo . . . Oh. Well, thanks very much . . . Yes, what's the opinion on that? . . . Oh. That's just dandy, adds up to voluntary manslaughter. Thank you very much, doctor." He put the phone down and looked at Delia. "The General. That—thing we saw yesterday just died."

"Thank God," said Delia.

"*In veritá.* It's the opinion of the doctors that it died of neglect and malnutrition, in other words of abandonment. If we ever find the Contrerases, it'll be a felony charge."

"And I don't for a minute suppose," said Delia, "that you've typed a report on the Carson girl."

"I've been busy."

"Well, let me have the apartment address and I'll do it."

"*Grazie,*" said Varallo meekly.

Gene Thomsen wandered in and said, "That apartment on Louise. Hell of a lot of smudged prints, nothing useful. But there was an address book"—he passed it over. "There's a Jean Carson listed, probably a relative."

"Yes," said Varallo. It was a Hollywood number; he tried it, but got no answer. "So leave it for the night watch."

Delia was rolling triplicate forms into her typewriter. She said, "I want to talk to you sometime about this Austen thing, Lieutenant."

"And when are you going to start using my name? Anything in that?"

Delia gave him a fleeting smile. "Force of habit. I'm not used to rank yet. Police females don't get familiar with the brass. I don't know. But there's a funny sort of feel to it, all I can say. Nothing to put a finger on, but—funny."

"Then we'd better go on looking at it," said O'Connor.

"Only I don't see where."

"You know," said Katz, who had been brooding over a list of names from Records, "the fellow I like for that rape is this Guido Fuentes, Charles. True, he's only got one count of attempted rape, but his last known address is Magnolia Street, and that's only three or four blocks from the Memorial."

"I've been looking for him," said Varallo. "He's said by his mama to be out job hunting, he ought to be home tonight. And I caught the afternoon news on the way back—it's going to ninety-five tomorrow."

"Thank you so much," said Katz. The phone rang on O'Connor's desk.

"O'Connor . . . Oh, isn't that nice. Of course it figures. The heat wave always sends the rate up. . . . We've got a new homicide, boys. Down at the Amtrak depot."

It was ten past five. They uttered simultaneous groans. "So I'll pull rank. The female is busy on a report. I'm going home early—I've got around today. You and Joe can go look at it."

"So you call Laura and tell her I'll be late."

"I'll call her," volunteered Delia unexpectedly, and Varallo swung around to look at her.

"Well, thanks."

The railroad station—formerly Southern Pacific but now Amtrak since the whole operation had been so disastrously nationalized—was in the extreme southwestern edge of town, very nearly on the border of Hollywood. When they got there, two squads were parked in front of the station and Morris and McLeon were keeping a little crowd at bay from a body there on the sidewalk.

"At least you've got an eyewitness," said Morris.

They had, and an excited one. He was Bill McManus, he drove a cab for Yellow, and he'd been parked along the curb there because the southbound Daylight was due in at five-fifty and once in a while somebody off it wanted a cab. There'd been another Yellow parked behind him, but its driver, Jim Ferguson, had gone into the station for a cold drink from the machine. He hadn't seen anything. Everybody else had been in the station.

"I saw it happen, only I didn't believe it," said McManus. "Broad daylight, I mean! There wasn't anybody in front, everybody inside waiting for the train, y' know, and then I see this couple come out, they was maybe twenty, thirty feet from my cab—I don't know, not close, but— Standing there talking, see, a girl and a guy. I was just sitting there. All of a sudden I hear a scream, I look, the guy is like hitting her," and he brought one arm up and down in graphic illustration, "like stabbing at her—

no, I didn't see a knife, but he had his back to me—and she was
screaming, she fell down, and I get out of the cab and yell at the
guy, he runs like hell, up that way, and he jumps on a motorcycle and takes off—up El Bonito there—"

He gave a very vague description. "It all happened so fast—he
was about medium sized, I think, maybe light brown or blond
hair—jeans I guess, a light colored shirt."

The corpse, dead of knife wounds, had been a pretty brunette
in her early twenties. She was wearing a white pants suit and a
few pieces of costume jewelry. There didn't seem to be any
handbag.

A couple of the trainmen said there had been. Gilbert Light
said she had bought a ticket on tomorrow's Daylight for San
Francisco, and paid in cash; she'd had a big brown leather handbag when she was at the window. He hadn't seen anyone with
her. The man at the luggage desk, Ed Elliott, had noticed her
too— "Because she was a real looker," he said frankly. "A dish.
But look, there was a little crowd in here, and everybody flocked
out when they heard the noise out here—and there could have
been some character who swiped her bag in the confusion. I
don't know if you know, there've been stray rumors about dope
peddlers hanging around here lately, you know we only got the
two passenger trains a day through, bring any people around,
and it's a kind of deserted area the rest of the time—"

That, of course, might have happened. They had indeed heard
the rumors, and sometime one of the street informants might
come up with something more definite. Varallo and Katz looked
at the dead girl, and Katz said sadly, "Well, if nobody reports
her missing, get the *News-Press* to run her picture and see if
anybody recognizes her."

# THREE

Saturday night was apt to be busy; of course it was a lot busier for Traffic, for the squads out roaming the streets, picking up the drunks and dealing with the brawls in bars. But Glendale wasn't like downtown L.A., or a lot of other places around; there wasn't much of that as a rule.

Rhys and Hunter didn't get a call until nine o'clock, when a squad called in a heist. It was an all-night pharmacy down on Central, and the lone clerk on duty gave them this and that. "Sure I'd know them again, just show 'em to me! Pair of guys in the twenties, around there, one about six feet, one shorter, white guys—they had a gun, and they were after the drugs as well as the money, cleaned out our stock of barbs and amphetamines, and I'd guess about forty bucks from the register. It'd been a slow night so far."

Rhys told him they'd like him to come in and make a statement, look at some mug shots. "Sure," he said. "Oh, and they called each other Eddy and Doug a couple of times."

"You don't say," said Rhys. The pro thugs were usually fairly dumb, of course. Back at the office, he wrote the report on that, and they sat around for a while waiting for anything else to come along. Nothing did until eleven-forty, when they got a call to the Memorial Hospital. Another nurse going off duty had just been raped in the parking lot.

That might suggest a few new ideas for the day men to work. They got down there in a hurry.

This woman was one of the RNs, a married woman named Joyce Collier, a good deal older than Sandra Maxwell and a sensible, matter-of-fact woman. She was also a much larger and heftier woman, and hadn't been knocked around as much. Naturally she was shaken and upset, her uniform torn and dirty, but she wasn't much hurt aside from the rape. She was sitting in a chair in one of the Emergency examining rooms dabbing a cold compress on her bruised jaw, and she answered questions volubly. Her husband had been called, would be coming to take her home.

She was on the three-to-eleven shift. "There was a crowd of us came out together, but Wilma and I stood there a few minutes talking—she's giving a wedding shower for my daughter—and everybody else had gone when we said good night. Wilma was parked the other side of the lot, she'd drive out the side entrance, and I'd just got to my car—good heavens above, that other thing last Thursday just never came into my mind, we've never had anything like that happen before, I'm so familiar with that lot— He jumped me from behind the bushes at the side there, and it was all so fast and unexpected, I hadn't time even to try to scream! He grabbed me by the throat and said something like, 'You scream, I kill'—in a heavy accent—and then he threw me down and I hit my head on the cement and passed right out. When I came to—I don't think I was out long, but thank God I don't actually remember the rape—he was just, well, you know, getting off me, and he started back through the lot, I think. I managed to get up to the Emergency entrance, and Dr. Whitely called the police—"

She couldn't give any kind of description, just that he was big and strong. "But this is the same joker all right, Dick," said Rhys. "That's just what he said to the Maxwell girl. And right here at the hospital again, that suggests a couple of ideas."

"Yeah," said Hunter. "Maybe he's got some kind of a hang-up about nurses."

"The sex nuts," said Rhys, "you never know what kind of hang-ups they might have." And he'd done the report on the heist; Hunter could do this one.

That was waiting for them on Sunday morning. O'Connor was supposed to be off on Sunday—he was probably up in the hills somewhere exercising that improbable dog of his, but he would also probably be in later. Bill McManus was due in to make a statement about the homicide at the railroad station; Delia could stay in and take that. Harvey and Boswell had gone directly to Records looking for more possible burglars.

Forbes, looking at the two reports centered on O'Connor's desk, passed one to Katz and said, "Well, well. Another rape, same place, same time. Makes you think. Rearranges our ideas some, maybe." He glanced at the other report. "Oh, for God's sake. They are so Goddamned stupid, the punks, it makes you tired. Look at this, Vic. I ask you. They walk into this place after the drugs, the money, and call each other by name. Eddy and Doug. My God. I didn't know Eddy was out—the damn parole board hardly lets 'em get settled in a cell."

"Don't tell me," said Varallo. "The Keelers."

"That's got to be just who. And Eddy's got to be still on P.A., he drew a one-to-three last year. Damn moronic punks." Muttering, Forbes sat down at his desk, looked up the number, dialed the Welfare and Rehabilitation office downtown. Within ten minutes they supplied him with an address in Burbank.

"If they weren't so dumb we wouldn't catch up to so many," said Varallo, "but it does make you wonder sometimes." They took Forbes's car; it was an old run-down apartment building on the west edge of town. Forbes shoved the bell, and in a moment Doug Keeler opened the door.

"Gee, you're early— Oh."

"Expecting a dealer to barter for the loot?" asked Varallo. The Keelers weren't users: just pro thugs. It was a shabby, cluttered little living room, but a good part of the clutter consisted of the boxes of prescription drugs, the barbiturates and amphetamines, miscellaneous drugs still neatly labeled with the pharmacy brand name. Also visible was an ancient S. and W. .38 revolver.

"Candy from the baby, for God's sake," said Forbes. Eddy Keeler, coming in from the kitchen with a cup of coffee in one hand and a doughnut in the other, was staring at them.

"How the hell did you drop on us so fast, anyways?"

They didn't bother to explain. They gathered up the evidence and brought it and the Keelers back to headquarters. There wasn't any point wasting time talking to them; the evidence was sufficient. Varallo phoned in for the warrant, they bagged the evidence for the DA's office, and Forbes booked them in to jail. Sometime they'd get a report written on it.

McManus had come in and was talking to Delia, waving his arms excitedly, while she scribbled shorthand.

Nobody had reported a girl missing who might match the corpse at the railroad station. But she might have lived alone; and if she'd been intending to leave for San Francisco, she could have quit any job she had here. People here who knew her might think they knew where she was. It had been too late to get to the *News-Press* last night, and they didn't print a Sunday paper; sometime today have the lab get a picture, get the *News-Press* to run it, and see what that might turn up.

"And the Carson girl ought to be able to answer questions now," said Varallo. "We'd better go and ask some. It'll be an assault charge."

"I haven't been able to get hold of that Jean Carson yet," said Delia, catching that. "I'll go on trying."

The Memorial Hospital was at the south end of town, at the corner of Central and Los Feliz. It was a busy area, two main drags and business crowding both. Varallo wandered around hunting a parking place; the meters were only a dime, the public parking for the hospital across the street nicked you four bits. Finally he found a slot on the narrow residential street immediately behind the hospital, and as they got out Forbes said, "Great minds with but a single thought."

Katz and Poor were standing in the parking lot behind the hospital talking. Varallo and Forbes went up there. "Well, a few new ideas," said Katz, nodding at them. "Another one right here. It makes you think about the hospital itself. Look at this lot." It was just one part of the parking accommodation reserved for the hospital staff, behind and to one side of the looming, tall hospital building. The ambulance entrance and the entrance to Emergency was at one side, up to the left as they faced the rear of the building here; there was a rear exit to the back street, a side exit down from the ambulance driveway. Space here for around fifty cars. Presumably the rest of the staff had parking reserved across the side street where there was a much bigger lot.

This lot ran right back to the narrow street behind the hospital. There was a low wall at one side, with some well-grown oleander bushes against it; there were four tall arc lights scattered at intervals.

"It wouldn't be as bright as daylight here," said Katz, squinting up at those. "It just strikes me that our boy might be pretty familiar with this set-up." He was teetering back and forth ruminatively, looking around. Beside Varallo he looked small: only squeaking in at five-nine, a spare dark man with shrewd, restless dark eyes.

"I don't know, Joe. The hospital staff, you're thinking about. Well—"

"The rapists come all kinds like other people," said Katz. "And a place this size, they must have quite the hell of a staff—three, four hundred people? Counting everybody. And all kinds of people, Vic—janitors, people to do all the rough work, besides all the doctors and nurses. I think we'll sniff around and have a look, anyway."

Varallo and Forbes left them to it and went into the Emergency wing. The nurse at the desk looked at the badges and told them the Carson girl would be discharged tomorrow; they could see her— "But she hasn't been doing any talking," she added dryly.

Gloria Carson was a pretty girl even with a black eye and a swollen jaw. She was flat in the hospital bed with the sheet drawn up tight, she looked pale and sorry for herself. At the sight of the badges she looked frightened.

"We'd just like to hear what you can tell us about this, Miss Carson. Who did this to you?"

"I d-don't know," she said in a thin voice. "It was—a strange man, I never saw him before. Well, I didn't see him at all because it was dark. It was the middle of the night. I was in bed, and I don't know how he got in—I suppose he jimmied the door or something—I woke up, I guess I heard a noise—and he was there—a burglar. A burglar. And I was too scared to scream, but I made a noise and he—and he started to hit me. Chased me into the living room—he kept hitting me and I guess—I passed out. When I came to he was gone—but I was hurting so bad I couldn't move—I don't know any more to tell you, that's all." She turned her face away and shut her eyes.

In the corridor Varallo said, "Quite a lot wrong about that. There wasn't any sign of forced entry. The place hadn't been ransacked. And there were lamps switched on in both the bedroom and living room."

"Um," said Forbes. "The boyfriend?"

"The boyfriend. And she doesn't want to get him into trouble."

"Well, we've got other jobs to do."

"Too true."

Back at headquarters, they stopped off in Records and had a look for anybody named Contreras with a narco pedigree. They drew blank, so Varallo called LAPD headquarters and asked there; they had a lot of computers and wouldn't waste much time hunting. The R. and I. office called back in ten minutes and gave him three Contrerases: Juan, William and Philip, no relation to each other. The first two just had small records of possession, street peddling; the third had been convicted of smuggling the stuff in from Mexico, was currently on parole from a three-to-five. The addresses were in Boyle Heights, Torrance, and Huntington Park.

"No rest for the wicked," said Forbes.

O'Connor came in at one o'clock and Delia at last was able to give him chapter and verse on Marion Austen, in detail. He leaned back in the desk chair, the .357 magnum bulging as usual, his square bulldoggish face serious, dark eyes thoughtful as he listened. "Nothing much, and then again maybe a little something," he said. "I see what you mean. The funny discrepancy between the doctors. Have you got that thing Cushing gave you?" She produced it from her desk. "Double Dutch to me," he said, looking at the single filled-in form sheet contained in the folder. "Let's see if Goulding's in."

Dr. Goulding, who had private means and could indulge his interest in police work without sacrificing comfort, had made himself a cozy, cluttered little office in a room down the hall from the small morgue, in the basement under the jail. They found him just finishing one of his noxious black cigars, his feet up on the desk, reading a detective novel.

"I was just about to get to the autopsy on your new corpse, Charles," he said, sitting up guiltily.

"We're not pushing you, she isn't identified yet. Has somebody been down to get a picture?"

"Burt was here just now—I should think he got something, her face wasn't touched. Damn good-looking girl." Goulding patted his bald head thoughtfully. "Pity. She doesn't look more than twenty-five."

"Well, we've all got to go sometime," said O'Connor. "Evidently she did something to annoy somebody. We want your opinion on something, doctor. Delia, you tell the man the story."

Obediently Delia told it over again, Goulding listening attentively, and passed over the sheet of notes Dr. Cushing had taken. Goulding lit another cigar and studied it. He rubbed his bald head some more and finally said, "It's been a while since I was in general practice, but all this is pretty elementary. I can only say that looking at this—record of blood pressure, heartbeat, pulse, so on—I'd have made the same deduction Cushing did. Anybody would. The heart undoubtedly enlarged, in a precarious state—but I'd have liked to see some tests run. Exactly as he wanted to. You can't always be dogmatic."

"And so what about the other doctor?" asked O'Connor.

"Well," said Goulding wryly, "we do come all sorts like other people, good, bad, and indifferent. But I must say I don't make out this Harvey at all. No physician in this damned world could have told the woman her heart was sound as a bell."

"He was just going to retire. He may have been—may be a very old man. Maybe incompetent," said Delia. "Do you think—"

"My dear good young woman," said Goulding, "any doctor as incompetent as that could hardly exist. It's hardly a matter of a tricky diagnosis or— Matter of using a stethoscope, damn it. A doctor half blind and deaf would have spotted this tired old wonky heart for what it was, in half a minute with a stethoscope." He took the cigar out of his mouth and sniffed it. "I've got to admit, there are always a few rankly incompetent physicians around, and a panel of patients happily convinced the dear doctor is such a fine knowledgeable fellow, if he looks paternal and uses a few long words. Known a few myself. All the same, you know, this is such an elementary thing"—he was looking perplexed. "Well, we don't know, do we? Obvious thing to do, find Harvey and ask him—take a look at him, see what kind of fellow he is. Have you had a look for him?"

"He wouldn't be in the new phone book, I suppose," said Delia.

Goulding snorted. "Never know when things come in handy." He rummaged in a desk drawer and produced a battered copy of last year's phone book, flipped to the Yellow Pages, and ran a finger down the list of physicians. "Four of 'em—John, Wendell, William, Guy. Wait a minute." Now he produced the new phone book from another drawer and had a look there. "So, one added and one taken away. New one named Sylvester—ye gods, what a thing to do to an innocent baby—but William's missing. There's your man. Go and take a look at him—lessee, yep, he's still listed at a private address, and still using the M.D. See what he looks like."

"Yes," said O'Connor. "It looks that way. So thanks very much, doctor. I don't suppose that autopsy will give us much."

"Neither do I," said Goulding, puffing his cigar contentedly.

Back in the office, O'Connor dialed the number listed for William Harvey, M.D., on Kenneth Road. He pushed the button of the amplifier as the call went through. A woman's pleasant voice answered, and he asked for Dr. Harvey. "Oh, just a moment, please."

In a moment a firm male voice said, "Dr. Harvey speaking."

"Is this the Dr. Harvey who used to have an office on Central Avenue?"

"Why, yes. Who is this speaking?"

O'Connor introduced himself. "You just seem to come into a sort of roundabout little mystery, doctor. It's about one of your former patients. A long-time patient, so you should remember her pretty easily—a Mrs. Marion Austen."

"Austen?" said Harvey blankly. "I don't recall that I ever had a patient named Austen. Why on earth are the police interested in my patients?"

"Just in Mrs. Austen. An elderly woman—seventy-four—she'd gone to you, not very often, for a number of years."

"No," said Harvey. He sounded entirely competent and confident, and also very definite. "I never had such a patient. I can probably prove that by looking up old records. I don't say I might not forget a name, someone who'd only come in once or twice, but a regular patient—no. I never knew a Mrs. Austen. What made you think—"

"So thanks very much." O'Connor put the phone down and looked at Delia. "Little mystery deepens?"

"Not necessarily," said Delia. She looked in her notebook and found the number: Mrs. Potter's son's house on Sunset Canyon Drive. A child answered, carefully polite, and could be heard shouting, "Gran'ma!" After an interval Mrs. Potter came on.

"What?" she said. "Dr. Harvey's office? Why, I don't think I ever heard. There'd be no occasion for Marion to mention— But I'm glad you're going to talk to him."

"We'd like to talk to him if we can locate him," said Delia. "Was his office in Glendale? We took that for granted, but—"

"My lord alive, I just couldn't say, Miss Riordan. All I know is, they'd gone to him over twenty years. Now up to twenty-three years back, around there, Marion and George were living in Atwater, it was just after that they moved back to Glendale, and I suppose he could have been in Atwater or around there."

"Well," said Delia, "thanks." She looked at O'Connor. "Atwater. He could have been anywhere in Hollywood, from there."

"Yes. I wonder," said O'Connor suddenly, "if he's any relation to our new boy."

"That'd be a switch." Jim Harvey had been with them such a short time—not quite three weeks—that they weren't thinking of him as a member of the team yet. He tended to join up with the other new boy Boswell when he could; he seemed to be reasonably efficient. Boswell, of course, had ridden a Glendale squad car for six years; Harvey had applied for the job from service in Burbank.

"I wonder if he's around." O'Connor went and looked, and found him with Boswell down in Records looking for possible heisters. "You number any family doctors among your relations?"

Harvey looked up, surprised. "Oh, my, you do flatter me, Lieutenant." He was as tall as Forbes or Varallo, a lantern-jawed fellow about thirty with a shock of dark hair. "Plumbers, electricians, even a farmer, and I can boast of one schoolteacher—my father. Nary a doctor. You looking for one?"

"A Dr. Something Harvey."

"Well, it's not that uncommon a name, you know."

Of course it wasn't. O'Connor went back upstairs and said to Delia, "All right, if they started going to him when they lived in Atwater, it could have been there or anywhere in Hollywood. If they went to him after they moved back here, it could have been La Cañada, Eagle Rock, even Pasadena." The other nearby communities, Burbank and Montrose, were included in the local phone book, and those Harveys they'd accounted for.

"Have we got a last year's Hollywood phone book anywhere? Or last year's Pasadena book?" Delia went to look at the shelf beside O'Connor's desk where a miscellany of reference texts were lodged: current phone book, atlas, dictionary, a book of local maps.

"Who keeps out-of-date phone books?"

"The junk that gets piled up in desks—" said Delia. She tried Varallo's first, drew blank, and was looking in John Poor's desk drawers when Katz and Poor came in looking pleased with themselves. "I think we may have hit a little jackpot, Charles," said Katz, sitting down and loosening his tie. "This second rape, at the hospital again—it sort of focuses the attention, hah? We've been poking around the hospital staff asking questions."

"What gets me," said Poor morosely—by the time he got to his desk Delia had moved on to Forbes's—"is how the hell any of these people can follow directions, get anything right—in a hospital I'd think things have to be pretty damn precise, and half of these people we've seen can't speak two words of English, for God's sake."

"Well, the doctors and nurses do," said Katz. "Maybe they use sign language or something. God knows we had to with a few we saw. There are, just as I said, a lot of clean-up people. Orderlies and maids and janitors, and a lot of people in a big laundry room in the basement. They'd be familiar with the shifts the medical people are on, and the whole premises. And one thing we came across is that there was an orderly fired from a job in Emergency just a couple of weeks ago, for being drunk on the job. One Arthur Parshegian. What we heard about him, he could fit what description we have—he's fairly big, speaks very broken English. He'd only worked there a couple of months, wasn't very satisfactory. I think we'd like to talk to him. They gave us an address, on Elk, it's an old place cut up into apartments, but he's not there. Bunch of other Armenians there say he still lives there, so— Just what in hell are you looking for, Delia? If you've run out of cigarettes—"

"Last year's phone books," said Delia. "Maybe the desk kept them." She went to find out. She wondered if they were all using a little imagination on this Austen thing: was there something offbeat about it? She rather felt as Mrs. Potter did, that Marion Austen had been bundled out of the way in quite a hurry: but when you came to think of it, it was natural enough in a way, you didn't leave a body lying around indefinitely, however sudden and unexpected the death had been.

She hadn't been able to reach Jean Carson.

Downstairs, nobody at the desk, in Communications or Records or the Traffic office, had any leftover phone books. "Damn," said Delia. They'd have to try the phone company tomorrow. She went back upstairs. O'Connor, Katz, and Poor were hashing over the rapes.

She tried the Hollywood number again, and this time Jean Carson answered. The high young voice went higher at Delia's question. "Gloria? Yes, I'm her sister—has something happened to Gloria? Oh, my God! Oh, that's just—the *hospital?* I've got to come and see her—please, which one is she in? This is the *police?* —well, yeah, I can see . . . Thanks an awful lot for calling to tell me, I really do appreciate it. Really." She hung up abruptly.

As Delia swung her chair around to the typewriter—of course neither Varallo nor Forbes had yet typed a report on the Keelers, and it ought to be done today— Varallo came in shepherding three people ahead of him. "Jeff not back yet? We split up to look—he must have got hung up somewhere. I've got to get a decent-sized set of wheels—had to call up a squad to transport this bunch. You can all sit in as witnesses. We usually end up doing things the hard way—the third name we were looking for, and he'd moved since he saw his parole officer, but a helpful neighbor knew where. This is Mr. Philip Contreras, Mr. Alfredo Contreras, Mrs. Maria Contreras." Delia automatically pushed chairs out for them.

They were all dark and slightly dirty looking, the men in jeans and gay shirts, the woman in a faded pink dress and soiled white sandals. "I don't know nothin' about anything they been doing," said Philip Contreras belligerently. "You can't lay any charge on me, I'm clean." The woman began to weep, sniffling dolefully. "They just land on me when Al loses his job and they can't pay the rent. That's all I know."

Alfredo Contreras was looking sullen and angry. He said to her, "I said we might get in trouble about it. Now you see."

She just went on crying. "Now," said Varallo, perching one hip on the corner of his desk, looking down at them, "you left your apartment here in Glendale about the first of last week, didn't you? And you left something behind. Call it an infant. Just whose child was it? Yours?" They both looked to be in their forties. "Come on, you'll have to tell us all about it sometime."

Maria Contreras sobbed into a dirty handkerchief. "The creature is not ours—no—it was begotten of the devil, a terrible creature, it should have been killed when it was born—but Luisa knows no better, she takes care of it like a doll, like a little animal pet—she would never hear to killing it—but now she is sick in hospital, I say to Alfredo, we can be rid of it—"

"All right, who is Luisa?"

"Our daughter, Luisa is our daughter, and she's a good girl, she was only foolish a little like girls will be, she is in love she thinks, this boy at the school, they run off and marry—but not in Church, only his papa is mad and makes, what you say, the *anulación*—"

"Annulment," said Delia.

"But he, this boy, we never saw, but he must be possessed by a fiend of hell—Luisa only fifteen, she bears this terrible creature, this monster—never should it see the light of day—"

"But," asked Delia involuntarily, "didn't the doctor—the hospital tell you that it should be put in an institution?"

"There is no hospital, no doctor—a disgrace, I take care of Luisa myself, at home, and when I see the terrible monster I wanted to kill it then, but I am afraid to bring the devil upon all of us, for it is a creature of his own, begot by a fiend—and then Luisa is stubborn and won't listen to me—I am afraid, all the time since, nearly two years—but now she is sick in hospital and can't do nothing, I say to Alfredo, we only go away. Don't do nothing to it, just leave, maybe the devil not know."

"My God," said O'Connor.

"The—it is dead," said Varallo. "And so—"

She crossed herself. "The good God be thanked."

"And so you will both be charged with manslaughter." She looked uncomprehending; Alfredo was still staring at the floor, Philip smoking indifferently.

"*Homicidio involuntario,*" said Delia.

"In jail? For being rid of the monster?" She shook her head. "I don't understand. I don't understand."

"What hospital is your daughter in? What's wrong with her?"

She said dully, "I don't know the name. The biggest one. Police come and tell us she is there. It is an accident, and she is bad hurt. And I say to Alfredo—"

"The things we do see on this job," said Katz, and his dark eyes were sad. Varallo drew a long breath and stood up.

"I'll take you over to the jail now."

"You can't lay a charge on me," said Philip venomously. "I don't know nothin' about it."

"We don't want to," said Varallo coldly. "You can go any time." He called them a dirty name and went out without haste. O'Connor said he'd start the machinery on the warrant, and Delia went over to the jail with Varallo to book them in.

When they got back, O'Connor said, "I've been on to the General. The accident was on the Ventura freeway a week ago yesterday. Five teenagers, all high on angel dust—the Contreras girl's the only one still alive, and she's got a broken back." He sat back and lit a cigarette. "Such nice people we get to associate with."

And Varallo said, "Hell and damnation. I forgot all about that Guido Fuentes. The one you liked for the rapes, Joe. I'd better leave a note for Bob and Dick."

"I think I'm liking this Armenian a little better now," said Katz.

At ten minutes to six, with everybody starting to drift out, a girl came into the office, looked around, and walked up to Delia's desk. "I guess you're the one called me. I'm Jean Carson."

"Oh, yes, Miss Carson. My name's Riordan. Did you see your sister?"

"Sure." She sat down and reached into her handbag for a cigarette. She was in her mid-twenties, a middling pretty, dark girl with a peaches-and-cream complexion and a very good figure in a sleeveless tan sheath dress. "Reason you hadn't got me before, I'd been at a party at Marge's—my best friend's—Saturday night and it was so late when it broke up, I stayed over. But listen, I got to tell you, about Gloria—she's such a little fool, honest! I tried to tell her, get her to see sense—listen, she's my kid sister and we're on our own, our folks got killed in an accident three years back. Argued at her till I was blue in the face nearly, her taking up with that bum, that louse—you'd think any girl 'd have better sense! In love with him, she loves him yet, she says! Well, I'd be damned if I'd stay in love with any bum that beats me up and steals my money! I just don't understand it."

"You think it was your sister's boyfriend who gave her the beating? So do we. Do you know his name?"

"Sure I know his name. Bruce Watkins. Ever since she met him, she's been crazy about him, wouldn't hear anything against him. I've been in an awful state about it—he's not only a louse, he's on dope and he's got a police record—but you just couldn't talk to her, she was going to get him off the dope, she was going to straighten him out and everything be fine—you couldn't make her see you can't change that kind! I—I don't know if you know she'd been living with him."

"Yes, it looked that way."

"Oh, I feel awful about it! We weren't brought up that way— Gloria knows better! We'd been sharing an apartment in Holly-wood, and I knew what she was up to when she got the job over here and moved—and at first she had a pretty nice apartment, and I can guess why she moved again, too—him getting money out of her so she had to find a cheaper place—"

"Did she admit to you that he beat her up?"

"She did not, but I know it and she knows I know. He's hit her before, lots of times, I know that. I don't understand it. I hope you can put him in jail for it, but I suppose if she won't tell on him—"

Delia just shook her head. There'd be no way to charge Bruce Watkins with assault, if Gloria wouldn't testify against him. *Through the Seventh Gate,* slid into her mind, *I rose, and on the*

*Throne of Saturn sate, And many a Knot unravel'd by the Road,*
*But not the Master Knot of Human Fate.*

"Well," said Jean Carson. She got up and started for the door.

Once again the day watch had left jobs for the night watch.
The first one wasn't much of a job. This Guido Fuentes, it appeared, wasn't exactly the loner you might expect a potential
rapist to be. The frame house on Magnolia Street was bulging
with people—Mama, Papa, assorted brothers and sisters from
about eight to twenty-five. When they understood why the police were asking about Guido, they were all voluble and anxious
to assure them that Guido was a good boy, just got in a little
trouble once, never again, would never do anything wrong.

Guido just looked a little simple, but perfectly amiable. It was
when Rhys began to ask him about last Thursday night, if he
could say where he'd been, that everybody let out a collective
happy sigh. The police thought Guido did something wrong on
Thursday night? Impossible! On Thursday night all the family,
not only this family here but everybody, they had all been at the
grandfather's house, it was his birthday and there was celebration, the good time and much wine and food and dancing,
and all were there, could say Guido was there—cousins, many
cousins, aunts, uncles—

"I suppose," said Rhys back in the car, "it'd be helpful to
speak Spanish, but I was never any good at languages."

"Judging from a lot of the people moving in here lately," said
Hunter dead-pan, "they seem to feel the same about English."

They both liked the sound of Arthur Parshegian for the rapes
a lot better. They found him in a frowsy two-bedroom apartment
in an old house that had been partitioned into units. He didn't
speak English very well, and he wasn't at all happy to be taken
back to headquarters and questioned.

He wasn't a very prepossessing specimen: about six feet, broad
and muscular, with a heavy jaw, a pockmarked skin, suspicious
deep-set eyes. Katz had turned up a record for him with L.A.,
not much, one count of burglary and he hadn't done any time,
had got probation.

"I not do nothing," he said. "Why you think? I not do nothing."

They started to question him. He'd been fired from the job at the hospital, had he been angry with the people there? Had he thought the nurses, the doctors, were prejudiced against him?

He shook his head violently; he seemed to have caught the one word, hospital. "Don't care," he said vehemently. "Work too hard there—clean, clean floors, poosh, poosh the big carts—and no like poosh carts with dead peoples on! No get job like, next! Head peoples there?" A massive shrug. "OK, boss around too much—go, come, carry, always the clean, clean, clean! One little pea drop off dish food, one little drop water fall out bucket, come, come, clean, clean! Is like madness."

"All right, can you tell us where you were last Thursday night —and last night?"

"Pliz? Nights?"

"Oh, hell," said Rhys. "And so damn many Armenians coming in these days—Spanish bad enough but I can imagine what—"

"Yes, I Armenian, how say here. Why?"

"Why indeed," said Hunter. "Look. Four days ago—you know days? Monday, Tuesday, Wed—"

"Oh, yes. Which you say?"

"Thursday. Last Thursday. Night. Where were you?"

Another shrug. "In room. Not do nothing. Coupla drink."

"Did you talk to anybody else in the house?"

"Why? Nothing say to they."

"All right. Last night. Yesterday. Where were you?"

"In room. Same. Do nothing."

"How," asked Rhys irrelevantly, "are you paying the rent? Have you got another job? Work?"

"Ah," said Parshegian expansively. "America such nice, good place! Work—not work—America gov'mint give money when not work!" He beamed at them. "Is good!"

"Oh, for God's sake," said Hunter.

But they liked him, provisionally. He was possible. Though when the women couldn't identify— They decided to keep him overnight for Katz and O'Connor to look at. They could hold him twenty-four hours without a warrant. He was annoyed about it, but they couldn't help that.

They'd just got back to the office when a new call went down: heist at a motel on Colorado.

There weren't too many motels in Glendale; it was out of the way for tourists; the few down on Colorado were the oldest in town. The first two the heisters had hit were the newest and fanciest, the Golden Key on Orange, the Ramada Inn just off the Ventura freeway; the third had been an older one over toward Burbank.

This one wasn't fancy, but looked respectable and quiet: the Green Tree Motel. There were about twenty double units. The squad was still there, Judovic talking with the desk clerk, who turned out to be the owner, Ernest Bundy. He was a big beefy man in his fifties, and he was hopping mad.

"Just walk in here, these two Goddamned punks—I swear to God, I don't know what's with people these days, the crime rate, right back to Sodom and Gomorrah and ancient Rome and for all I know Atlantis, take whatever you want, steal, kill, burn, I swear to God—"

They got him calmed down a little, and he told them about it. There were two vacancies, and he had the sign out; he and his wife lived in the front house, with the motel office in front of their living room. He hadn't really expected anybody to come by this late, but when the bell rang, naturally he went out to welcome a customer.

"Look," he said, "I'd recognize 'em. I would. It was fast—the tallest one had the gun, he just shoved it at me and said hand over the money, man. He was about five-ten, a hundred and sixty, little moustache, black hair. The other one was maybe five-eight, heavy built, clean shaven—well, he needed a shave—they both had leather jackets and jeans on. The gun, I give you three choices. A J. C. Higgins model 80, a Hi-Standard Duramatic, a Colt Huntsman."

"What?" said Rhys. "How could you—" Nobody else had given them anything on a gun.

Bundy gave them a rather evil grin. "Listen, gents, I been a gun buff all my life. I spent twenty years in the Marines—MP. I'll come in and look at some of your mug shots, if you got these punks on record I'll know 'em. It'd be no good routing your lab out, they both had on gloves. And guns I know. Reason I'd pick those three, it was the hell of a long barrel, like those have got. And"—he flexed his muscles—"I'm not as young as I was, but if the damn thing had been a revolver I might have tried to jump the guy, but an automatic's a chancy thing, there could have been one up the spout and they can be hair-trigger."

"Maybe this time they heisted the wrong man," said Rhys. "What did they get?"

"Day's receipts—being Sunday. About a hundred and eighty bucks, Goddamn them."

That, of course, interested the day men considerably, on Monday morning. Forbes went over to bring Bundy in to look at mug shots. And, Glendale being just part of the sprawling complex that was Greater Los Angeles, he might eventually be taken down to Parker Center, LAPD headquarters, to look at their much larger collection. Until and unless they finally dropped on somebody, the information about the gun was just academically interesting.

Katz and O'Connor brought Parshegian over and started a session in an interrogation room. After glancing at Rhys's report, Varallo wondered what they hoped to get out of him. And with Fuentes cleared out of the way, where was there to go on the rapes?

Delia was out somewhere, on something.

There was no point, of course, in looking up Bruce Watkins. The girl wouldn't testify. Women.

There were still a few possible suspects on the burglaries, the other heists, from Records. He was about to go out looking, on the inevitable legwork, when one of the policewomen from Communications brought in a manila envelope. The autopsy report on the stabbing victim.

There wasn't much in it. The girl was anywhere between twenty-one and twenty-five, five-five, brown and blue, a hundred and twenty. She hadn't been a virgin, but had never had a child. No evidence of alcohol in the stomach, any drugs. No evidence of recent sexual intercourse. The stomach had been nearly empty; she hadn't had a meal for several hours. She had been stabbed seven times with a fairly narrow knife, about seven eighths of an inch wide and tapering. The heart had been penetrated deeply with one blow; the other wounds would have been dangerous, not necessarily fatal. No particular anatomical knowledge was indicated.

Well, if they ever got her identified—corpses usually did get identified—some lead might show up.

# FOUR

O'Connor and Katz spent an hour talking to Parshegian, with some difficulty, and they both thought he was very possible for the rape jobs. They asked for a search warrant for his apartment, and it came through about ten o'clock. Among his rather sparse possessions there was a fair selection of pornography, some of it explicitly violent pornography; and that made him look all the likelier, of course.

When he grasped what they were talking about, he just went on denying it vehemently. And of course there was no solid evidence at all, for a charge. Neither of the women could make a positive identification; the fact that he was familiar with the premises, the hours of hospital shifts, said nothing.

He was just a possibility. They had to let him go, at least halfway convinced that he was the boy they wanted.

They emerged from that session to find that there'd been another burglary reported, the householders discovering it when they got up; Varallo and Forbes had gone out on it. Varallo had left the autopsy report on O'Connor's desk; he read it, passed it to Katz, and said, "Nothing in that. Well, she ought to get identified sooner or later."

Delia had been received with impersonal courtesy at the telephone company building on South Brand, and supplied with what she asked for. The accommodations were not particularly comfortable: she had found a cubbyhole off the main lobby with a public phone, a very narrow shelf, and a high, hard stool and had been doing her research there, her notebook balanced on the open phone books, collecting a list of all the possible Dr. Harveys.

The possibilities, of course, opened out. Mrs. Austen had been, like most residents here, mobile, driving her own car, and again like most people in L.A. and environs, hadn't up to this year thought anything of driving twenty or thirty miles on mundane errands. In the last year's Hollywood book there were six Dr. Harveys just in the Atwater section and downtown Hollywood, and he could have been much farther afield, West Hollywood, downtown L.A.—or over the other way, Eagle Rock, Pasadena, Altadena, and that would be in a different book.

She went back to the main desk and got that book, and collected seven more Dr. Harveys from that area. And another thought occurred to her: that he could have moved. Twenty years and more, by what Mrs. Potter said—if he'd had his office in Atwater when the Austens first went to him, and moved to Eagle Rock or West Hollywood or Sierra Madre, ten to one they'd have gone there to see him on the rare occasions when they needed a doctor.

And as long as she was here, better do the job thoroughly. She asked for the valley book too, and conscientiously went through that, checking all the communities in the San Fernando Valley west of Burbank. Altogether, from the three books, she came up with twenty-seven Dr. Harveys, scattered from Sherman Oaks to San Marino, Atwater to Westwood. Well, it was a big city, and Harvey not that unusual a name. Now to find which of them might have vanished from this year's books, or rather professional listings, and could be presumed to have retired.

Delia sighed, sat back from the big cumbersome books and lit a cigarette; she had borrowed a tiny glass ashtray off the main desk. She was ready for a little break, after all the fine print. She thought inconsequentially, perched there on the high stool, that the reason she'd been feeling a little unsettled lately, when she came to analyze it, was what you might call ambivalent. Because she'd got where she wanted to be—detective rank, a career cop, and the youngest female ever to make it. But on this force. Promotion slow in the LAPD, she'd qualified for the rank nearly a year before the slot opened up here. And the crime rate was up everywhere, but in this largely quiet suburb the pace wasn't anything like as fast and furious as at any LAPD precinct. They were busy, but not anything like as busy as she'd been used to being the last six and a half years before landing here: the overtime, the assignments overlapping, the paperwork piling up—and of course, up to a couple of years ago, all the extra courses, the homework. Adding to the useful skills. It wasn't exactly that she was just coasting along here, they had enough to do, but the pace had slackened very considerably, and that was probably why she was feeling—oh, let down.

She shook herself out of the little mood and went back to the phone books. Of the twenty-seven Dr. Harveys in the out-of-date books, surprisingly, six were missing from the new ones: John, Andrew, Arthur, Carl, Dudley, and Miles—Hollywood, Atwater, San Marino, Eagle Rock, and Pasadena. Dead, retired, moved to another area? Methodically she checked private listings and discovered addresses for, of course, a number of John, Carl, and Arthur Harveys: minus the M.D., who could say which were the right ones? Only Miles had appended the M.D. to his private listing, and Andrew and Dudley were missing altogether.

She looked at the list tiredly. It was after twelve; this had been a tedious job. Go and pick up some lunch, and then carry on with the doctors by phone? But she also wanted to see that cleaning woman, Rena something, who had been one of the people to find Mrs. Austen's body. She had worked for other people at that apartment, they would know where to contact her.

Delia yawned and stretched. She reached for her handbag on the floor beside her, got out her compact to powder her nose and check whether her hair needed tidying—

And suddenly, shockingly, without reason or volition, she was back there—six years back—the vaulted lobby of the old Presbyterian church in Hollywood—

—Rehearsal for Isobel's wedding, she was going to be the maid of honor, and she'd had to take time off—swing shift out of Hollenbeck Division—in uniform all ready to go straight to the job afterward—

"What the hell have you been doing to yourself?" He had maneuvered her into a corner of the lobby, looming over her, his voice rough and abrupt. "You've cut your hair off—my God, you look like hell—"

She hadn't expected him to be there; he was in his last year at Arizona University, and Isobel hadn't thought he would make the wedding, he was supposed to be on a summer dig in Guatemala.

"For heaven's sake, there's a dress code." She bristled at him, hackles rising, knowing why; she'd been bitterly sorry about her hair, the plain short cut, she'd wept like an idiot the night after she'd had it done, it made her look and feel so dowdy, the utter plain Jane.

"Ah, but it was such lovely hair, darling," he said sadly. "The nice chestnut lights in it—it's not my Delia without it—and that damned ugly uniform—"

"Don't be silly, Neil," she said crossly. "I couldn't go around with my hair loose down to my shoulders, you've got to remember the uniform's a sort of symbol, and if we expect people to respect it—"

His eyes were angry and then angrily amused. "Oh, don't you sound like a damned little prig—the honor of the school!— You do look like hell, do you know that? Like something out of Russia. The uniform, the damned uniform—you trying to forget you're female?"

And people all around, Isobel and Adam, the bridesmaids, ushers, Mr. and Mrs. Fordyce, she'd always liked them so much, nice people— "You're just as obnoxious as usual, aren't you? I can't help it if you disapprove—you don't own me, you know, whatever you—"

"Oh, no, more's the pity. I don't suppose you'll wear the uniform for the actual ceremony—or do they allow civilian dress on occasion?"

"Well, of course I've got a long dress for tomorrow, idiot—" Such a pretty dress it had been, pale turquoise—but she'd have looked so much nicer if she'd still had the long hair; dressed up for the first time in so long, high heels, she had felt a little silly in it.

"Goddamn it, I wish I hadn't come, to see you looking like this —not my girl, my Delia. Damn it, Delia, you know me better than to think I'd object to a girl having career ambitions, even funny ones—but this isn't you, not my daydreaming sentimental Delia." His hand was rough on her shoulder. "That college teacher wanted you to try your hand at writing, didn't she?"

"Just silly. So many people think they can write."

His eyes were grave and then suddenly laughing. "You remember the night at the beach when we got to quoting poetry at each other? *'Oh, Love, could Thou and I with Fate conspire To grasp this sorry scheme of Things entire—'*"

"Don't, Neil. It's a long time ago—it's too late."

"And everything decided, and you're all of twenty-one, no, just turned twenty-two. Damn it, I hate this for you—it's not your thing—letting that arrogant old bastard browbeat you into this—"

"Nobody's browbeaten me into anything, and it's nothing to do with you."

"Oh, no, you'd never listen to a word against him, would you? And it's not even Freudian, because you just don't know any damn better. You've been too close to it all your life to see it straight. I wonder, for God's sake, if he's forgotten you're a girl?"

And the organ suddenly booming, the minister bustling in, people gathering toward the body of the church— He turned and walked away from her, and the set of his wide shoulders looked stiff and angry. And she mustn't let Isobel see how angry she was. . . .

Delia snapped her handbag shut and slid off the stool. She carried all the phone books back to the main desk and thanked the girl there. Outside, the merciless heat struck her like a physical blow. She didn't really want much lunch.

She walked down the block to a hole-in-the-wall snack shop and had a chocolate malt. She collected the car from the public lot and drove over to the East Dryden Street apartment Marion Austen had owned. The unit at the back numbered Eight bore a name-slot beside the door, COSTELLO.

They were a garrulous elderly couple, both gnarled and bent. The old woman fumbled at an address book nearsightedly. "I know I've got the address besides the phone number, I always send her a Christmas card—such a nice reliable young woman, and I don't know what we'd do without her now I'm no account at doing so many things—still make shift to wash dishes and keep up the laundry, it's nothing with these automatic washers, but as to scrubbing floors and washing windows, well, I've sort of got beyond that— There, I knew I had it. . . ."

Delia didn't think they had taken in who she was at all: just someone who wanted Rena Perry's address. Which was all to the good.

It was in Burbank, on a residential street of mixed single houses and small apartments. Rena Perry lived in one upstairs unit of a middle-aged four-family building. Delia was half expecting to find her out: it was the middle of a week day; but a minute after she pushed the bell the door opened. She introduced herself, without producing the badge or mentioning police; it would only delay things and produce confusion. There wasn't anything in all this, really. "It's about Mrs. Austen's death. A little legal paperwork still getting cleared up. If you wouldn't mind answering a few questions—"

"Oh!" said Rena Perry. She looked doubtful, a little startled. "You from the lawyer, then?" She looked at Delia interestedly. "Well, any way I can help you—come in, sit down. You're lucky to catch me, I'm taking off on a little vacation. Been saving up for it."

The apartment was old, but this living room, with a collection of shabby old furniture, was scrupulously neat and tidy. Rena Perry looked around thirty-five, not a pretty woman but attractive in a humdrum sensible way: a little over medium height, just slightly plump, with a round cheerful face and curly light brown hair in an old-fashioned poodle cut. She waved Delia to a chair and said, "I'll get us some iced tea—won't take a minute, and it's hot enough to burn the devil, isn't it?" She bustled out to the kitchen, bustled back with tall glasses rattling ice cubes. "Give you sort of an illusion of feeling cooler, anyway. What was it you wanted to know?"

"Well, you were one of the people who found Mrs. Austen's body, weren't you?"

"My goodness, yes." She had a warm contralto voice, friendly sounding; her grammar slipped occasionally but she gave the overall impression of a frank and forthcoming woman, maybe not overburdened with brains but sincere and warm-hearted. "It was an awful thing. I really liked Mrs. Austen, she was a nice woman. I'd worked for her nearly seven years. Oh"— she smiled at Delia— "I guess maybe you think it's funny, me just going around doing housework for people, I could get something better. I took typing in high school, guess I could've brushed it up, but I don't think I could stand a regular office job. My sister Lois, when she came down here after she got out of high—we're from up around Lompoc, Dad had a big truck farm there—she got a job in an office and liked it fine, of course since she got married and has a couple of kids she only works part time now, receptionist for a dentist here, Dr. Dally down on Alameda—but I couldn't stand being cooped up, I guess I stayed on the farm too long. After Dad died and I came down here, I tried a couple of different jobs, but you know, I found out I can really make more money just working by the hour for people—I've never been afraid of hard work, and I get four dollars an hour—people find out I do good work, they're glad to pay it. You can pick your own hours too, I've got about twenty people I work for regular, and I don't have to punch a time clock."

"Yes, I see," said Delia. "Is it Miss or Mrs., by the way?"

"Oh, Mrs., but I divorced him a while back—it just didn't work out. But what was it you wanted to know about Mrs. Austen?" She was curious, a little wary.

"Nothing much really. It happened pretty suddenly, didn't it? I understand it was in the evening sometime—how did you happen to be there?"

"Sudden you sure could say. I liked her real well, you know. Like I say, she was one of the first people I started to do house-work for—I had a regular job back then, but I could use some extra money, and I put an ad in the paper and she called me. She said she figured she owed it to herself, get out of the hardest work, when she could afford it. I went there every Friday for a couple of hours and did the usual things, wash the kitchen and bathroom floors, and I did the windows once a month—helped with the spring cleaning. And then later I got jobs at two of the other apartments there, that nice old couple can't do much for themselves anymore, this arthritis is awful, isn't it? And those Robertsons, they're out a lot and both work—that place is usually a mess. I'm there most of Fridays, go to the Costellos and Robertsons in the morning and then Mrs. Austen in the afternoon. But now, of course, the lawyer said not to bother while he, you know, gets things straightened out. So the Robertsons gave me a key—the Costellos are always home, of course."

"It was on a Friday she died, wasn't it?"

Rena Perry sipped iced tea. "That it was," she agreed. "I'll never forget it. She seemed her usual self just at first, I got to her place about one o'clock. I went to the Costellos first that morning, finished there about ten, and Mrs. Austen let me into the Robertsons' and I went through there, dusted and cleared up, washed the breakfast dishes and cleaned the bathroom and vacuumed, and then I had the sandwich I brought with me and got to Mrs. Austen's about one. I was doing the kitchen windows that day. And it could be she felt the attack or whatever it was coming on, because just before I left she said she had a favor to ask me. She said she'd been having some dizzy spells just that day, maybe her glasses needed changing, and could I come and stay the night because she was afraid she'd take a fall. Well, I'm not one likes to be out of my own place, but she said of course she'd pay me, so I said I would." She finished her iced tea and gave a sharp sigh.

"So that's why you came back," said Delia.

"That's right. I went on—oh, I should say I left there about three o'clock, and just as I was leaving she said she was going to lie down and take a nap. I went on to this other woman I work for, Mrs. Castleman over on Buena Vista, and I finished there about five-thirty, and came home and had dinner. I guess it was around seven or a bit later I got back to Mrs. Austen's, with my night things you know, and there was Mrs. Fowler from the next apartment standing there, she said she was afraid there was something wrong because there wasn't any lights on and the door was unlocked. So we got Mr. Fowler and went in, and there she was—just like she was asleep on the bed. She must've died while she was taking her nap. It did seem awful sudden, we were all sort of shook up, you can imagine. I was sorry, I liked Mrs. Austen."

"It was Mr. Fowler who called her friends? And then the lawyer—Mr. Adler?"

"That's right. There wasn't anybody else *to* call, you know, she didn't have any family at all. He came right away."

"And who knew what doctor to call? I understand her old doctor, the one she'd been going to, had retired. But she'd just recently seen another one?"

"I don't know anything about another doctor," said Rena

Perry, her brow wrinkling. "But the lawyer asked, he was looking in her address book, but I could tell him because I remembered the name—I remembered the Friday before she'd said she
had an appointment, and it was such a funny name it stuck in
my mind. Cushing."

"You never heard her mention the other doctor she used to go
to? Dr. Harvey?"

Rena Perry shook her head slowly. "I don't recall her ever
going to a doctor, or mentioning one, all the time I worked for
her."

"Well," said Delia. "Thanks very much."

"You're welcome, I'm sure," said Rena warmly. "Not that I
could tell you anything new about it. My goodness, it is hot, isn't
it? Like I say, I'm going to treat myself to a little vacation, up at
Lake Arrowhead or some place cooler. I been working pretty
hard, guess I deserve it."

These were very ordinary people, very ordinary circumstances,
reflected Delia, getting back into the new Chevy and switching
on the air-conditioning. There couldn't be anything wrong about
all this, could there? Just the funny discrepancy between the
doctors. And another thing that just occurred to her, when and if
they found Dr. Harvey that might be cleared up very easily. She
might simply have mistaken something he'd said to her. Everyone said she had been a sensible and intelligent woman—but she
had been seventy-four. And people did make mistakes, did mis-
understand things.

Bundy didn't make any mug shots, and volunteered to go on
downtown and look at the larger collection there. It was Poor's
day off, and there were still a few burglars and heisters to hunt;
everybody was out of the office but Varallo and O'Connor at
twelve-thirty, and they were just leaving to have lunch when
something new got called in and they were chased down to
Roosevelt Junior High on South Glendale Avenue. It was, said
Sergeant Dick on the desk, a donnybrook of some kind, a couple
of kids knifed and an ambulance called.

"Now what the hell?" said O'Connor. At least, it wouldn't be
the kind of wholesale trouble too many public schools were having these days, with the forced bussing and alien kids brought

into strange neighborhoods, both sets of kids on the defensive and ripe for trouble. The county hadn't been able to foist the bussing on incorporated suburban cities like Glendale.

Patrolmen Tracy, Gallagher, and Adams were waiting on the front step of the main building to brief them. "Not that we can tell you much," said Tracy. "The kids just clammed up. There were about fifteen of 'em mixing it up when we got here—we pulled 'em apart and two of them were bleeding so we sent 'em down to Emergency. Steiner went with them. By then the principal was back—he'd been to a meeting or somewhere, probably the reason we got called, a couple of women teachers lost their heads when he wasn't around—and they're all waiting for you in his office. I don't suppose it amounts to much, but it does add up to assault, after all."

The principal was a fat, bouncy little man named Jacobs. On one side of his office were clustered about ten kids in a tight, silent little group, kids about twelve or thirteen. On the other side, a lone blond boy sat hunched in a chair looking at the floor. That one was a lot bigger, fifteen or so, a good-sized boy running to fat. His clothes were torn and he looked as if he'd had a working over. In the silent little bunch, all the kids were white except one.

"Well, well, this is all most unfortunate," said Jacobs, "and I've no idea what started it"—he looked at the black boy doubtfully—"but boys do have their little differences and prejudices—I've heard a little from Bob here, this is Bob Smith," and he indicated the fat blond kid.

"You police?" asked a shrill voice. They looked at the other kids. "It's the cops—" and there was a sort of general surge forward. "So we gotta tell about it now," and one of them took a step ahead of the rest. He was a freckled redheaded kid with a fierce, determined expression. "Cops 'll listen—ole Jacobs don't know what's goin' on most o' the time—but you cops got to be on the side o' good guys, don't you? It's on account of Jerry. You gotta see it wasn't Jerry's fault! Because they been doin' it all semester, these damn senior guys—Bob Smith an' Paul Giddings an' Jim Stover—they been stealin' a lot o' kids' lunch money an' anything else they had, say they'll beat us up good if we tell anybody—an' they did beat up Jackie Farrell real bad when he tried tell Miss Fitch, only she dint believe him because that ole Paul's so smart in her math class—an' Jackie was too scared tell anybody again—" He took a long breath. "An' we tole Jerry not to mess with them but he hadda take out after that Paul—an' when they all started beat him up we hadda do somethin'—I got Bill an' Tom an' Larry an' some others just sorta come up—we hadda do somethin'—"

"I got to say it was all my fault," said the black boy.

"It most certainly was," said Jacobs severely. "Civilized children in a civilized school do not carry knives, Jerry. Er—this is Jerry Cohane."

The black boy rubbed his ear, looking a little embarrassed. "I had a reason, sir," he said. He was a tall thin boy, maybe thirteen, with sharp features; he was very black. His shirt was torn half off him and his nose had been bleeding, but he looked more self-possessed than any of the rest of them. He looked earnestly at Varallo and O'Connor. "I tell you just how it happened, you want to listen."

"We're listening," said O'Connor.

"Like, I mean, my dad's a deacon at our church and I know what's right 'n' wrong," said Jerry Cohane with some dignity. "But you gotta stand up for yourself. I been goin' to Le Conte Junior High in Hollywood, an' there're some tough guys there, but man, we gonna move to Glendale, everybody say oh, brother, wow, Glendale, snotty all-white town, you gonna get it good, man. And I don't want any trouble with anybody, but you gotta stand up for yourself. I got that knife, an' anybody gave me any trouble I just let 'em see I can protect myself, that's all. But" —he looked around at the little crowd of youngsters—"they all been OK to me, real friendly, no trouble. Only they told me about these senior kids, how they been doing—and I make up my mind, they come try to steal my money, I show 'em I can be just as tough as they can. My dad says guys like that aren't tough at all, just bullies, they back down if you stand up to 'em."

"And they did, and you did, and they backed down?" asked O'Connor.

"Yes, *sir*. Today was the first time they come after me, and when I show the knife I guess that Paul and Jim figure it's just bluff, they jump me and try to take it off me. But you gotta stand

up for yourself," said Jerry. "Oh, my dad is gonna be mad as sin
at me about this."

"For carrying the knife," said Varallo.

"And fighting. Not bein' a Christian. He'll say all about turnin'
the other cheek." Jerry reflected for a long moment. "I guess," he
said, "things was a lot different when Jesus was down here
preaching, you know?"

It took some time and paperwork and it would all be for nothing, or very little; but they had to go by the book. They took
Jerry Cohane and Bob Smith in, and called the parents. They
checked with the hospital, and the other two boys weren't much
hurt, could be released to their parents.

Mrs. Smith came in, a fat woman with a nasal voice, and told
them it was all a mistake of some kind, Bobby had always been
one for mischief but he never meant nothing bad, really, and she
couldn't call her husband, he drove a truck for a laundry and she
didn't know where he was. They explained about the juvenile
court hearing, probably next week, and let him go with her.

The Cohanes didn't show up for a while. "Dad's probably at
the church," said Jerry. "He works nights at a factory makes air-
plane parts." They got him a Coke from the machine down the
hall and he thanked them politely. He sat drinking it in silence,
and when he finished it he went over to drop the can into
O'Connor's wastebasket and wiped his mouth thoughtfully. "I
just thought of somethin'," he said. "I can tell him I was de-
fendin' the meek an' lowly. Could be that'll get me off the hook."

When the Cohanes had come and gone, Varallo sat back in his
desk chair and laughed. "Now that's a smart kid. Play both ends
against the middle. And we never got any lunch. *Dannazione!*
I'll be damned if that hadn't gone right out of my mind—that
Reynaldo. Fresno never got back to me, damn it. Well." He
picked up the phone.

"Probably nothing in it," said O'Connor.

"Just being thorough." After a delay he got the sergeant he
had talked to before, who apologized.

"Say, didn't anybody call you? I left a message, but we've
been kind of busy here with a nut sniping at people. This Rey-

naldo—we located his mother, but she says he's not there, hasn't seen him for months and doesn't know where he is."

"Oh. Well, that's that." Varallo passed that on to O'Connor. And if Reynaldo was one of the motel heisters, his mug shot was in their books and Bundy would probably have spotted him.

Burt came in and said, "Occasionally we do spot one for you. This new burglary—the guy lifted off a back screen and obligingly left us a nice clear set of prints. I just made them for you. He's one Derek Berger, just off P.A. from his first adult charge—another burglary. There's an address in Burbank."

"I don't know why we can't enjoy the air-conditioning in peace," said O'Connor, annoyed. But Boswell and Harvey came in just then and he basely pulled rank and sent them over to look for Berger. He wasn't there; the neighbors said he'd moved last week. So they contacted Sacramento to get a make on his car and put out an A.P.B. on it.

At five o'clock Patrolman Harper called in with a new homicide. A householder over on Oak Street, annoyed at the strange car parked in front of his house since Sunday morning, had finally taken a closer look at it and there was a body in the back seat. A woman.

"The hot weather," said O'Connor sourly. "It always shoots the homicide rate up." He got up and put on his jacket, tightened his tie. "For my sins, I've put in sixteen years at this damned job, and when I'm eligible for a pension in nine more I'm thinking about going up the coast to some peaceful little farm town away from the jungle—room for Maisie to run, and the boy too—maybe grow a vegetable garden."

Varallo laughed. "That I'll believe when I see it. I can't see you in a small town, *amigo.*"

They rode over in the Gremlin; it was across town, a couple of blocks up from San Fernando Road. The squad was waiting, and there were a few curious people standing around front lawns up the block, which was a block of small single houses. The householder was an agitated middle-aged man named Swoboda. All he could say was that the car hadn't been there when he went to bed Saturday night, and had been there on Sunday morning.

It was an old Pontiac four-door sedan, tan under a liberal coat of dirt. All the windows were down. The woman was lying on the back seat, face up. Just at first glance it looked as if she'd been strangled. Not raped; she was wearing a light blue pants suit, and it was neatly in place on the corpse.

There wasn't much they could do on the scene. They called the plate number in, and summoned the morgue wagon and the lab. Five minutes later they got a make on the car; it was registered to Maureen Miller at an address on Pacific Avenue. Burt and Thomsen showed up in a lab truck, and when the morgue wagon came they got a back door open by depressing the handle with a ball peen hammer, and with some difficulty got the body out without, hopefully, destroying any possible prints. The body was limp.

"Saturday night," said O'Connor. "Rigor's come and gone." She had been a woman somewhere in her thirties by her looks, with brown hair; you couldn't tell now whether she'd been pretty, the face bloated and eyes bulging. Burt fastened plastic bags over her hands in case there was anything helpful under her nails, and the morgue wagon took her off. The car would be towed in and gone over; but Thomsen shoved the button on the glove compartment with his pen, it popped open, and on top of a little miscellany there, all correct, was the registration.

"Maureen Miller," said Varallo. "If that's her."

"Well, I'm not going to do anything about it tonight," said O'Connor through a yawn. "See what Goulding and the lab say. Hunt up her friends tomorrow."

Varallo took him back to headquarters and dropped him off, and drove up across town to the house on Hillcroft Road. His roses were blooming profusely, and heat or no, on his day off he was going to have to prune all the dead blooms.

In the kitchen, he found Laura getting out ice cubes. "I heard you drive in. It's still too hot to eat. Let's have a civilized drink before dinner—with lots of ice—and then I've got cold meat loaf and potato salad and you can always make a sandwich before bed."

"That's fine with me, *amante*." He kissed her again, his lovely Laura with the brandy-brown hair. In the living room, with the air-conditioner humming, blonde little Ginevra was playing with a big stuffed cat; belatedly realizing he was home, she came squealing to be picked up. There wasn't a sound from the nursery; Johnny was a good sleeper. "Half an hour, and bed for you, young lady," said Laura.

They sat quite a while over the drinks as the sun got lower, talking desultorily. Presently Laura asked, "Are you all still liking Delia Riordan to work with?"

"Oh, she's a good girl," said Varallo sleepily. "All business, no nonsense."

"I like her very much," said Laura. "She's a nice girl. Of course, a bit like an iceberg—only the one tenth showing, as it were." Varallo laughed. "Well, it's so. I think she's rather deep, that girl. Of course, that old father of hers—he must have been quite a character, strong influence on her—and never knowing her mother—"

"He still is a character as far as I know. Yes, I suppose so." He wasn't much interested. He yawned. "Tell you what. I've got to do something about those roses on Wednesday, then suppose you get all dressed up and I'll take you out to dinner at that fancy new place on Pacific." The Andersons next door were always willing baby-sitters.

"Fine with me, but can we afford it?"

"Oh, the hell with money," said Varallo.

About nine o'clock, as Rhys and Hunter were sitting idly talking about the rapes, a man came into the detective office and looked at them doubtfully. "The guy downstairs said to come up here and see the detectives. Are you the detectives?"

"Yes, sir. What's it about?"

"Well, my God, it's Rosalie," said the man. He had a paper crumpled in one hand; he came up to Rhys's desk and spread it out. "I never saw it till twenty minutes ago. I go across the street like usual, middle of the evening, for a sandwich and a cup of coffee, somebody's left a paper, I pick it up. And my God, there's Rosalie. Murdered! I don't believe it, but it is. Who the hell would want to murder Rosalie?"

"Good," said Rhys. "We hoped the picture would get her identified. What's your name, sir, and who was she?"

"I'm Jack Sinclair, I work at Acme Towing on Los Feliz," he said. He was a stocky dark fellow about twenty-six. "Her name's Rosalie Wegman, I knew her from Talberts' Chevy agency. I hadn't seen her in a year or so but that's her all right—" Burt had got a good clear picture; it wasn't very flattering, but of course the girl was dead.

"That's fine, Mr. Sinclair. A Chevy agency?"

"Yeah, that's right. I worked there a couple of years, only the car business is fallen off, they laid off a couple of us mechanics and half the salesmen. Rosalie was the cashier there, did the books."

"Ever date her?"

"No, I just knew her at work—she seemed like a nice girl, friendly. I got married just the first year I worked there, I wasn't—"

The phone rang on Hunter's desk and he took it up. "I want the police," said a careful voice. "Is this the Glendale police?" The call would be relayed up from the desk.

"Yes, sir. Detective Hunter speaking."

"My name is Talbert, Herbert Talbert. I have only just seen tonight's *News-Press,* and I am calling to tell you that the young woman pictured on the front page is a Miss Rosalie Wegman who used to work for me."

"Thank you very much, sir. We'd like to know anything you can tell us about her."

"I'm afraid I don't know much about her personally, officer, but any help I can give you—"

"May I have your address, sir? One of our detectives will probably want to talk to you. Thanks very much for calling." He hadn't taken his hand off the phone when it rang again.

"Glendale Police Headquarters, Detective Hunter."

"Oh. I thought I'd better call, the paper said—it's about the picture—I know who it is." A high female voice this time. "Her name's Rosalie Wegman."

"May I have your name, miss?"

"I'm Sharon Taylor. I didn't know her very good, she hadn't worked there long, but of course I recognized her."

"Yes, Miss Taylor. May I have your address? You worked with her? Where?"

"At Denny's restaurant—I mean, she was the cashier and I'm one of the waitresses, but—"

Rhys had finished talking with Sinclair, who was on the way

out. In the next fifteen minutes seven more people called to identify Rosalie—the manager of Denny's restaurant, two other
waitresses, three salesmen who had worked at Talberts' agency,
and a girl friend.

"It's funny," said Hunter, "that nobody who knew her seemed
to look at the paper till the middle of the evening. It's been on
the street since four o'clock."

"People watch a little TV after dinner and then settle down
with the paper," said Rhys. At which point they got called out to
a dead body, but it was nothing to work, just made more paperwork: an elderly man dropping dead as he came out of a movie
theater downtown. There was identification on him; they had to
break the news to the family. It had probably been a heart attack. The autopsy would say.

On Tuesday morning, with Forbes off, there were two more
burglaries reported overnight. As well as the dead body, and
Rosalie. It had been a middling busy night for Rhys and Hunter.

O'Connor and Katz had already gone out on Rosalie.

At ten of nine Burt came in with a handbag. "From the Miller
car," he said. "Nothing but smudges on it."

Varallo had been typing an initial report on that, and left it
without regret. "So let's have a look. Female opinion, Delia?"

She came to look. It was a small blue plastic bag, fairly new.
He upended it on his desk and just a few things fell out of it. "It's
an evening bag," said Delia, "not a workaday one, Vic."

"Yes." There was a change purse; it held a twenty, four ones,
and some change. A powder puff and lipstick. A full package of
Tareyton cigarettes and a disposable lighter. And a birthday
card, crumpled in its envelope. It was a sentimental, saccharine
little card with a verse about friendship, and it was signed in a
round careful scrawl, *all the best always, Dorrie.* There was also
a bunch of keys.

"I suppose," said Varallo, "we'd better start to do something
about this."

"I should think so," said Delia.

"So, come on," said Varallo, getting up with a sigh.

# FIVE

Denny's was a chain of restaurants, medium-priced quick-service places sans liquor licenses, and they were open from 10 A.M. to midnight. When the manager of the local one had called in, he had left a private address, and it was there that O'Connor and Katz talked to him on Tuesday morning. His name was James Hardin; his wife let them in, at a rambling old California bungalow on Myrtle Street, and left them alone in the living room. He was a nondescript man about forty-five.

"I can't tell you much about the girl," he said. "She'd only been with us a few months. She was very efficient, friendly with the customers, well liked—seemed to be a nice girl. Well, I wouldn't know anything about her family. I can't get over her being murdered, of all things—hardly believed my eyes when I saw the paper last night. Oh, yes, of course she'd told me she was quitting the job—I was sorry to lose her. She said she was thinking of going up to San Francisco, she liked the climate better."

"Yes," said O'Connor. "She'd already bought her ticket, she was going up on the Daylight on Sunday."

"What?" said Hardin. "She hadn't any business doing that, she was supposed to stay on the job till the end of the month, give me time to find a replacement. She seemed like a responsible girl—"

"She'd definitely agreed to that?"

"Well, I took it for granted. I really didn't know much about her, and it's put me in a little bind, have to fill in myself until I find somebody—" He was annoyed.

They had her address from the girl friend who had called in. It turned out to be a tiny single guesthouse on the back of a lot on Doran, an old frame house in front. It was on a corner, and the guesthouse faced on the side street. At the front house, Mrs. Mildred Lossner was much taken aback at the badges, the news of the murder; she didn't know a thing about it, she saw the *Ledger* instead of the *News-Press*. She was incredulous and shocked. "That young girl! Murdered! The things that happen nowadays—" She was an elderly, white-haired woman with a cane, evidently living alone. She was cooperative, answered questions readily.

Rosalie Wegman had rented the little house for nearly two years. It had originally been built, many years back, for Mrs. Lossner's son when he first got married, and now he had a couple of married children. But it brought in a little rent, she asked a hundred and twenty-five a month for it, seemed sinful but money not worth much these days. She really hadn't seen much of the girl, the other entrance on the side street as they could see, but of course she'd have had friends come to see her from time to time— "I'm a bit hard of hearing myself, so it didn't matter to me, but you do have to think about neighbors and I'd asked her not to play her stereo loud or anything like that—but a pretty, lively young girl, she'd have friends, she'd be out some evenings and her friends in—oh, I didn't know any of them at all, I didn't pay attention to her going and coming—" And yes, Rosalie had a car, one of those VW bugs.

Rosalie had told her she was moving, a week ago today, but she hadn't thought she'd gone yet, so she hadn't been into the little house. When it was empty, she'd see about getting it cleaned, advertise for a new tenant. She handed over the keys. "I just can't get over it, such a pretty girl, so friendly and happy—"

It was a very little place, a tiny living room, bedroom just big enough for a double bed and three-drawer chest, a cubbyhole kitchen, a bathroom about three feet square with a shower, no tub. But it was a good deal cheaper and afforded more privacy than a regular apartment. She couldn't have rented the shabbiest, smallest apartment anywhere here for that money.

And it was obvious that she'd been getting ready to leave, imminently. One shabby old leather suitcase was standing at the foot of the bed, already packed; a second was open on the bed, in the process of being packed. She had been doing a neat, efficient job: shoes carefully bagged, underwear, dresses, blouses, and pants carefully folded. There was a plastic cosmetic bag waiting on top of the bedroom chest, nothing in it yet: a selection of cosmetics still in the medicine chest, face powder, a plastic cup holding half a dozen lipsticks, face cream, liquid foundation, eye makeup, shampoo. In the narrow wardrobe with sliding doors were hanging half a dozen dresses, a couple of pairs of slacks, some blouses; more shoes stood on the floor. Next to the packed suitcase was waiting a large canvas totebag with a zipper; probably the rest of the clothes would have gone into that.

O'Connor took down one of the dresses and looked at it. "I think Katy would say, a little flashy." It was a hot pink sheath with a mandarin collar.

"Hm?" said Katz, wandering in from the kitchen. "She'd nearly cleaned out the refrigerator—whatever else about her, a pretty good housekeeper, everything cleaned up. Just about a pint of milk left, orange juice, a couple of eggs. Few cans, half a box of cereal. You come across an address book?"

"Negative."

"So it was in her handbag. Practically everybody's got an address book." Katz looked at the suitcases. "And in all probability, the handbag snatched just after she was stabbed, in the confusion when that little crowd came out of the railroad station to see what had happened."

"Probably so."

"Well, this place hasn't much to say. Let's go see that girl who called in."

Her name was Shirley Feldman, and she was a checkout clerk at the big Safeway down on South Central. As O'Connor pulled into the lot he cast a look at the tall rectangle of the Memorial Hospital catercorner across Los Feliz.

Shirley Feldman was a tiny little thing, dark and pretty. She flushed excitedly at the badge in O'Connor's hand and said, "Oh, sure, anything I can do to help you—it isn't time for my break, but I can ask the manager—I told him about it already—"

He'd have liked to sit in on the questioning, avidly interested. He let her go, and of course there wasn't anywhere to talk in the market; they went outside and sat in O'Connor's Ford with the air-conditioning on, she in the back seat and O'Connor and Katz twisted around to watch her.

"Had you known Rosalie long, Miss Feldman?"

"Oh, yes, I knew her in high school—we both graduated from Burbank High. She was twenty-four, the same age as me. Well, I knew her pretty well, sure, but we weren't best friends or anything like that. She knew a lot more people—she'd worked around a lot. She liked change, she'd get bored with a job and switch to another, you know? She was good at figures, she never had any trouble finding jobs."

"Could you tell us anything about any boyfriends?"

"Well," said Shirley, "she dated quite a few men. We'd double-dated some, a few times. Sure."

"So you can give us some names?"

"Well, Fred Buckman, he's a mechanic at a Shell station. And Gil Rogers, he's one of the projectionists at the Roxy Theater. Howie Stone, he's at a VW agency, he got her car for her last year, the one she was driving gave out on her. But—" she hesitated. "I don't want to give you any wrong ideas, but Rosalie was always—sort of changing around, she never went steady with anybody that I knew about. I hadn't seen her in about three weeks. I—well, you see, I've just got engaged, and we're going to be married next month, we can't afford a big wedding but it'll be in the church, and there are a lot of plans to make. I talked to her on the phone about nine or ten days ago, and now I remember I'm pretty sure she said something about a new boyfriend, but I didn't pay much attention, because—well—you know, she did have a new one pretty often."

"Yes, I see," said O'Connor, and added casually, "did she sleep around?"

She looked away, uneasily embarrassed. "I—I don't really know. She wouldn't talk about anything like that to me, because she'd know how I feel about it. I mean, some girls think that's perfectly OK if you really like the fellow, only I don't think that way. But, well, Rosalie got around a lot more than I did and knew a lot more people—I really don't know, I just wouldn't like to say."

"What about her family?"

"Oh, her parents were divorced years ago. Her mother got

married again a couple of years ago and moved up to Santa Barbara—oh, I wouldn't know what her name is now. I never knew
anything about her father."

"Hell," said O'Connor absently. They ought to notify the relatives.

"I can tell you about some other people who knew her—some
of the girls we both knew. I don't know if any of them had seen
her later than I had. There's Terry Enright—and Patricia
Mathias—of course some of the girls we both knew in school are
married, we'd sort of lost touch, but I think Rosalie had double-
dated with Pat—"

It filled in a little background, but wasn't immediately helpful.
"Maybe one of these people will know who the new boyfriend
was," said Katz.

"And maybe," said O'Connor, "he didn't have one damn thing
to do with it, Joe. Well, we can go and ask."


The apartment building where Maureen Miller had lived was
a newish modern one on Pacific Avenue, close to downtown:
about sixteen units, with carports across the back. Varallo and
Delia went in and looked around. No manageress on the
premises: a good many places like this were owned by big man-
agement corporations. The eight downstairs doors were labeled
with names, none of them hers. They climbed a narrow stair and
went looking down a narrow hall; at the end they found a door
whose name-slot said MILLER. Varallo tried the biggest Yale key
and it opened the door.

It was the average apartment of its class and age: living room,
kitchen with space for a table and chairs, a square bedroom with
a bath off it: a fair-sized walk-in closet. There were some individual touches: a latch-hook wall hanging of a forest scene over
the couch, a couple of hanging plants in macramé hangers in
front of the living room window. The furniture was nondescript
but in good taste, not shabby. The kitchen was immaculately
clean, no dishes left out, the counters polished.

Delia left Varallo nosing around the living room and went
back to the bedroom. "Here's the workaday bag," she reported.
It was on a straight chair beside the bed, a big practical beige
leather bag. It was stuffed full of the usual clutter a handbag

collected: there was a wallet with her driver's license, Social Security card, a Visa card, a Sears credit card; there was a stray
dollar bill and a little change in that. Receipts, used tissues, an
old compact, a couple of ballpoint pens. Delia put it down and
looked in the closet. That was very neat too, shoes tidily put
away in bags, a cardboard blanket chest on the shelf, clothes
separated into blouses, dresses, pants. On the whole quite smart
clothes, not expensive but good timeless design, nothing flamboyant. There was one good winter coat, black wool with a lynx
collar. And rather unexpectedly, no fewer than five long evening
dresses: black, coral, turquoise, beige, pale green.

She came back to the living room and said, "I wonder why she
wasn't carrying her regular wallet with her driver's license when
she was out in her own car."

"We may find out," said Varallo. He had found an address
book beside the phone on one of the pair of end tables flanking
the couch. He handed it to her, open. "Among about twenty
names, see Doris. I rather think we start there, because—"

"Yes," said Delia. Doris Fogel, an address on Burchett, a
phone number. "Because of the birthday card. Because that was
an evening bag, and it was the one she was carrying Saturday
night, so it looks as if she got the card then—it hadn't been
through the mail. So possibly she saw Doris some time that
night."

"Elementary." Varallo was dialing the number. She sat down
beside him on the couch. "Mrs. Fogel? This is Detective Varallo
of the Glendale Police. We'd like to talk to you about Mrs.
Maureen Miller. . . . I'm sorry to have to tell you that she's
dead. She was found dead in her car yesterday afternoon. . . .
Yes, ma'am. Well, we're not sure yet. . . . Will you be at home
for the next hour or so? Thanks very much, Mrs. Fogel, we'll be
with you shortly." He hung up the phone. "Just short of hysterics," he said to Delia. "Emotional, sentimental, shallow female, at a guess. Well, whatever happened to Maureen it didn't
happen here. We'd better go and see what Doris can tell us."

They were driving the Gremlin. On the way up Pacific, after a
little silence, Delia asked suddenly, "Why did you pick the job,
Vic? I heard something about you holding rank on another
force—"

Varallo laughed a little ruefully. "You and Laura. When we got married and came down here, she said I was a damn fool to join this force and start all over at the bottom. But it was the job I knew. Yes, twelve years on the force up in Contera, and I resigned as captain." She didn't ask why. "And it's a safe job. That is, a secure job. Whatever happens, there have to be police. It can be pure drudgery, of course, and God knows most of what we see is the dregs—the muck at the bottom of humanity, and the senseless tragedies. But somebody has to deal with it. And on any job, there are things you don't like."

"True," said Delia thoughtfully.

"You get so you leave it at the office, and forget it until the next shift. And there are other things in life than the job you're doing."

Delia didn't say anything to that; she was silent the rest of the way up Pacific.

The address on Burchett was another apartment, newer and bigger than the one Maureen had lived in; it was built around a courtyard with a pool. Doris Fogel lived in one of the rear units; she opened the door to them promptly. She was a tall thin blonde with protuberant, pale blue eyes, and she had been crying. She'd evidently just got up when Varallo called, and had hastily put on a pink nylon housecoat over her nightdress, a pair of fluffy feathered mules. She had dabbed on some lipstick; she was shaken and upset, but she cast a faintly interested look at Delia; most of her interest was on Maureen.

"I can't believe she's dead—you just struck me all of a heap—you mean somebody killed her? Somebody—oh, my God. Maureen never did anything to make anybody want to kill her! Ever since you called, I've been trying to take it in—" She was crying gently again.

"We don't know much about Mrs. Miller," said Delia. "Had you known her long? Do you know where she worked?"

Doris Fogel nodded. "Yes, sure, we knew each other ever since we both worked at the Game Room in Hollywood, I was one of the waitresses and she was the hostess. It was before she got divorced—her husband was a lush, always losing jobs. The last three years she was hostess at the Alpine up in Montrose, and I'm at the Heather Inn in Atwater—yeah, both of us hostesses." That, of course, explained the evening gowns. "Oh, my God, I just can't think of Maureen dead—"

"When did you see her last?"

She fumbled for another tissue in her pocket. "I—it was S-Saturday night," she choked. "Oh, my God, it was her birthday— she was thirty-four. Oh, my God. See, the two of us both being divorced and, you know, alone, even with the good jobs and all— well, it can be a drag—we sort of teamed up, we were good friends, liked the same things. We'd go to each other's places sometimes on our days off, shopping, like that. And oh, my God, Saturday was her birthday—we're both off on Saturdays—and we went out to dinner, I took her out for dinner for her birthday—"

"It looks as if she was killed on Saturday night," Varallo told her.

She crumpled the tissue in both hands and looked at them wildly. "Saturday night? Right then? I thought maybe some- body broke in— Oh, my God."

"You went out to dinner," said Delia gently. "What time?"

Her mouth worked convulsively. "I—I—we went to Damon's. It wasn't—wasn't much of a celebration, but we both got dressed up—and—we were going to take my car and then at the last min- ute we decided to take hers, I've been having a little trouble get- ting mine started, I guess—a new battery—"

So she had forgotten to take her driver's license.

"I suppose we got there about seven—and I gave her her birthday card—wished I could've got her a real nice present, but she said it didn't matter— It must have been about nine-thirty when we came out." She paused. "But it couldn't be—oh, my God."

They waited, and Delia asked, "Do you know if she dated any man regularly?"

Doris shook her head. "She wasn't keen on getting married again. I wouldn't mind, find a nice guy with a little money—but that's what I was telling you— It's a real drag, being alone." Her voice was dull now. "But—well—Saturday night—you see, we came out and started back—for her place—and it all seemed kind of nothing, just out for dinner on her birthday—and I said why didn't we go somewhere and have a couple of after-dinner drinks, make it a better celebration—and she laughed and said why not. So we went to this place on San Fernando Road, it was a nice place, not a cheap bar, the Casino it's called—neither of us had ever been there before—and we had a couple of brandies. And we got talking to these two fellows sitting at the next table— I mean, they were friendly and there wasn't anything wrong, the blue jokes or anything like that. Just nice ordinary fellows—the one I was talking to, his name was Joe Esquibel, and he asked me to go somewhere and dance. I didn't want to leave Maureen, but she knew I like to dance, she said go ahead, she was going home pretty quick anyway—I guess it'd be about eleven-thirty then. So I—so I did—this Joe Esquibel, I don't know where he works or anything, but he seemed like a nice guy, we went to this place has a dance floor and combo, up on Verdugo Road— and he brought me home about 2 A.M., he was a perfect gentle-man, no funny stuff, no passes. Everything just ordinary."

Varallo exchanged a glance with Delia. "That was the last time you saw her?"

She nodded. "She was just—sitting there with this other guy when we left. There were other people all around. She said she was going home in a few minutes."

"Do you remember the other man's name? He mentioned it?"

She swallowed. "Yes, he did, but I was talking to Joe—it was Ed. Ed something. I don't remember the last name. I don't re-member much about him—it was pretty dark in there—well, I guess he was about thirty—kind of dark hair, I guess—he talked just ordinary, no accent or anything—well, he just had on slacks and a light-colored shirt, I guess. You don't think *he* could've done anything to Maureen? Oh, my God—"

She wouldn't, of course, be able to identify him. It had been dark in the bar; she didn't remember anything else about him.

In the car, Delia said in exasperation, "How any two females could be so stupid—and on the surface quite respectable women, not the type to go casually sleeping around. To drop into a bar and pick up a couple of strange men—honestly. You'd think any-body would know better."

"Yes, the informal manners people use nowadays—there is such a thing as elementary caution."

"I suppose we go and ask questions at the bar."

"It won't be open yet. I think I do, see what kind of place it is.

You can finish the report and put all this in. I'll drop you back at the office."

O'Connor and Katz got to Howie Stone about two-thirty. They had heard this and that about Rosalie from several other people by then, so they weren't surprised at what Howie had to say. He was a good-looking brash fellow in his late twenties, the typical salesman; they found him at the VW agency on Colorado. He was shocked to hear about Rosalie—a damn nice girl, he said. He hadn't seen the story in the paper. All the nuts around these days, it's a damn shame. "Well, I got to know her when we both worked at a Chevy agency a couple of years ago. Well, yeah, we'd dated some."

"Anything more?" asked O'Connor.

He shrugged. "Well, look, you know how it is. Rosie was a pretty easy-going chick, but there wasn't anything serious with either of us. I guess she pretty well played the field. When I say sure, we had a thing going for a while, it wasn't serious, see what I mean. It was off and on."

They'd heard much the same thing from the other two boy-friends mentioned by Shirley Feldman. Neither of those had acted at all nervous; of course the *News-Press* story had said there was a witness to the crime, and conscious of innocence they wouldn't be nervous. This one was acting much the same.

"Did she stick to one at a time as a rule?" asked Katz.

He gave them an automatic winning smile. He wasn't the type given to introspection or deep thought. "I—well, I just wouldn't know. We'd go out somewhere, end up back at her place, and then I might not see her for a week or ten days—I was dating a couple of other girls, no reason she shouldn't— It wasn't anything serious."

They headed back for the office, and Katz said resignedly, "The good-time girl. She got around. And so far nobody but Shirley mentions the new boyfriend. It could be that he got serious and she didn't feel the same way, and that's why she was clearing out to Frisco. Talbert would be scandalized, wouldn't he?" They had seen Talbert, a precise elderly man who could only tell them that she'd been an efficient employee: had left the job, he supposed, for a better paying one.

"Well, we may hear some more from the waitresses at Denny's, the other girls she knew."

It was called the Casino Bar and Grill, and it looked a bit classier than some other places along San Fernando Road. Inside, it wasn't very big, but was comfortably furnished with big leather chairs, a vinyl upholstered banquette booth in each corner, fat candles in glass jars on all the tables; there was a mahogany bar with high-backed bar stools, and a TV suspended above it at an angle, turned off now. The place was just open, and there were only a couple of customers in, both male, both eating sandwiches.

The bartender was casually friendly, blinking at the badge, not disturbed by a cop coming in. "Well, the night barkeep'd have been on, if it was late Saturday night," he said. "Sure, we got a good many regulars come in all the time, but also a lot of casuals, naturally. This is a quiet spot, officer, we don't get trouble here—like the noisy drunks, the fights. The owner likes it nice and dignified, kind of a family place. He's here now, you want to see him?"

The owner was a bland, dapper middle-aged man named Sellers. He listened to what Varallo had to say, shrugged, and said, "Well, we try to keep the decent atmosphere here, but we can't be responsible for what the customers do after they leave, no? That's a hell of a thing, but what can a woman expect, when she picks up a stranger? I don't suppose it'd have been one of our regular customers, they're all respectable types—drop in a couple of times a week, spend a couple of hours over a few drinks. But you can ask Olly if he noticed anything, he's the bartender comes on at seven."

Varallo reflected that he'd be doing a little overtime here tonight. It was Rhys's night off and Hunter would be sitting on night watch alone. And he hoped somebody had remembered that Richard Bland was due to be arraigned this afternoon and had gone over to the courthouse to cover it, offer the formal evidence.

Delia finally finished the initial report on Maureen and got back to the doctors. The Johns, Carls, and Arthurs listed at private addresses with no M.D.s appended; one of whom would, hopefully, be the Dr. Harvey practicing last year, not professionally listed this year. Common names, and this wasn't a sampling of the entire L.A. area—and when a man retired, he sometimes moved his residence. But make a stab at it. There were twelve Johns, nine Carls, and fourteen Arthurs. She started with the Johns, and got an answer to six calls of the twelve. A couple of women were highly amused at the notion that their particular Johns should be mistaken for M.D.s. One man was completely incredulous and said, "Lady, are you kidding? I'm a lineman for Ma Bell, see?" The other calls were unanswered; she'd have to cover those again. She started in on the Carls, and on the third call was rewarded by a brisk masculine response, "Dr. Harvey speaking." She explained what she was after, thinking that he sounded rather young to be her quarry, and he said, "Oh, I see. I was only in private practice for five years or so. I'm now on the teaching staff at UCLA Medical. And I can say definitely that I never had a Mrs. Austen as a patient."

"Well, thank you very much," said Delia. It was nearly four o'clock, and her left hand was cramped from holding the telephone. Poor and Boswell had brought in a burglary suspect to question, and now let him go. Poor had just said that they still had this Smotherman to locate, he supposed they'd better go and do it, when Patrolman Tracy came in looking annoyed, with a big redheaded man in tow, and said, "Here's that burglar you're after. Berger. The A.P.B. on his car—I just spotted it up on Broadway."

He was annoyed, of course, because it was the end of the Traffic shift; he'd been on his way in when he spotted the plate number, and now would be delayed getting off shift for fifteen minutes or so, making the report. "And I suppose you'll want to tow the car in, it's parked in the six hundred block of West Broadway. Here are the keys."

They already had the warrant on Berger; Poor took him over to book him in, and Delia called downstairs and talked to Burt, who was annoyed at being deflected from examining the Miller car. But he and Thomsen went out and brought in Berger's car, and most of the loot from his latest burglary seemed to be in it, which was nice. They started bagging it for evidence.

Delia was late getting home, the traffic was murder and the sun glaring on cement as she drove into it, heading west, had produced a slight headache before she turned onto Waverly Place. She wasn't much interested in what there was for dinner. She came in the back door, thinking about a long cold shower, and at the foot of the stairs glanced into the living room.

Alex and Steve were there watching an old rerun on TV, but of course they'd heard her come in. Alex swung the wheelchair around and looked at her shrewdly—still handsome, cocksure old Alex with his crest of silver white hair. "You look a mite tired."

"I am," said Delia. "I am damned tired of dealing with all these idiots who get themselves into trouble because they don't use good sense—or haven't any to use."

He laughed. "People were always like that. Part of the job."

"Dinner any time you want," said Steve comfortably.

She went upstairs, thinking that Alex's birthday was next month—he'd be eighty years old. She hadn't any idea what to get him. Have to think of something. . . . Maureen Miller and her birthday celebration; you would think any woman with any sense at all— That silly sentimental birthday card . . . Birthday presents. That target pistol—it was still in its box on top of the bureau. Oh, well, she thought—men.

Dick Hunter was sitting on night watch alone; Rhys was off. He wondered if Bob was helping his mother deliver another litter of puppies—she bred Cairn terriers and Bob had mentioned that one of them was expecting puppies. He yawned—it was dull alone in the big office—and thought he'd like a dog but not a silly little one like that, and besides you couldn't keep a dog when you worked and lived alone. It wouldn't be fair to the dog. He'd been dating a pretty nice girl lately, Claire was pretty and lots of fun, but he didn't know if he wanted to settle down and turn into a family man just yet—he was only twenty-nine, there was time enough. Bob Rhys didn't seem to be in any hurry either, a couple of years older.

He'd brought a paperback with him to pass the time, but he couldn't get interested in it, and he didn't get any calls at all until nine-thirty. Then it was a call to the Memorial Hospital, and he thought, God, the rapist again. He got there in a hurry, and found McLeod's squad in the lot and a little crowd of people in the entrance to the Emergency wing.

This time the rapist had missed. And of course he'd been off schedule; it had only been a few minutes past nine.

This nurse was named Ruth Boyd, and she was working in Emergency. She was a short heavy woman, at least in her fifties, she was indignant and at the same time thrilled at the excitement, and more than willing to tell the story all over again to Hunter.

"Times it pays to carry a little too much weight, and I'm just thankful it was me he jumped and not one of the younger women. But heavens, when you think, he must have been out there lying in wait, and how many nights he'll have done that, with nobody suspecting— It was my shoes," she explained to Hunter. There were a couple of interns, four or five other nurses, a couple of burly men in white coats, standing around; she sat on the narrow padded bench just inside the ambulance entrance and fanned herself with her handkerchief, though the air-conditioning was on. "I had a suspicion they'd be giving me trouble— they're new shoes—so I brought along a comfortable old pair, you see. And it hasn't been a bad night, we only had those three accident cases and the coronary, but I'd been on my feet all the while and they were bothering me pretty fierce—and two hours to the end of the shift—so I just slipped out to my car to change into the old ones."

"Oh, I see," said Hunter. "And he was waiting." That made a new little picture, didn't it?

"I'd just got to the car when he jumped me from behind," said Mrs. Boyd. "But he picked the wrong woman this time—he didn't know I'd spent five years in the psychiatric ward at the General. You have to have eyes in the back of your head and be ready to move quick, some of those patients, I tell you! He knocked me against the car, so I didn't lose my balance, and I kicked backward as hard as I could, and heard him grunt—I think I got him on the shin—and he let go, and I turned around and began to scream as loud as I could and when he grabbed me again I bit his arm—to the bone, I'll bet." She sounded complacent. "And I think I'd have got away from him too, but just then the ambulance pulled in and Al and Gary saw what was going on and jumped out and ran over—and by then Dr. Eddowes and Dr. Michaels had heard me and came running out—"

But everybody had been so concerned for Mrs. Boyd that the rapist had got away. "I see the doctors coming up," said one of the ambulance attendants, "and I took out after the guy—he heard us coming, and let her go and ran, see—he went out toward the back street, and he was just too fast for me, he was long gone." Everybody else had been clustered around Mrs. Boyd. Her uniform wasn't even torn.

"But listen," said Dr. Eddowes, who was a boyish-looking fresh-complexioned intern, "I had an idea. Stories in those detective magazines, how the police in New York send out cops disguised as old ladies to catch the muggers—I had the idea, why don't we put a couple in nurses' uniforms to act as decoys out there? Let 'em come out alone, after the shift ends, and see if he'd go after one—" He was looking appraisingly at Patrolman Robert Bruce McLeod, who was a solid six-footer with impressive shoulders. McLeod looked alarmed.

"But I got a good look at him," said Mrs. Boyd. "When I turned around, I got a good look at his face—I was parked nearly under one of the lights. I can tell you what he looks like, he's got dark hair that grows in what they call a widow's peak, and his face sort of runs away to a little pointed chin—and his teeth stick out. I'd surely recognize a picture of him. And I'd think he has a very bad case of pyorrhea, because his breath smelled just rank."

"That's the dedicated nurse for you," said Dr. Eddowes fondly. "Keep the head and evaluate the patient though the heavens fall."

Varallo got back to the Casino Bar and Grill about eight o'clock. Being technically off duty, he could order a drink. Working leisurely on a brandy and soda, he talked to the bartender, Olly Lanza. Evidently Sellers had briefed him; he knew all about it. He was a big broad swarthy man with prizefighters' shoulders and a cauliflower ear. He said, "Varallo, hey? Well, greetings, *paisano*. You sure don't look it, but I suppose all your *antenati* came from up the Swiss border, hah? The big blondes up there. Well, Sellers told me about this deal, and I'll tell you

something, *paisano.* You know that name—Joe Esquibel—it's trying to ring bells in my head."

"Is that a fact?"

"I just can't connect it up, but I know I heard it. Somewhere,
sometime. I'm thinking about it. It'll come to me. The rest of this
—my God, these damn fool women. Now this is a nice quiet family place, Varallo, we get decent types in here mostly, but it is a
bar. And you know, it's all fine and dandy the females should
vote and go in for careers and all the rest of it, who's got any objection—but when it comes to these libbers yelling about equality
it gets just downright ridiculous. They can go around saying
there's no difference between the sexes from now till doomsday,
it don't hardly make it so."

Varallo grinned and said, "*Viva la differenza,* in fact."

"My wife says they are all just plain nuts, give up the natural
superiority of females for just the equality. She could be right. I
got more sense than to argue with a woman. But the point is, a
woman is still asking for trouble to take up with a strange man
and go off with him, the way this one must have. Look, the way
I say, we get the regulars in here, but also the stray customers
just in off the street, and I figure this pair must have been that
kind. But who knows? You want, I'll introduce you to a couple
people—there are some of the regulars in."

"What's to lose?" said Varallo.

"Wait a sec, I get you a refill on the house."

The regulars were, of course, ordinary honest people. A young
couple, Pete and Helen Frost, who lived a couple of blocks
away, didn't own a TV. Rodney Harris, an old fellow living with
in-laws who met an old crony here, another old fellow named
Sidney—they were both retired railroad men. They were all cooperative, but none of them knew a Joe Esquibel.

"But it rings a bell with me," said Olly Lanza. "I heard it
some place, *paisano.* And I'll do some thinking on it, and ask
around the people who come in. I find out anything, remember
anything, I'll get back to you. Hell of a thing, woman getting
killed like that—even if she asked for it, in a sort of way."

Young Vincent Charles was teething, and uncomfortable, and
letting the world know about it. Katharine was shut up in the

nursery with him, but his yells penetrated the walls, and O'Connor groaned and pulled the pillow over his head. He was academically sorry for young Vincent's troubles, but he did, after all, have to earn a living for all of them.

Maisie, who had a sympathetic disposition and had reacted the same way when the baby had first been introduced into the household, began to howl agitatedly from the living room.

"Oh, for God's sake," mumbled O'Connor. He wouldn't be fit for anything tomorrow—

Suddenly he sat up and said into the dark, "My God." Tomorrow be damned—and him a lieutenant of detectives—he hadn't been operating on all cylinders today. Rosalie had had a car, and why the hell he hadn't thought to put an A.P.B. out on it—

# SIX

On Wednesday morning, with Varallo off, the detectives were just drifting in and sorting out priorities for the day when the first call came in, and it was a rather surprising one—the Brand Art Library.

"Now what in hell would there be to steal at the library?" wondered O'Connor. It had been called in as a burglary.

Forbes and Delia went out on it, to find out. That library, which housed the art and music collection of the city system, had once been the imposing mansion built by one of the early city fathers; left to the city many years ago, it had more recently been turned into a small park, the white-domed mansion looming over some seven or eight acres of terraced lawn, a Japanese teahouse, an artificial stream with a bridge, a couple of baseball diamonds, a small picnic area. It was all expensively walled, and when they got up to the top of the hill and came to the tall ornamental gates, Delia asked, "How did anyone get in? It's locked about nine o'clock, isn't it? And these—"

"What?" said Forbes. "Oh, the gates. Yes, I think so." He was acting a little absentminded this morning.

At the main building they were met by an excited, agitated, angry group of librarians—five women all talking at once until they were overridden by the masterful raised voice of the head librarian, Mrs. Esther Rosen, and her assistant Miss Vera Dykstra.

"It is the most extraordinary outrage," said Mrs. Rosen, "and I must say the most meaningless—really you can only call it vandalism, and what the chief librarian is going to say—we discussed installing burglar alarms about six months ago, but really what would justify the cost?" She was a vast, dark forceful woman, highly outraged. "Juvenile delinquents," she decided. "Just making destruction and trouble!"

But it looked like something queerer than that, when they asked some questions and had a look. This library didn't house any books apart from art reference volumes; what was collected here was a good-sized art library, thousands of tapes and records of music, a few paintings, and thousands of prints of paintings. People could come, said Miss Dykstra, and borrow pictures, on the same basis as library books, to see what kind they liked in their homes, or for study purposes. They had a stock of frames of all sizes to fit all the prints. People also, of course, borrowed the tapes and records. All the tapes, records, art books were worth something; and throughout the place were the usual office machines, a couple of IBM typewriters. None of that had been touched. What had been stolen were thousands of the prints, from the big room where they were kept by themselves.

It was a room about twenty feet square, lined with steel cabinets, and all the drawers in all the cabinets were pulled out, there were outsize manila envelopes all over the floor, a few prints were left scattered on the floor. The women were still checking, but nothing else seemed to have been disturbed, no other room entered.

Miss Dykstra was in a fury, looking at it. "We can't even make a list of what's missing until we get the coded master list from the state, of what was here! And it's all worthless—comparatively speaking, that is—just reproductions of prints—on good stock, but anybody could buy them for about ten dollars apiece! The only framed pictures they took—well, really! I don't set myself up as a judge of art, but all eleven of them—six oils and five watercolors —were on loan from local artists, who aren't at all well known, and I'm afraid highly overrated by themselves."

Mrs. Rosen, asked for a general estimate, gestured at the steel cabinets and said simply, "The prints are stored flat, in protective covers. Each drawer would hold approximately fifty. You can see—"

They could. There were fifteen cabinets, with twelve or fourteen drawers each, and they were all mostly empty. "Good lord," said Delia. "I suppose it's a sort of general representative collection—"

"Whatever anyone might want," said Miss Dykstra savagely. "Old masters to Dali, Degas, Picasso—cave paintings, Homer, Wyeth, Grandma Moses, El Greco—you name it. Just reproductions. The original paintings were collectively valued at fifteen hundred dollars, but that"—she looked at them sardonically—"was the artists' own evaluation."

It was rather queer. Forbes called Burt, and they looked around. It was easy enough to spot where the burglar had got in: a ground-floor lavatory window had the outside screen lifted off, the window broken and raised. It was a good-sized window, big enough to admit an adult. Furthermore, in getting in the window he had inadvertently yanked out the cord of an electric clock on the wall, and it was stopped at eleven thirty-one.

It was a senseless sort of burglary, but it had to be worked. Burt and Thomsen came out, took one look at the array of steel cabinets, and did some cussing. Forbes and Delia drove back down the hill to the gates. They were at least twelve feet high, imposing wrought-iron gates, and while the stout stucco wall around the whole property wasn't that high, it was well shielded by thick, high growths of oleander, cotoneaster, prickly cactus.

"And the nearest houses," said Delia, "are nearly out of sight of the building, but if anyone noticed lights up there in the late evening, they wouldn't think anything about it—a meeting of the library board or something."

"Wouldn't think about what?" asked Forbes.

"A man could get over the gates easily enough with an extension ladder—and the bars are far enough apart that all those flat prints could be slipped through. But what a funny thing, Jeff— the worthless reproduction prints. You know, I'd lay a bet on two men."

"Hm?" said Forbes.

Delia looked at him. Forbes was usually on the ball. "It must have been quite a load to carry, and it's a good four hundred yards down the hill." They could have left a car right outside the gate, but it still would have been quite a job. "It would have been easier for two men—and I doubt very much that it was juveniles."

"Yes," said Forbes. He sighed and passed a hand over his long jaw and gave Delia an apologetic grin. "My mind isn't working straight, sorry. The fact is, I just got engaged and—well, er—"

"Oh. Well, congratulations."

"Thanks. She's a wonderful girl," said Forbes devoutly. "Her name is Joan Broderick—very bright girl too, a legal secretary. I've got about eight days coming to me, we thought we'd add it to my vacation in July and—"

"Very nice," said Delia. She hoped the girl really was a nice one; Forbes deserved a satisfactory wife. "This job. I think if we get any leads, it'll be from the lab."

"Probably." He stepped on his cigarette. "And that is going to be the hell of a long job, dust all the stuff in that place. I tell you what, you'd better go back and do the report, and I'll hang around to help Rex and Gene."

Delia agreed readily. But she didn't drive back downtown right away, because in there, just now, something new had come into her mind. It was the tapes had put it there. Mrs. Potter and Marion Austen and Sylvia Bates all talking interminably to each other on the tapes, telling each other every little thing, Mrs. Potter had said. And Mrs. Austen had seldom gone to a doctor, but she had made that appointment with Dr. Cushing for the beginning of that week—had she mentioned why, on her tapes to her old friends? Doctors, thought Delia, were always so cocksure, so definite; whatever Cushing or Goulding said, it seemed to her that it could be, that heart condition coming on since last December, and producing some symptoms she'd been worried about. The reason she went to see the new doctor.

The sprawling ranch house on Sunset Canyon Drive was large and new; Mrs. Potter's son must be doing well. Mrs. Potter opened the door to Delia after thirty seconds, and welcomed her in. "Well, there, I was just telling Sylvia about you on a tape, Miss Riordan. Taking advantage of Ann being out running errands. Have you found out anything about Marion?"

The living room was huge, beautifully furnished. Delia sat down on the couch opposite the big chair where Mrs. Potter had been sitting, the square black tape recorder balanced on the arm. "Not much. Did Mrs. Austen tell you about her appointment with the new doctor, Mrs. Potter? Dr. Cushing."

She looked surprised. "Why, no, I never heard about that."

"You said you used to tell each other every little thing. When did you have a tape from her before April twenty-sixth?"

"Well, now, let me get my schedule and look." She went down the hall, came back with the cheap notebook. "I had a tape from her on the twenty-third, made on the twenty-first, and she never said a thing about going to see a doctor—or on the last tape she made, on the twenty-eighth, either. Not a word. And of course she would have—I don't understand it—" She was worried, puzzled.

"I've been thinking about it," said Delia. "Now you tell me that— She'd never gone to doctors much. Do you think—you knew her, Mrs. Potter—if she'd been having some symptoms that worried her, if she was afraid she had something seriously wrong—would she have gone to a doctor for a checkup without mentioning it to anyone? Because she'd be afraid of what the doctor might say?"

Mrs. Potter looked disturbed. "I don't think Marion would have felt that way—she was a sensible woman—not a fearful woman. But—" she wiped her mouth with her handkerchief, and her eyes were thoughtful. "But she was a considerate woman too."

"Yes," said Delia. "She wouldn't have wanted to worry you. And if the doctor had said it was nothing to worry about, she'd probably have told you later. But he wanted to do all those tests, and hadn't said anything definite, so she hadn't mentioned it at all. What would you feel like yourself, in a case like that—if it was you?"

Mrs. Potter took off her glasses and began to polish them on her handkerchief. "You mean, suspecting there was something serious, and finding out I was going to die pretty soon. Well, if I was sure about it, I wouldn't lie about it, cover up, because it's better for the family to know. But Marion—no family, nobody really close but me and Sylvia, the Burrisses right there in town, and all of us as old as she was—I just don't know, Miss Riordan. She might have felt, least said, soonest mended—not wanting to worry us. That's so."

"Yes," said Delia. "She didn't want to distress any of you. Whatever the doctor eventually said, she was just going to keep it to herself."

Mrs. Potter wiped her eyes unselfconsciously. "It'd be like Marion to keep up a good front. Not to worry anybody, if there wasn't anything anybody could do. All I will say is, she wasn't a church-going woman, but she believed absolutely, the way I do, that we don't really die. I'd heard her say many times that she sort of looked forward to being rid of all the physical nuisances we have in this life, washing dishes and doing laundry—and seeing George and her parents again. She wasn't at all afraid of dying."

"Yes," said Delia, "but the will to live can be pretty strong"— irrelevantly she thought about the creature begotten of the devil —"and sometimes when it comes to the actual point, people feel different than they'd expected to. That could be another reason, you see. If she was afraid, perhaps she just couldn't bring herself to think about it, much less to talk about it."

Mrs. Potter shook her head slowly. She looked very distressed. "I just couldn't say. I just don't know. Have you talked to Dr. Harvey yet?"

"No, we haven't been able to locate him."

"That's strange. I don't recall Marion saying he was going to move away, just that he was retiring. But you've given me something to think about. Maybe I've just been imagining things, because her death was so sudden. I'm sorry if I've made you any trouble."

"No trouble." And there was absolutely no reason, no evidence, for the niggling small feeling at the back of her mind that there was something queer about Marion Austen's death—that it was, somehow, the wrong shape. No reason at all.

O'Connor had put out an A.P.B. on Rosalie's car, after getting the plate number from Sacramento. And locating and talking to people who had known Rosalie, names they'd got from Fred Buckman, Gil Rogers, Shirley—he and Katz finally found one of them who knew about the new boyfriend. Her name was Edna Crane, she worked at a music and record shop in Burbank, and she'd known Rosalie for just a year or so. She already knew about the murder— "Honest, I cried my eyes out. Rosalie! She was a good friend of mine, we took to each other right away."

She certainly looked to be more Rosalie's type than Shirley Feldman. And she'd heard about the new boyfriend.

"I'd never met him, but she was gone on him for real, I never knew Rosie to be so serious about a fellow. She told me about him, oh, around a month ago. His name was Ken Erwin, she met him at a disco, he was with somebody she knew there. She said he was a really great guy. He was a camera nut, always taking pictures. But listen, what you said about her moving—I talked to her on the phone a week ago Monday night, and she never said anything about going to San Francisco."

"Do you think she might have been going away with him?" asked O'Connor. "You know where he worked?"

"Yeah, he had a funny job, but she said it paid real good. He's a chef at some classy restaurant, I don't know which one. Do you think he could be the one who killed her?" She peered at them fearfully, brushing back untidy brown hair.

"We don't know. Do you remember who it was who introduced her to him?"

"Gee, I don't—I think she said he was with Stella and Bill, I don't know them, when she came in the disco with Patty Mathias. *Do* you think it was him?"

Back in the car, Katz said, "Are we being a little too logical here, Charles? The fellow with the knife in the railroad station might never have seen her before. Rumors about the narco deals around there—he could have seen her pay for her ticket, followed her out and tried to grab her purse, and lost his head when she struggled. If he's a user, they do overreact."

"All right," said O'Connor, "where's her car?" Belatedly remembering the car, he had gone and looked around the station—though if it had been left there, it would probably have been reported as abandoned by now—and it was nowhere there. "How did she get to the station?"

"Look, if we know one thing," said Katz, "we know that X didn't have a damn thing to do with the car. He got away on a motorcycle. Ten to one she parked at the station, and at the time none of us smart detectives had the sense to deduce she had a car and look for it. We could have got her identified right then by sorting out which cars there had people attached. And in the meantime, some punk hanging around there hopped it."

"Damn it," said O'Connor, "I don't remember if any of the reports mentioned—it was right at the end of shift, but I think Bob
went back to talk to the Amtrak men—"

Back at the office, he scrabbled through unread reports in his
In basket; O'Connor detested paperwork. "Well, there you are,"
he said presently. "Not all of us quite so dumb, Joe. Bob went
back to the station that night, and he thought about a car. But
there wasn't anybody there then but the Amtrak people, with no
trains due in, and only their cars around."

"Yes, and that'd have been about three hours after she was
killed," said Katz. "Plenty of time for somebody to hot-wire it."

Because of course, thought Delia, finishing the rather tasteless
sandwich at the bright and busy little snack shop on Central,
people did react to death, and the thought of death, differently.
Whatever they might say or think about it; and they'd say one
thing and feel another. The will to live stronger than most people
realized. She could well believe that Marion Austen, for whatever reason, deliberately hadn't mentioned those possible symptoms, the doctor's appointment, to her old friends. And it might
have been because she wasn't afraid of death at all, or because
she was so afraid that she was trying to push it out of her mind
and forget it. People acted out of character sometimes.

Like Dr. Leslie Borchard.

She poured herself more coffee. And what had made her think
about that, for heaven's sake? Death, of course . . . Two years
ago, when Neil was home— He had called and asked her out to
dinner. Called at the office, and that was strictly against the
rules, and she'd been so nervous that Sergeant Hagen would realize it was a personal call, she'd said yes to get rid of him. Lied
to Alex about having to do the overtime. Come to think, the only
times she'd ever lied to Alex was over Neil.

She didn't remember the restaurant—the Brown Derby, Cha-
sen's? He had just got the appointment as assistant head of the
university team, on that Peruvian dig. And he had looked older,
and tired; he was smoking too much. But he hadn't argued and
snapped at her, he just wanted to talk, and they got back to the
place where they were comfortable and happy with each other,
the way it had always been before he began asking her to marry

him. They knew each other so well— He had talked about Dr. Borchard, his old chief, a man he admired. "God, I hate like hell to get a step up because he's dead. And it was such a shock to everybody—he always said suicide was a cowardly thing. God, he was only fifty-nine—a brilliant man, if I'm ever half as good— he leaves a big hole, he'll be missed. And nobody even knew he'd been seeing a doctor. They found inoperable cancer, and next day he checked into a hotel room, wrote a letter to his wife, and took an overdose of morphine he'd stolen from the lab."

Delia said gently, "Maybe the bravest thing he could do, do you think?"

"I don't know—I wonder if I'd have the guts to do something like that—but it made it rougher on the family, I think. His wife was knocked out—the daughter expecting a baby—" He was stirring the contents of the ashtray with a dead match: he was always fiddling with things, nervous habit. "And then old Jowett telling me it meant the job would pass to me—I felt like a Judas, which was damn silly, I know."

He had just wanted to talk. And later on, when they were ready to leave, she had said something about his looking tired, and he stabbed out his latest cigarette and drew a long sighing breath and said, "It's been a long year. I'll be glad to get out of the classroom and back to some real work on the dig." And then suddenly his eyes smiled a little. "I don't suppose you'd like to come with me? It wouldn't take you long to resign. The climate's lovely up in the hills, and the natives speak a variety of Spanish —and you wouldn't have to wear that damned uniform." She'd come straight from work, of course, no chance to change.

"Oh, don't start that again, you know how I feel—and you don't mean it now."

He laid one hand over hers on the table, his familiar square strong hand, brown and ringless. "I'd always mean it, Delia. You've really made yourself into something you were never meant to be, but my old Delia's there underneath, all the same. I think. My daydreaming girl who likes beach parties and sentimental poetry. Maybe in a few years' time it'll be different."

And in the parking lot, he shut the door on her as she rolled down the window. "Don't forget to lock the door. It's late, and this is the city jungle." He leaned on the window ledge, and in the dark there was an edge of amusement in his tone. "Are you afraid that arrogant old bastard would have a stroke at the mere sight of me?"

"It's just, he doesn't understand your kind of person—just as you don't understand him."

"Oh, I understand him all right, and it's nothing to me what job a man picks for himself. What I don't understand is him trying to make you over to feed his damned ego. Doesn't it ever occur to him that a girl might want to get married? Just because you don't want to marry me—"

"I don't want to fight with you, Neil. Don't spoil the evening."

"Ah, no—it's been a good evening—bless you for coming. We could always talk to each other, couldn't we?" He stepped back. "Think of me sometimes, darling."

And driving home, she had thought wryly that it wasn't that it never occurred to Alex that she might want to get married. But— she knew him by heart—he took it for granted that if she ever did, naturally she'd pick some upstanding career cop, preferably LAPD.

When O'Connor and Katz ended up at the office for the last time that day, Poor had just come back from supervising Ruth Boyd's session with the mug shots. Regrettably, she hadn't made any. She was doubtful about taking the time to go downtown and look at more. Burt, Thomsen, and Forbes had spent the day up at the Brand Library dusting for prints, and now had so many to process that it would take a month of Sundays; that was a very queer job altogether. Delia was sitting over the phone again, probably hunting that doctor—O'Connor wondered if there was anything in that Austen thing.

"So, do we try to do it the hard way?" asked Katz.

O'Connor just scowled at him. They had now found Patty Mathias, and she said Rosalie had met Ken Erwin at the disco about a month ago, he'd been there with Stella and Bill. She knew Rosalie had really gone all out on him, but she didn't know him herself, didn't know where he worked. Well, Stella Shapiro and Bill Todd.

"Where do we find them?" asked O'Connor, and she giggled.

"Like, I guess, you don't, you know? They eloped last week

and went off on a long honeymoon, Bill just won a bundle on one of those silly game shows on TV."

DMV had no record of a driver's license for him.

There wasn't any listing in the local book for a Kenneth Erwin: there was, in fact, a rather short list of Erwins, and a few phone calls covered them: nobody knew a Kenneth. He could, of course, live anywhere in the Los Angeles area. A classy restaurant: there were ten thousand, Santa Monica to San Marino. "No way, Joe. Wait for the A.P.B. to turn up the car."

"I don't think the car's got anything to tell us."

"But I still feel the boyfriend has something to do with the murder."

Varallo had got all the dead blooms pruned off, and maybe it was wishful thinking, but it had seemed a little cooler today. In the late afternoon he took a long shower—he could get by without another shave—and put on his newest sports clothes, and Laura got dressed in the long blue dress he liked, and they went out to dinner at the new place called the Blue Danube. It was a nice place. They had a couple of drinks before dinner, and enjoyed the evening.

And as they drove home, Laura said a little sleepily, "Delia called me this afternoon. Suggested we meet for lunch tomorrow."

"Oh? You going?"

"Um-hum. I like her. But she seems—lonely."

When they came in, Mrs. Anderson said everything was fine. "But that cat—I think he fancies himself as a nursemaid. He hasn't stirred from the baby's side all evening, and he growled at me when I changed the diaper."

"He thinks he's a watch cat," said Varallo.

On Thursday morning, with Delia off, Dr. Goulding came in with the autopsy report on Maureen Miller; Varallo looked at it over O'Connor's shoulder. It was short and sweet. She had been manually strangled, hadn't been raped. Stomach contents thus and so, alcohol percentage— "Well, we knew they'd both had a few drinks, but she was nowhere near drunk."

Goulding sat down, patting his bald head absently. "Feeling a little pleased with life," he said. "She'd had a good meal a few hours before. It looks to me—not to tell you your job—as if somebody just lost his temper for a minute and grabbed her. It's an easy way to kill somebody without meaning to."

"Yes," said O'Connor, and took up the phone and talked to Burt, who said they could forget about the car. There'd been no clear latents to lift in it except hers, and the steering wheel had been polished clean, which made you think. "Twice," said O'Connor, and passed that on.

"You can read it like print, Charles," said Varallo. "That place, the Casino, stands all by itself about the middle of the block, with its own parking lot at one side. That's undoubtedly where she was parked, because there's no parking at the curb for nearly that whole block. She meant to go home, soon after Doris took off with her nice new acquaintance. So, she went out and the other fellow followed her—there wasn't any disturbance inside, just people coming and going—and let's say he wasn't the perfect gentleman Joe Esquibel turned out to be, he made the advances, and she told him off—there's no evidence of any struggle, it could be he just grabbed her by the throat and that was that. And when he found she was dead—maybe other people coming out just then—he put her in the car and drove a couple of blocks and left it. The place where she was found isn't three blocks from the Casino."

"And he wiped his prints off the steering wheel because he knows they're on record somewhere," said O'Connor.

"Yes, there is that."

The phone rang on O'Connor's desk and he picked it up. "O'Connor . . . Well, that's a step in the right direction. Shoot 'em up. What do you know, we've got Rosalie's VW. Patrolman spotted it over in Hollywood just now and nabbed the driver." Katz, who had been looking over some reports, heard that and came over. A minute later a navy-uniformed patrolman came in escorting a young fellow who was protesting all the way.

"What is this, anyway? What am I supposed to have done? I thought you were supposed to read people their rights before you arrest them—"

"Like I've told you six times, you're not arrested," said the patrolman. All he would know, of course, was that Glendale wanted the car and driver. "Baxter, Lieutenant. We had the A.P.B. when you put it out yesterday, and I picked the plate number up half an hour ago at Vermont and Los Feliz. The car's parked over in the precinct lot," and he handed over the keys.

"The Gestapo stealing my car," said his capture bitterly. "What the hell this is all about—" He was a nice-looking fair young man in neat and clean sports clothes; he looked around at all of them with anger, bewilderment, indignation. "What *is* this?"

"I think," said Katz maliciously, "I'm about to be proved right, boys. The car didn't have anything to do with it."

"All right," said O'Connor, "thanks very much for the cooperation, Baxter." The LAPD man gave him a careless salute and went out. "Now, let's get to some facts. What's your name?"

"Baker. Gerald Baker." He produced a wallet. In it there was a valid driver's license for Gerald Robert Baker at an address on Edgemont in Hollywood: he was twenty-one, and it was a good picture of him. There was also a Social Security card, a student union card for USC, and a library card. "I don't suppose it matters to you, but this is going to play hell with this morning's rehearsal of our semester play—I'm the villain. What the hell are you cops up to?"

"You were driving a VW belonging to a Rosalie Wegman," said O'Connor. "We've had an all-points bulletin out on it, which is why you were picked up—"

"Now let's get just one thing straight," said Baker. "I was driving a VW belonging to me. I paid the girl four hundred bucks for it last Saturday."

"Have you a bill of sale, Mr. Baker?"

"Of course I haven't got a bill of sale—naturally it's up in Sacramento with the pink slip and the white slip and all the rest of the red tape. At least, if the post office hasn't lost it. I mailed it all in on Saturday."

Varallo laughed. "Suppose you sit down and tell us about it, Mr. Baker. How did you come to buy the car? Had you known her long?"

"I didn't know her at all." He sat down unwillingly in Poor's desk chair. "I needed some transportation, the MG I'd had was on its last legs, ready to be junked. I hadn't much money to spend on wheels, and I hadn't found anything yet." Seeing they were disposed to listen, he calmed down a little. "I was out with my girl and another couple, a week ago, Friday night that is— there was a movie playing over here we wanted to see. Afterwards we stopped at a Denny's for sandwiches. This girl was at the cashier's desk there. She'd evidently heard Chet and I talking about cars, about my being in the market, and when we went to pay the bill, she said she had a VW she wanted to sell."

"Oh, yes, how simple," said Varallo.

"I said I might be interested, and she said it was parked in the lot outside and I could try it if I wanted. She gave me the key. So Chet and I went out and looked it over. It's got a lot of miles on it, but it's in good shape—Chet had a look at the engine. We drove it around a few blocks and it sounded fine, handled OK. It's strictly transportation, of course, and we figured it was worth about what I could afford. So we came back and I made the deal. She was asking five-fifty, but I beat her down without much trouble."

"And when did you take delivery?"

"The next day. She said she was leaving town and I could come and get it about four o'clock. She gave me the address here. I don't know this town too well, and Chet was studying for a final, he couldn't drive me, so I got Carolyn to bring me over— my girl, Carolyn Boland. I gave the Wegman girl a check—it just about cleaned my account—and took delivery, and Carolyn followed me back to Hollywood. Clear enough for you?"

"Eminently," said O'Connor sadly. Rosalie had decided to clear out in a hurry, all right, leaving her boss in a bind or not. "About five o'clock she was down at the railroad station. The way the buses run when they feel like it, could she have made it?"

"Well, it was just twenty-five blocks down Brand and across," said Varallo. "I should think—"

"Oh," said Baker. "Excuse me, but I think I can tell you about that. There was another fellow there, when we went in. That little guesthouse where she was living."

"Oh?"

"That's right. It was a little embarrassing," said Baker with a short laugh. "The door was open and as we came up we could hear him—well, I don't know what you'd call it, pleading with her or whatever—please wouldn't she listen, please marry him, she knew the other one wouldn't marry her, he loved her so much and wouldn't she marry him—like that. Embarrassing," said Baker, looking embarrassed. "When she heard us at the door, she shut him up."

"Did you get a look at him?"

"Hardly. She said something like, you wait in the bedroom, lover boy, and he went like a trained dog. She's a good looker, but thank you, I don't like the type. Well, I wasn't interested in her love affairs—I only had a glimpse. About my size, I guess, medium coloring."

"What about the railroad station?"

"Oh, yes. Well, it was Carolyn being polite. After I'd given the girl the check, Carolyn said she hoped it wouldn't inconvenience her, being without a car until she left—something like that—and the girl said no, it was just till tomorrow, and then she sang out, sort of—" he hesitated and chose, "mocking, 'lover boy'll drive me down to the station, won't you, Barney?' "

"Barney!" said O'Connor, taken aback.

Katz sat back and laughed. "Never underestimate the females, Charles. We knew she had a lot of boyfriends. This is just another one."

Varallo got up. "You've been put to a good deal of inconvenience, Mr. Baker, and I think you've just given us some interesting information. I'll drive you back to Hollywood to collect your car. You see, Miss Wegman got herself murdered that afternoon and we were naturally interested—"

"Murdered!" said Baker. "Well, I will be damned."

O'Connor and Katz looked at each other as they went out. "Barney," said O'Connor.

"And what he's reported to have said—yes, interesting," agreed Katz. "Don't tell me we have to see all her friends again to ask about Barney."

"Maybe the first one we ask will know him."

"No bets. It usually comes the hard way."

On Thursday morning, as Delia was dressing for her lunch date, Isobel called to thank her for the baby's present. Her voice was as warm and affectionate as ever, and as they talked, a kind of sharply hurtful nostalgia struck Delia, for the times when there *was* time, to sit and talk— She and Isobel doing homework together, back in high school, always at the Fordyces', and up to that last year Neil coming and going, superior big brother with his own car—after that he'd been away at the university— Summer days at the beach together when Neil was home, with the rest of the crowd from high school—sometimes parties at the Fordyces' house, other places, the girls they'd both known from high school. Even the two and a half years at Los Angeles City College, time to talk and go places together, shopping— She'd lost touch completely with girls she had liked, Marcia Hunt and Harriet Catlin and Geraldine Fulmer—hadn't thought of them in years.

Isobel just the same, easy and friendly, the same Isobel, but inevitably they had grown away from each other. Going in different directions—

And Alex curious as always—he had ears like a cat—she heard the wheelchair moving in the living room, close to the hall where the phone was. When she put the phone down, he was sitting there with his mouth drawn to a grim line; he would have heard her say Isobel's name. Was he still afraid of Neil, she wondered sadly. He should know it was too late now, that was over and done.

She dressed more carefully than usual, in a more feminine dress than usual, the coral with the full skirt, and the one pair of high heels she owned. She drove over to Glendale to meet Laura at Pike's Verdugo Oaks, a nice restaurant, quiet and spacious.

She liked Laura, and she felt that Laura liked her. They talked, casual and noncommittal—they were still at the getting-acquainted stage. But Delia said, over final cups of coffee and cigarettes, "I've just begun to realize that the job has got me away from most of my old friends—well, I suppose it's a matter of different interests really—"

Laura said, "Oh, well, any job can dominate you if you let it. And you can always find new friends." She smiled at Delia; she was an attractive woman, with her bright chestnut brown hair and milky complexion. "When Vic and I came down here, we didn't know anybody, but you do make new friends in time. Look, it's your day off, why don't you come back to the house and admire Vic's roses? Such a silly thing—they were there when we bought the place, and he got mad at this special one for not blooming, and bought all the books—"

So Delia drove back to the house on Hillcroft Road, and met Ginevra, who smiled at her delightfully and climbed into her lap with a picture book to show her the little kittens who lost their mittens, and Johnny, who was teething but really very good about it— "Not," said Laura with a chuckle, "like young Vincent, Katharine's been up with him every night this week, but he's going to be a lot like Charles!"—and Gideon Algernon Cadwallader, who deigned to let her stroke his handsome tiger stripes.

It was a lovely, friendly, restful afternoon, and when she started back for Hollywood, later than she had intended, she was feeling happier and more contented in herself than she had in a while. She had all the marketing to do for Steve; he had given her quite a list.

At five-twenty an urgent call came up from the desk: a heist in progress at Churchill's Restaurant. Varallo and O'Connor were the only ones in.

They got there in five minutes: Churchill's was a fairly classy place in the Fashion Center on Glendale Avenue, four blocks from police headquarters. They found Patrolmen Bauman and Painter there, a flurry of waitresses, the cashier in floods of tears. The heist man had got away about thirty seconds before the squads got there.

The cashier was a pretty girl, and she sobbed at them, "Oh— oh—I'm sorry, I tried to keep my head—he was here in the lobby, he said he was waiting for his boss—and then when there wasn't anybody here, Mr. Pargeter went into the dining room, he showed me this gun and said give me the money or I'll blow your head off—but I saw Mr. Pargeter in the door, he saw the gun and I knew he'd call the police—but when I gave him the money he ran out the door—"

Pargeter, the manager, couldn't tell them much about him; had only seen him from behind. "He was pretty tall—I think he had light hair—oh, I didn't notice what he was wearing—"

The job sometimes also involved making bricks without straw.

# SEVEN

They would never pick up the fellow who had heisted Churchill's; nobody could identify him. He had got away with about
three hundred and eighty bucks; that place had a good lunch
trade, and wasn't a cheap snack shop.

Overnight, they got another burglary to work. And O'Connor,
glancing over the night report at eight-ten on Friday morning,
let out some heartfelt cusswords. "For God's sake, another motel
hit—and this time they put the clerk in the hospital. A woman—
evidently she put up a fight." He and Varallo went out on that in
a hurry. It was, of course, Katz's day off. John Poor and Delia
were briefed to check back on Rosalie's friends looking for Barney. But before they left the office, a call got relayed up from a
Mrs. Mildred Lossner.

"I thought the police might want to hear about it," she told
Delia. "I hadn't heard anything myself, being a bit hard of hearing, but my neighbor Mrs. Wills told me that all week the
phone there, where Rosalie Wegman lived, you know, in my little guesthouse, it's been ringing and ringing twenty and thirty
times a day. Her house is on the side street, you see, the guesthouse is only about ten feet across her drive, and she'd hear it."

Delia was interested. "Thanks for letting us know. Mrs.
Lossner, if we should want to have someone there to intercept a
call, would it be all right with you?"

"Why, I suppose so."

"We'll let you know." Delia told Poor about that. "Somebody
anxious to get hold of Rosalie. And what about this new boyfriend? If they had such a hot affair going, where is he? He must
know some of her other friends besides the couple who eloped,
and heard about the murder by now."

"I don't know," said Poor doubtfully, "he might not have.

None of the other people we've talked to know much about him, where he works or lives."

"But she was killed last Saturday. He must have expected to see her before now—I'll bet those calls are from him, and," said Delia, "from San Francisco. I think he expected her to join him there—and if that's so, you're quite right and he didn't know any of her other friends, to call and ask where Rosalie is. And there's no way to locate him. But I'll bet that's the way it is."

"Well," said Poor, "whether it is or not, this Barney seems to have been one of the last people who saw her—supposedly he took her to the railroad station that day. We'd better see if we can locate him."

And Delia thought, friends. She had never seen those Burrisses, the other old friends of Marion Austen's—but they couldn't have much to offer, could they?

Miss Nelda McKenzie looked at Varallo and O'Connor with grim exasperation and said, "Do I look as if I hadn't got good sense?" She did not, being a tall and gaunt woman in her sixties with a hatchetlike profile and a forthright manner. They had found her in the main lobby of the Memorial Hospital paying her bill for emergency overnight treatment. "And it was just a mercy," she said, "that my checkbook wasn't in my handbag." She had a broken arm and a cut on the temple, had just been released, and Varallo told her she needn't call a cab, they would drive her home.

"Very kind of you, I'm sure," said Miss McKenzie tartly. "It's always nice to get something for our taxes. I ask you, am I fool enough to start an argument with a man holding a gun on me? But I worked hard to get that place paid for, insurance against my old age, and I resent these lazy bums walking in to steal my money. When they left, I went after them as far as the front porch, to see if I might be able to spot their car, get some evidence for the police, and the bigger one saw me and came back and hit me—knocked me down the front steps. I'm afraid all I can tell you about them is that they both had heavy Spanish accents, and the taller one had a moustache—" It was the same description they'd heard before. "And they took my purse too, with my credit cards and a little cash, it was lying on the counter, I'd

just come back from mailing some letters at the main post office—"

"You'd better call and let credit offices know," said Varallo.

"I fully intend to," she said, "as soon as I get home." She
could tell them that the heist men had been wearing gloves.
They drove her home. It was a very modest motel far down on
Colorado, about twelve units of old frame cottages.

"Bundy didn't make any mug shots," said Varallo, looking at
the motel premises thoughtfully. "But they're conscious of
fingerprints, so the odds are they've got records somewhere,
Charles. They must have made a hell of a lot bigger haul at
those two big places, the Golden Key and the Ramada Inn. Why
these second-rate places?"

O'Connor said moodily, "Any damned motel these days, the
rates are up, at the end of the day there'd be a fairly good haul.
And at those bigger places, which might have occurred to them,
there are apt to be more people around than a single desk clerk.
They're playing safe."

"Yes," said Varallo, "exactly. It rather says to me that they're
small-timers, not really experienced heisters."

"Well, for God's sake," said O'Connor, "they're getting experience, aren't they?"

Delia talked to Shirley Feldman, Patricia Mathias, and Edna
Crane; none of them knew any Barney connected with Rosalie.
"But she knew a lot of people," said Edna.

Yes, thought Delia, the good-time girl, with a lot of casual
friends—she'd have been a casual sort of girl, take up with anybody any time, the standard not particularly high and not much
caution.

She stopped for a malt at a place in Burbank; it had cooled off
a good deal today, thank heaven; and perched on the counter
stool she had a sudden fleeting thought about those other two
women. She had thought before, about that, how foolish could a
couple of erstwhile respectable women be, talking to a pair of
strange men in a bar, but now she remembered how Doris Fogel
had said wistfully, it was a drag, being alone— Yes, probably
Maureen, even with the job to keep her busy, had been lonely on
occasion too, living alone in that impersonal drab apartment.

And where, probably, they would both have been normally cautious, fairly conventional women, with the couple of extra drinks, celebrating the birthday, they had acted a little out of character.

She used the public phone there to announce herself, and went to see Mr. and Mrs. Clyde Burriss. For, she told herself, no very good reason.

It was a comfortable old stucco house on Sonora Avenue. He was a tall, bald old man in his late seventies, his wife, Helen, a stout white-haired woman in a wheelchair. She seemed to be partially paralyzed but mentally quite sharp. Again, Delia let them think she was from the lawyer's office, and they talked to her readily, ramblingly. They said the Austens had bought the house next door about twenty-five years ago— "Doesn't seem that long, but it was, of course we've lived here nearly forty years. And they weren't young then, but we were all a lot more active back then, of course—used to get together to play cards, do a show together once in a while, not that any of us were great ones for gadding around or night life. George liked to work in the yard, and so did Helen, they used to exhange plants and so on. Since Marion moved to the apartment, we didn't see her quite so often, but we'd have her over to dinner or go see her, until Helen had the stroke."

"I just wondered," said Delia, "if she had mentioned seeing a new doctor." Another thing that had occurred to her was, why and how had Marion Austen picked Dr. Cushing? Had he, possibly, been recommended to her?

"Why, no," said Burriss, "she hadn't. Did she?" He knew the doctor she used to go to had retired. They had Dr. Henry Martin; they'd never heard of Dr. Cushing. "I kind of think," he said, "the old doctor turned his patients over to somebody else, they generally do that, don't they? I don't know the name, if she ever mentioned it, and I don't think she did."

"Clyde, maybe the young lady would like to see a picture," said Mrs. Burriss. "You'd never have taken Marion for seventy-four, you know. She always kept herself up." He ambled out of the room obediently, came back with a little leatherette photograph album. She took it from him, fumbled the pages with her one good hand. "There—that's Marion. That was taken last year, just before I had the stroke, she'd come to dinner and Clyde took it out in the rose garden in back. You'd never think she was seventy-four, would you?"

Oddly enough Delia had never considered what Marion Austen might have looked like. Now, looking at the little colored print, she found Marion Austen assuming three dimensions for her. She stood smiling beside an upright, smiling Helen Burriss: a slim woman of medium height, wearing a sleeveless blue dress, high-heeled white sandals, looking smart and not much more than middle-aged. Her hair was gray, but silvered and smartly coifed; she wore fashionable silver-rimmed glasses, tailored and uptilted.

"It was quite a shock, her dying so sudden," he said. "When that woman called—well, I couldn't leave Helen, I couldn't think what to do, but then I remembered her lawyer's name, I knew he'd know what had to be done."

"It was a grief to me," said his wife gently, "that I couldn't get to her funeral—I can't get out at all anymore. I knew there wouldn't be many people there, they weren't the kind of people always had scads of friends. I always thought so much of Marion, she was a lovely woman, a woman would do anything for you. She was so good to me when I was in the hospital, she came every day and was so good— Why, the very last time we saw her, it was just the Tuesday before she died, she came and brought us a cake, she knew how I loved her bundt cake."

*Some we loved, the loveliest and the best That from his Vintage rolling Time hath prest, Have drunk their cup a Round or two before—* Impatiently Delia shoved old Omar to the back of her mind.

The Burrisses didn't know any more to tell her than she already knew about Marion Austen's death, and she didn't know why she'd wasted the time to see them. She had decided—hadn't she?—that this was a mare's nest. Marion Austen not mentioning any possible worry over symptoms, not to worry her friends. And of course there had been the dizzy spells on the day she died. Mrs. Austen, lying down to take a nap as Rena Perry left, and never waking up. And maddeningly, Delia still felt that there was something a little offbeat about it, somehow.

She wondered if Poor had come across Barney anywhere.

When she got back to the office, Varallo and O'Connor were there talking about the motel heists. Since Bundy hadn't made any mug shots downtown, they had teletyped NCIC asking about any current wants on a similar MO, and come up blank. The National Crime Information Center had been a good idea, a national pool of current information available to all police, but when a crime was cleared or shelved, all the information was cleared out of the computers. At the moment, NCIC didn't know anything about heisters hitting motels.

Poor came in and said he'd talked to six or seven of Rosalie's friends and nobody knew Barney. "And I've got to say ditto," said Delia. "Did you see my note about the phone calls?"

"Yes, and I agree with you that it could be Erwin," said O'Connor, "but since when have we had the manpower to put somebody sitting by a phone waiting for it to ring? If it is him, and you're right, the chances are he was already in San Francisco last Friday night and couldn't have been the one to kill her."

"But he might know Barney."

"Oh, for God's sake," said O'Connor, "the stupid floozy is no loss, her and her boyfriends."

Burt looked in the door; he had a paper cup of coffee in his hand, his objective in climbing the stairs. He said, "It's being one hell of a job to process all the latents we lifted up at the Brand Library, we have to weed out all the regular employees, but we lifted a lot of fairly good ones, eventually we may have something for you. Just thought I'd remind you that we're finished with the Miller car, whoever's entitled to claim it can get it released."

"We haven't heard if there are any relatives," said Varallo. Burt went out. "Well—" After a minute Varallo dialed Doris Fogel's number; she probably didn't go to work until four or so.

She said drearily, "Oh, both Maureen's parents were dead, I don't think she had any relatives but a cousin back east. I don't know if she ever made a will."

"You were about her closest friend?"

"I guess you'd say so."

"Somebody will have to—clear things up. If you want to stop by and pick up the key to her apartment—and her car is here—"

"Oh, I suppose—I'd be the one to do it. All right, I will." She had started to cry again.

"I don't want to sound absolutely idiotic," said Delia, "and after all you're all more experienced detectives than me, but you did look in Records for Joe Esquibel, didn't you?"

Varallo looked at her indulgently and said, "We are trained to go by the book, aren't we? We even asked L.A. and Pasadena. Nothing on him."

"What did we expect?" said O'Connor. "Doris told us he was a perfect gentleman, didn't she?"

Forbes was sitting at his desk by the window apparently daydreaming. His engagement was common property now, and they were all amusedly aware that probably Forbes wasn't going to be operating on all cylinders while the romance was new. They were all hoping she was the right girl for Jeff.

"At least it's cooled off a little," said Poor.

"And the weekend coming up," said O'Connor. "What do you want to bet—" He was drowned out by a siren shrieking, coming closer very fast, and suddenly there was a spatter of gunfire as the siren seemed to be headed for the front door downstairs. They all leaped up and ran to the tall front windows, O'Connor instinctively reaching for the .357 magnum. The siren passed, still making an ungodly clamor, and they just saw the rear of the squad doing about seventy as it passed the building on Wilson. There were more shots.

O'Connor, Varallo, and Poor erupted out of the office and down the stairs. When they got to the front steps, they could see the squad about three blocks up, nearly to Brand, slewed around in the street, and another car on its side ahead of it.

They fell into O'Connor's car and bucketed up there. The patrolman was Gordon, and he was just efficiently snapping the cuffs on a man. The other car was an old beat-up Ford. "He hasn't got a scratch," said Gordon rather breathlessly. "I'm sorry about the wholesale shooting, Lieutenant, but I wanted to stop him before he got up to Brand—he started it."

The man was a Latin type about twenty-five, medium height and stocky; he was wearing old jeans and a faded Hawaiian shirt. He just glowered at them. "Not do nothings," he said.

"What's the story?" asked O'Connor. Already, of course, a little crowd was collecting.

"I was just taking a swing through the parking lot at the Fashion Center," said Gordon, "when I saw this guy come running out, with a man chasing after him—fellow spotted me and waved, and said this joker had a stolen credit card. So I took after him—he was just pulling out onto Glendale Avenue—just to get the plate number if nothing else. He spotted me after him, and I'll be damned but he waves a gun out the window and starts firing at the squad! So I put on the siren, and he's firing at me again when we turn on Wilson—my God, I hope he didn't hit anybody on the street—and I thought, Christ, if he gets up onto Brand—I tried for his back tire, and I got it just as we came past the station—"

"Well, let's see what we've got," said O'Connor. "We'll have to get this heap out of the street—" They went over to look at the car. The driver's door hung on one hinge. In the street just below it lay a gun. "Now just fancy that," said O'Connor, picking it up. It was a J. C. Higgins model 80 automatic. Inside, on the front seat, they could see a couple of boxes of ammunition. O'Connor ducked into the window to get at the glove compartment, and emerged with the registration.

"Pedro Ramirez," he said, looking at it. "Raleigh Street. This you?"

The man shook his head. Gordon started to march him over to the squad. Thomsen drove up in a tow truck and said, "What the hell goes on? My God, I'll have to call up a crane to get that moved."

The crowd had increased. "Where was he coming out of?" O'Connor asked Gordon.

"Magnin's. At the side."

"OK, take him back to the station. John, you can go along and keep an eye on him." O'Connor and Varallo got back in the Ford and O'Connor swung it around to the side street, round the block, and back up Glendale Avenue to the Fashion Center. Probably not ten minutes had elapsed since the start of the whole action; in the parking lot, at the side door of Magnin's department store, a couple of men were standing talking, gesticulating, looking down the street. O'Connor braked and got out, badge in hand.

"You know anything about what happened here?"

"Police—did they catch him? My God, when I heard the shots —yes, yes, I do—did they get him?"

"We've got him, and nobody's hurt. What happened?"

"Thank God for that. Excuse me, my name's Teitelman, I'm the general manager here. That man was in the ladies' lingerie section, picked out a lot of stuff, and handed over a Visa card. The sales clerk ran a routine check on it, and there was a stop on it, put through not an hour before, it was stolen. She came and got me, and I told her to call you, started to question the man, but he just ran out—and I saw the patrol car—"

"Have you got the Visa card?" asked Varallo.

He produced it promptly. It belonged to Miss Nelda McKenzie. "Oh, all those helpful computers," said O'Connor happily. "Thank you so much, Mr. Teitelman."

They went back to the office and found Poor, Forbes, and Delia watching the captive, now supplied with a cigarette and a cup of coffee. He stared up at them and said, "Not say nothings to fuzz."

"Now, you don't want to go to jail alone, do you?" asked Varallo gently. "Come on, be a good boy and tell us who your pal is."

"And where you got this," said O'Connor, showing him the Visa card. He eyed it resentfully. "Come on, this was in the lady's handbag you picked up last night at the motel you knocked over. The owner reported it stolen so nobody could use it—you might have expected that. Why did you try to use it?"

He licked his lips. "I see people with such cards. In shops. Take things, no pay money—just card. Carlos he threw away— but I think—pretty things for Lucita. Don't know why man made trouble—other people no have pay."

"Well, of all the silly things," said O'Connor. "After all the trouble this damned pair has made us—oh, take him over and book him in, John."

"We don't know his name."

"What's your name?" asked O'Connor crossly. The man looked uncomprehending.

"*El nombre?*" said Delia.

"Esperanza. Roberto."

"Take him over. Let's see what shows at this address, Vic."

Five minutes after Varallo and O'Connor had gone out, a call came in from a squad: a new homicide. Delia and Forbes went out to see what it was, and it was one of the sorry little things cops see.

The house was up on Cumberland, a manicured, expensive, well-kept house. Patrolman Adams was gallantly trying to cope with a woman having hysterics in the living room. Forbes took one look, went out to the squad, and called for an ambulance. The woman was screaming and incoherent, and it was incongruous because she was very smartly dressed and made up, but the green shantung sheath was torn away from one shoulder where manicured hands had ripped, and her eyes were frenzied. They held her down until the ambulance came, and the attendants strapped her on a stretcher and took her off in a hurry.

"It's in the bedroom," said Adams. "God. It's funny how people react. She kept her head until just after I got here—she was crying, but that was all. I'd no sooner put in a call to the front office— Oh, God, this is a thing. The kid. The poor kid."

They went to look. Down the hall in a pretty bedroom—a bedroom for a young girl, white canopied bed, a skirted dressing table, a flowered carpet, Degas prints on the walls—the young girl lay on the bed, half her head shot away and blood and brains all over. The gun was still in her right hand.

There was a note lying on the little white desk across the room, a note scrawled on school notebook paper in splotched ballpoint ink. "This is the END because Ill never get a date for the senior prom now and Ive never been pretty or popular like other girls, probly Id never get married and be happy or anybody love me I cant bare it and maybe everybody be sorry for me now."

She had probably visioned the pathetic corpse lying romantically on the soft white comforter, the remorseful tears of parents and cruel friends, but she hadn't known what even a .32 could do at contact point.

There wasn't much to say about it. They went through the

necessary motions. The house belonged to a Richard Hartigan, who was a lawyer downtown; that they got from a next-door neighbor. Forbes phoned him, and he came home.

He was a big man in immaculately tailored clothes. For a long time he didn't seem to find anything to say. Presently he said to them, "But she's fifteen. Fifteen." Forbes asked him about the gun several times before he responded numbly, "Forgotten it was there. There was ammo—in the same drawer—it wasn't loaded."

Delia told him about his wife, that they'd be taking the body. About an inquest. She didn't know whether he was listening.

When she stopped talking, he focused on her with some difficulty. Slowly and politely he said, "But she's only fifteen."

In the end they sent him down to the hospital too.

They got back to the office at five-thirty, too late to start a report on it. Do that tomorrow. Delia was tired, and her head was aching slightly. She might take off early. Forbes went down the hall for a cup of coffee, and when the phone rang on her desk she picked it up automatically.

"Oh, Miss Riordan," said Mrs. Potter. "I've got something rather queer to tell you. I don't know, I suppose you're not going to do any more about it, now we've both decided what the truth was. But you know, that about Dr. Harvey—what he said to her— still bothered me. And I decided to call Sylvia a couple of hours ago. Bob always says the phone service is the cheapest convenience we have, but I never was brought up to making long distance calls at the drop of a hat. I wanted to hear what she thought about it, and I thought it was funny that you couldn't find Dr. Harvey. Well, I got Sylvia, and I told her what you'd said, and she agrees with us it's a thing Marion might have done —just not said anything about her troubles, not to worry us. But you see, Sylvia had lived here until about five years ago, and I thought she might know something about Dr. Harvey. And she did. She says it wasn't spelled that way."

"How do you mean?" asked Delia.

"Like Harvey. It's pronounced that way, but I guess it was French to begin with and they kept the spelling, and it's spelled H-e-r-v-é—you know, with an accent mark. And his first name's

John. She didn't go to him herself, but she knew that. Isn't that a queer thing?"

Surprised, Delia said it certainly was. Mrs. Potter sighed. "Well, I don't suppose I'll stay on much longer—no reason to, and seeing the way the town's changed makes me feel a little sad. But I just thought I'd tell you that."

"Yes, thanks very much," said Delia. When she put down the phone she got out the phone book, and found him right away. John Hervé, and he'd appended the M.D. It was an address on Redwillow Lane in La Cañada.

She dialed the number, but there wasn't any answer.

At the Raleigh Street address, Varallo and O'Connor had found two young women, both good-looking, but only one of them spoke any English. She was surprised at cops coming, but not unduly alarmed. Her name was Elisa Ramirez, and she told them the other girl—a pretty dark little thing—was Lucita Sanchez. "Only she's goin' to marry Pete's cousin pretty soon, they just both come over a couple months ago. Oh, don't worry, they both got papers OK, come over all legal—Pete and me, we're what they call sponsor them, see. Pete helped Roberto get a job in a restaurant, he's just a bus boy but it's a start. Why you want to know about Roberto?"

The other girl looked from one to another, curious, puzzled.

"He's not in any trouble, is he?" It was a man, stocky and clean-shaven, coming in from the bedroom off the little living room; he was just putting on a clean shirt.

"You're Pedro Ramirez?"

"That's right. Has Roberto had an accident? I let him drive that old heap, been meanin' to junk it—I suppose I shouldn't, till he gets a license, but he couldn't pass the test till he learns more English—"

"Has he," asked O'Connor, "maybe picked up some new pals since he's been here?"

"What? Why? Well, I guess he's pretty good friends with another fellow works at that restaurant, Carlos Calderon. Well, it's Casey's up in La Crescenta, but what's all this about? Where's Roberto, and what are cops—"

"He's done you a little favor and junked your car for you," said O'Connor. "He's in jail."

They drove up to the restaurant in La Crescenta and found Carlos Calderon just coming to work. He was the bigger one, the one with the moustache. When they told him about Esperanza, that they had the gun, the Visa card, he stopped protesting innocence all of a sudden.

"That *imbécil condenable!*" he exclaimed in exasperation. "*¡Pedazo de alcorne que!* He's too dumb to live, that one—try to use that card—*¡oye, vaya historia!*"

"So you admit it was the pair of you have been pulling these heists."

He hunched his shoulders in a huge shrug. "You catch up, what else I do? But, last time I take up with a dumb *bracero* just outta the hills, you bet!" He was philosophical; he said, "Anyways, don't hafta work inna joint. I done a li'l time over Arizona once."

They would look up that record tomorrow, just to get it in the evidence. Tomorrow, let Bundy have a look at them; and, said Varallo sardonically, even though it looked all tied up, with the admissions and evidence, better do it the regulation way with a line-up, or otherwise the appointed lawyer might muddy the issue.

When they came back from the jail, Forbes told them about the suicide.

Rhys and Hunter got a call to a heist just after they came on shift. It was at a realtors' office out on West Glenoaks; the owner, Clinton Reeves, had stayed late to do some paperwork, and as he came out to his car a man had held him up. He was mad about it, because as he said there wasn't one damned thing the police could do about it. "Empty gesture calling you. I couldn't begin to give you a description, except that I think he was young—not much more than a kid by his voice. It's damned dark out there, away from the street lights, you can see." The kid had got his watch and about twenty dollars.

"Well, if he's not a pro," said Rhys, "your watch may turn up in a pawnshop—we can put it on the hot list."

Reeves laughed. "I don't know the serial number—it's just an old Bulova."

They went back to the office and Rhys was just starting a report on it when they got a call to the Memorial Hospital.

"My God, another one?" said Hunter. They got down there fast, and found the parking lot empty and silent; but a nurse beckoned them excitedly from the ambulance entrance—the squad was in the parking lot, driver's door hanging open.

In the entrance to Emergency, they stared at the figure hunched on the padded bench, nursing one eye. "What the *hell?*" said Rhys. There were six or eight nurses standing around looking anxious and excited.

Dr. Eddowes looked up with a happy grin, somewhat marred by a cut lip. He was nattily attired in a nurse's white uniform dress, beige nylons and white oxfords, and on the seat beside him was a curly blond wig looking a little the worse for wear. "I told you," he said. "Put out a decoy. I mean, he didn't seem to be at all particular, he was jumping anything female he could catch alone, just out there in the lot. So I fixed myself up as the decoy. You should have seen what a fetching female I made—my sister's going to be mad if that wig can't be fixed up. The middle of the evening's generally slow, and everybody was primed to keep an eye on me. Out I went about twenty minutes ago—Betty here had her hand on the phone to call cops as soon as anything started happening—and I fussed around a car there a few minutes, and bingo, right on schedule he jumped me. I was expecting it, but I wasn't expecting him to be quite so big—" Eddowes was about five-ten, but slenderly built. "Had the hell of a fight with him for about forty seconds, until Whitely and Michaels got there. When they piled on him, he got out from under some way and ran—"

"Oh, hell," said Hunter.

"Not to worry," said Eddowes. "He's only across the street. He ran into the house on the corner and locked the door, but Whitely and Michaels and four ambulance men and your patrolman are all around the place, he won't get out. And God help us if we get coronaries or accident victims until you take him."

They left him still nursing his eye and ran across the parking lot and the street. The corner house was a little old frame place showing no lights. McLeod was on the front porch. "I could have that door down in a minute," he offered.

"So do it."

McLeod put his shoulder to the door, it gave a crack and bent, and he heaved at it again. Both Rhys and Hunter had their guns out. McLeod leaned on the door again and it fell in, and simultaneously there rose hoarse shouts from the back yard. "There he is!" "Tally-ho!" "Grab him, Al!" Rhys and Hunter ran around the house. A writhing mass of bodies heaved on the ground, and came apart, and rose. Its center was a hulking fellow with four men hanging onto him from both sides. Fortunately Hunter had a pair of handcuffs on him.

When they got those on, they dragged him across the street to the Emergency wing to have a look at him. Two ambulance calls had just come in, and the attendants dashed out. "That's him!" said Ruth Boyd triumphantly. "I told you what he looks like!" She had indeed described him accurately, from his widow's peak to his pointed chin and buck teeth.

Eddowes looked at him interestedly. He had for some reason put on the golden wig again, slightly crooked, and he looked like a drag queen after a night's debauch. "My God," he said, "if I'd got a look at him I don't know I'd have risked tangling with him. But at least you've got him."

"What's your name?" asked Rhys. The prisoner was silent, watching them sullenly.

A man came running in the door, a young wild-eyed man in pajamas and bathrobe. "Help! My wife—the baby—it's coming early—" Eddowes sprang up, the alert efficient professional at once, and the incipient parent shied back and yelled, *"What are you?"*

Rhys and Hunter collapsed in mirth. Eddowes said, "Oh, hell," snatched off the wig, and ran for the parking lot.

When they got around to frisking him, the one thing on their capture was a card from the Welfare and Rehab office downtown, bearing the name of James Fielding: probably a parole officer. They brought the rapist back to headquarters, called O'Connor, called down to Welfare and Rehab, and got Fielding's home phone.

Fielding came out; he lived in Toluca Lake and hadn't far to come. He got there just after O'Connor. He said wearily, "When are the courts going to forget about the McNaghten rule? You've got him for rape, of course. He's been on parole for two months."

"What's his name?" asked O'Connor.

"Oh, excuse me, I didn't know we were starting at square one," said Fielding. He was a square and stocky redhead about forty, with an engaging crooked smile. "Marvin Weiss. He's just out of Susanville on his fifth charge of forcible rape."

"What was he doing in a house in Glendale?"

"His uncle owns it. He offered it to him rent free until he could find a job. He has held jobs off and on, mostly off," said Fielding. He looked at Weiss impersonally. "The pedigree goes back, friends, to age six when he tried to set fire to his little sister. The family had just emigrated from Vienna then. It goes on, attempted assault, assault, child molestation, rape, and rape, and rape. And on. And every time he has come before a court the judge has meticulously examined the head doctors with reference to the McNaghten rule."

"Christ," said O'Connor in sole comment. The courts, of course, were slow to change rules, and in the main that was a good, wise thing. But the simplistic reasoning behind the McNaghten rule needed some updating now that they knew a little—just a little—more about what made human people tick. What the McNaghten rule said was, if he knows the difference between right and wrong he isn't insane. And with human people, it wasn't always that simple.

"Of course he belongs permanently up in Atascadero with the criminal insane," said Fielding. "By the way, you needn't mind discussing him while he's here—he has a trick of shutting himself off completely, I don't think he's hearing us at all. But he's got an IQ, so the head doctors say, of around a hundred and ten, which is a little above normal, and he graduated from high school, if that means anything these days with the help of their bilingual program. Technically speaking—semantically speaking—he knows it's morally wrong and against the law to commit assault and rape. So time after time he's been found sane and sent to serve time as an ordinary felon."

"We have all seen it," said O'Connor somberly.

"Yes. Well, you'll be collecting the evidence for the DA," said Fielding. "I only wish to God I could think that this time he'll get a judge with some common sense who'll take a look at his record and commit him where he ought to be. But I won't hold my breath."

"At least he'll be out of circulation awhile."

"Oh, Lieutenant, face the facts," said Fielding. "Even a lot of murderers, on the plea bargains, get three-to-tens nowadays. And you can't have our prisons overcrowded, men doubling up in cells—inhumane treatment. He'll likely get a three-to-five, and the parole board will let him out in fifteen months. To do it again to some other women."

"Mr. Fielding," said O'Connor, "go home. You annoy me so damn much that I'm not going to get any sleep tonight."

Fielding got up leisurely. "That can't be cured."

When they'd both gone, with Weiss stashed in jail—it was nearly the end of shift—Rhys said, "I wonder if that baby came OK." Just for fun, he called, and eventually got Dr. Eddowes.

"Oh, yes, it was a nice healthy little female," said Eddowes. "Seven pounds four ounces. Her name's Julia Mary."

"Did the papa finally decide you're a straight male?"

"I suppose I'll never live that down," said Eddowes.

On Saturday morning, the rest of them heard about Weiss. The P.A. officer, Fielding, came back with chapter and verse on his record, and Varallo and O'Connor discussed exactly what they should package up for the DA. There were two more burglaries reported, and Poor and Boswell went out on those.

Forbes was sitting staring absently at his typewriter; Delia regarded him amusedly. Probably Forbes would stay a little absentminded until he married the girl.

Fielding left at ten-thirty. Delia had tried to call Dr. Hervé again, and again got no answer.

Thomsen came in as she put the phone down. "Slow but sure," he said to O'Connor. "It was the hell of a job, the number of latents we picked up—of course a lot of 'em probably belong to the general public, not on record anywhere, and we had to sort out all those librarians. This is the Brand Library job. But we finally came up with something for you. One solitary print, nice and sharp—sixteen points of identification. Off one of those steel cabinets. It belongs to a fellow named Eugene Dowling, he's got quite a little burglary record with us and LAPD."

"Thank you so much."

"He's off P.A. since March. You can try the latest known address."

# EIGHT

O'Connor was waiting for a call from the DA's office. Varallo and Forbes went out to look for Eugene Dowling. The latest address was an apartment down on Fletcher Drive; by the record Burt had Xeroxed for them, Dowling worked in construction when he wasn't burgling, made decent money. "And why in hell," wondered Forbes, "would a pro burglar go for all those art prints at the library?"

"Your guess as good as mine." It was still warm, but not unbearably so; as usual they would have a respite from now through June, until the real summer heat descended.

It was an old red brick apartment not far from the entrance gates of Forest Lawn. They found the name-slot labeled DOWLING on the second floor. Varallo shoved the bell, and twenty seconds later the door opened. "Yeah?"

Varallo held out the badge and said, "We'd like to talk to you, Dowling." Burt had Xeroxed the mug shot too, and this was Eugene Dowling—burly, going bald, bulldog jaw, small deep-set eyes under beetling brows.

"Now what the hell about? I haven't done nothing." He gave way reluctantly, and they went into a cluttered, dusty, dirty living room. Nothing had been added to the tired old pieces of furniture that came with the place. Another man was sitting on the couch, a smaller man but much the same type, with the same thinning reddish hair and prognathous jaw. There was a plate of hot dogs and potato chips on the coffee table and a six-pack of beer.

"About," said Varallo, "the burglary at the Brand Library, Mr. Dowling."

"I don't know nothing about that," said Dowling.

"Well, we found one of your fingerprints there, you see, on one of the cabinets where the burgled materials were kept."

"Uh, well, that place, see, I was in there just last week to, uh, look at the books. I guess—"

"I'm afraid not, Dowling," said Varallo. "The public isn't allowed in the room where we found your print."

"Oh, hell," said Dowling.

"My God, Gene," said the other man querulously, "You mighta been more careful! That's the third time you got dropped on by leavin' prints! You didn't find any o' mine, did you?" he asked them anxiously.

"Just who are you?" asked Forbes.

"It's my brother Mike," said Dowling morosely. "Damn it, I never seem to have no damned luck at all lately."

Varallo and Forbes took a quick look around; without a search warrant they couldn't open doors or drawers, but they didn't have to. In both the bedrooms there were stacks of the library's art prints propped against the walls. "You'll be coming in to answer some questions," said Forbes.

When they got back to the office, O'Connor had gone down to see the DA, Delia told them. They sat the Dowling brothers down in a couple of chairs and Varallo said, "So let's hear all about it, Dowling. Why the hell did you pull off that job? You hadn't tried to fence all that yet, why?"

"Oh, for God's sake," said Dowling despondently. "This is just my luck. So you get it tied up to us, it's all blown to hell."

"Why," asked Forbes, "did you pick the Brand Library, of all places, Dowling? I suppose when you tried to fence the loot, you found—"

"Hell, no," said Dowling. "We wasn't going to fence it. It was insurance, like."

"Insurance?" said Varallo blankly.

"Yeah, that's right. See, this job I been on—it's a big condo up in the foothills, and I heard the contractor and the architect talkin', about how there's gonna be a big depression again and money no good and no jobs and all. And just after that, there was this story in the *Times,* about the way people invest in things you can always get money for, and it was all about people buyin' pictures. You know, art. Some pictures worth thousands and thousands of dollars. It said this one guy, he owns some big gallery where he sells pictures, he says it's just like insurance, collect pictures. Famous artists, you know. Well, I sure as hell don't want to starve to death, there is a big depression, and I been thinkin' about it. There's one o' those galleries here, down on Brand, and I went and looked it over, but there's an alarm system and grilles on the windows, it looked a pretty tough job. So I thought of that library place. It says Art Library on the front, I was up there on a picnic once. There wasn't any alarm system I could see, and— Hell, you could say it was the easiest job I ever pulled off! It took the hell of a time to carry it all back down to the car—it'd of taken all night to get it all, but see, I reckanized some names. There was labels, like, on them drawers, and I see the names. Picasso was one, he's a real famous artist, I know. And another one named Rem-brant, and a guy named Vango."

"Vango?" said Varallo.

"Van Gogh," said Delia *sotto voce*.

"I figured—"

"But you know, Dowling," said Varallo, "those aren't real paintings. Not the kind people collect. They're just copies— they're not worth anything."

Dowling said in astonishment, "They ain't? Just *copies?* Well, I'll be good and Goddamned! Now that is sure the hell of a thing —if you ask me that's a real con game—an art library just havin' copies of pictures!" He was highly indignant about it.

Forbes prodded them up and started them over to the jail, and Varallo sat back in his desk chair and laughed and laughed and laughed.

"Honestly!" said Delia, giggling uncontrollably. "It makes you wonder how anybody could be so stupid—"

"There is no known limit," said Varallo, "to the stupidity of the small-time pros. Reason the fictional plots about master criminals are so unrealistic. The master criminals are operating all legally as politicians and international bankers, not on our level. I'd better get the machinery started on the warrant." And just then Poor came in with a burglary suspect, so after he'd applied for the warrant he went to help out on the questioning.

Forbes hadn't got back when the phone rang on O'Connor's

desk. It was Patrolman Tracy calling in on an outside line, and he said, "I thought I'd better check. I just got called to a disturbance here, and I think he's a nut of some kind but he's no trouble —he's sitting in the squad crying—but I understand from the householder that it might tie up to a homicide you're working. He was trying to break into a little rental place at the back of a front house, it's a Mrs. Lossner over on—"

"Yes, all right, we know it," said Delia. "Who is he?"

"I don't know, I haven't frisked him yet. I just thought I'd better check—"

"Yes, you'd better bring him in." Some kind of a break in that case?

Forbes came back just before Tracy came in with his catch, and they looked at that one interestedly. He looked to be not much more than twenty or so, a rather weedy weak-chinned fellow with dirty blond hair, in jeans and a soiled T-shirt. He had been crying, and was still distraught, trembling all over like a nervous horse.

They offered him a chair, but he wouldn't sit down until Forbes eased him into it coaxingly. "He had a motorcycle," said Tracy. "Kind of a beat-up one. It's still up there."

"Oh, really," said Forbes.

He looked up at them and said in a thin voice, "I didn't want to make any trouble. I just thought, I might find her there again —if I went back to look—I just wanted to find Rosalie—"

"Oh, you were looking for Rosalie?" Varallo and Poor had just let the suspect go, and come to listen.

"I thought she might have come back. I love her so much—I'd never want to hurt Rosalie, not really—even when she laughed at me—"

He didn't make any objection when Forbes searched him, and came up with a driver's license and Social Security card for Bernard Erwin, at an address in Burbank.

"When did you see Rosalie the last time?" asked Varallo quietly.

Erwin looked at him vaguely. "She laughed at me—she said she wouldn't marry me—if last man—I begged her not to go away —but she wouldn't listen. She laughed." He began to cry again in great convulsive sobs.

They left him alone at that side of the room. "Whatever's behind this, he doesn't belong in jail," said Varallo. In the end, they called up an ambulance and sent him down to the psychiatric wing of Emergency.

It was after twelve. "This one we follow up," said Varallo, looking at the identification, "but let's snatch some lunch first, Jeff. He's not going anywhere."

It was after one when they found the address, on an unpretentious residential street in an old section of Burbank. The man who answered the door, a middle-aged nondescript man, gaped at the badges and identified himself as Ralph Beck. They told him about Bernard, and he was surprised and shaken. "That's terrible—I know he's been worried lately, he couldn't find a job, and of course he was upset over Ken leaving. That's his brother, Ken's nearly ten years older, always kind of protected him—well, they're my nephews, my sister's boys, they been renting the apartment over the garage about two years. Ken's been doing fine but I got to say that Barney's always been something of a weak sister, know what I mean—"

"We've been looking for Ken Erwin, just as a witness. We couldn't find any listing for him anywhere." The first place they had looked, of course, was the DMV, and there was no record of a driver's license.

"Well," said Beck, "the phone's in my name. What you want Ken for?"

"Where's he gone?"

"Why, he's gone up to San Francisco. He had a good job here, chef at that Great Scot restaurant, but he'd saved up a bit of money and he and a friend of his, Don Ferris, they're going to open their own restaurant up there. Don went on ahead and found a building and all, and Ken left about ten days ago."

"Driving?"

"Why, no. What's all this about? Ken can't get a license, he's got tunnel vision and don't drive," said Beck.

"Did you ever hear anything about his girl? Rosalie?"

Beck shook his head. "The boys don't go around confiding in me. Listen, about Barney—is he really bad, off his head? I suppose I better wire Sarah—his mother, she lives in Tennessee."

"Mr. Beck, do you mind if we have a look at their apartment? We haven't got a search warrant but—"

"No, that's OK. I get you a key. I suppose I ought to go and find out what those head doctors think. Did you say, the Emergency place at the Memorial?"

"That's right."

The little apartment over the garage at the back of the lot was very dirty and cluttered. There were dirty dishes piled all over the minute kitchen counters, and clothes strewn over the bed in the second, smaller bedroom; the bed was an unmade tangle of soiled sheets.

And the knife was lying on the little coffee table in the front room. It was a switchblade, opened out for use, with a blade not very wide and tapering to a sharp point. The blade was heavily encrusted with rusty brown stains all down its length, and a part of the handle.

Varallo said, "Well, there we are. Answers, all of a sudden. Barney fell for Ken's girl, and she just laughed at him. You can read it, just from what he said to us."

Forbes massaged his long jaw. "He's got a motorcycle. Baker said she asked Barney to take her to the station. On his motorcycle?"

"Rosalie wasn't a particular girl, she wouldn't have minded—it was only across town. She went in and bought her ticket, and when she came out he was arguing and pleading with her again, and she laughed just once too often—he went off his head and stabbed her. Yes," said Varallo thoughtfully, "and she probably meant to mail Baker's check to the bank for deposit, and transfer the account when she got up to San Francisco. I don't suppose we'll ever know what happened to her handbag—unless somebody's fool enough to try to cash that check."

"And I wonder if he'll ever come to trial," said Forbes.

"See what the head doctors say."

They eased the knife into a plastic evidence bag and went back to the office, dropped that off at the lab. Varallo called the hospital and eventually talked to a doctor who knew something.

"Well, he seems to be in a cataleptic state now. I couldn't venture on any prognosis. Oh, that you can be sure of—he's not faking it."

O'Connor had just got back from the DA's office, and listened to that interestedly. "Simple when you know. I suppose in time Ken Erwin would have heard about the murder, and come in, and we'd have heard about Barney."

"I wonder," said Varallo. "He might have decided that Rosalie had just changed her mind, and let it go. Damnation, I meant to ask Beck for his address. Well, there's time. Where's Delia?"

"I've got no idea, I just got back."

Delia and John Poor had gone out to look at another homicide. It was an old apartment on Louise Street, and when they got there Stoner was waiting, took them up to the second floor. "I don't think any of these women went in, I told 'em not to," he apologized, "but there wasn't any way to secure the scene and I don't figure it's too important. It's open and shut."

There were four women standing around in the hall outside an apartment door broken in and off its hinges. "This is the manageress, Mrs. Colquhoun—"

"Nora Colquhoun," she said, quivering several chins at them. She was pleasurably thrilled at all the excitement.

"Mrs. Reade, Mrs. Violente, Mrs. Gunther."

"Oh, it was awful!" burst out one of them. "I live right next door, and she was usually quiet, no loud parties or anything, but this was just awful—since about half an hour, forty minutes ago—"

"I even heard it down at the end of the hall—"

"Some man yelling at her, and her screaming back, loud enough to hear plain, he kept yelling she was a—a Goddamned little snitch, brought the cops down on him, and calling her all sorts of dirty names—and her crying and hollering she never would—and a lot of bangs and crashes—"

"I called down to Mrs. Colquhoun, asked her to call the police—"

"The detectives will want to talk to you all later," said Stoner firmly. They dispersed very reluctantly, dying for a look into the apartment. He followed Delia and Poor in.

"The girl's name is Gloria Carson. When I got here I had to break in the door, they'd said it sounded like a fight, he was assaulting her. Only I was too late." The girl, looking small and frail, was lying quietly alongside the coffee table. She was wearing shorts and a T-shirt, and one thong sandal had fallen off and was upside down across the room. Poor squatted over her. "Oh, she's gone," said Stoner. "Looks as if she got knocked against the corner of the table."

"Depressed skull fracture," said Poor, "for a bet." He stood up.

"When I got in, the guy was raving—higher than a kite, drugs, not drink, but he passed out in a couple of minutes and I got an ambulance and sent him in. There was ID on him, he's a Bruce Watkins, Hollywood address. Christ, these stupid, stupid people, getting hooked on the dope—all the trouble they make—"

Delia was feeling a little tired of the stupid people too. So this was Gloria Carson. Gloria who wouldn't listen to a word against her own true love, whatever he was and however he treated her, so she was lying here dead of her stupidity. There'd be plenty of evidence here for the lab to collect, and evidence from the various witnesses. And when Bruce Watkins came to trial, his lawyer would probably plead diminished responsibility because of the drugs, and he might get off with a comparatively light sentence. It was all very depressing. There would be an inquest on Gloria some time next week, as there had been inquests this week on Rosalie and Maureen, the cumbersome machinery of the court getting started.

Stoner went back on tour, and Delia and Poor called the lab. When Thomsen got there, they went back to the office to write the report. And all those women would have to be brought in to make formal statements.

Poor was telling Varallo and O'Connor about it. Delia sat down and looked at her typewriter with distaste. She really did not feel like typing the report. It was five-twenty. And she thought, better leave a note for the night watch. To call Jean Carson; she wouldn't be home from work, now. She was just as glad not to have to break the news.

Today she was glad to leave the office. It was much cooler; she rolled the driver's window down, grateful for the rush of cool air on her face. The traffic wasn't bad, though the intersection at Riverside was always a bottleneck.

She ran the car into the garage and went in the back door, down the hall to look into the living room. And, unexpected and shocking, a frightening thing happened to her. They were there in front of the TV, the only family she had ever had—dear stubborn Alex, stout comfortable Steve—and for one nightmarish moment as she looked at them she saw them as two rather foolish and narrow-minded old men, men who had never had many interests or emotions in life beyond the petty drudgery of the job. Her world wavered and her heart turned over—and then just as suddenly everything was on an even keel again and they were just Alex and Steve, familiar and loved.

"Dinner in fifteen minutes," said Steve. "Everything's ready."

"Yes, fine," said Delia. "Alex, what do you want for your birthday?"

Rhys read Delia's note, when he and Hunter came on, and grimaced. Part of the job, they often had to break the bad news; they never enjoyed it. He called the Hollywood number and broke the bad news to Jean Carson. He was going on tactfully to tell her about the mandatory autopsy, the inquest, but she just said, "Oh, God. Oh, God," and hung up on him. Well, she had been told.

Saturday night was sometimes busy; tonight they sat here all evening and got no calls at all. They discussed the rapist, still amused at the spectacle Eddowes had made. It was boring sitting there with nothing to do, and they were both yawning when just at eleven o'clock there were footsteps on the stairs and three people came in, a man and two women.

"The man at the desk said to talk to you—the detectives."

"Yes, sir. What can we do for you?" All three of them looked very distraught and worried. The man and one woman were in their forties, the other woman much older. They were all well dressed, looked like upper-class people.

The man was abrupt and businesslike. "My name's Brian Cunningham," he said, and laid a card on the desk: CUNNINGHAM, BREWSTER AND CAHILL, ARCHITECTS, RESIDENTIAL AND COMMERCIAL, it said. "I'll tell you as quickly as possible because you've got to get right on this. This is my wife, Betty, my mother, Mrs. Gregory Cunningham. My parents used to live here, but when my father retired they moved to a mobile home in Palm Springs. Of course they come up on visits, and they've been here since last

Thursday. Tonight after dinner my father was going up to La Crescenta to visit an old friend, James Barnes. He left the house, we live on Cabrillo Drive, about six-thirty, intended to be home by ten. When he hadn't arrived by ten-thirty, I called Mr. Barnes, and Dad hadn't been there at all."

"But where is he?" burst in the older woman. "What could have happened? An accident—"

"He's got identification on him, of course. If there'd been an accident, we should have heard about it by now." Cunningham was keeping his seething agitation under control; his wife laid a hand on his arm, and her eyes were anxious.

"Yes, sir, you'd think so," said Rhys. "Or, of course, if he'd been taken ill on the way. What's he driving?"

"A brand new VW Rabbit, dark tan," said Cunningham promptly. "My mother had the plate number in her address book—trust Dad to think of everything, just in case she ever needed— It's JTL-nine-oh-nine. It's registered to Gregory Cunningham, nine four two Aladdin Way in Palm Springs."

"That's very helpful, Mr. Cunningham. We can put out an all-points bulletin on the car right away. If you'll let me have your home phone—as soon as we find out anything—"

"But where can he *be*, Brian? And he hasn't got his high blood pressure medicine with him, he has to take it every six hours— We would have heard about an accident, wouldn't we?"

"Now, Mother. We're doing all we can. You'll be on it, then," he said to Rhys and Hunter. He was a conventional, self-controlled man, but there was deep fear in his eyes.

"We'll be on it, Mr. Cunningham. We'll be looking. There's nothing you can do but go home and wait. We'll be in touch as soon as we find out anything."

But when they had gone out, they looked at each other and Hunter said, "I've known hospitals to make some goofs now and then."

"First place to check." If Gregory Cunningham had had a stroke or heart attack—or an accident—in the five hours since six-thirty, he would have ended up in Emergency at the Memorial, even from La Crescenta. They might have had a busy night down there, and it wouldn't do any harm to check there first.

Rhys called, and seeing that they had a little personal in down there now, he talked to Dr. Michaels. He listened and said definitely, "No, Mr. Rhys. We've had a couple of accident victims in, and an attempted suicide an hour ago—Eddowes is still with him—but they're all properly identified and relatives have been notified."

"Well, what does that leave?" Rhys asked Hunter.

"Possibilities. He'll be in his late sixties, early seventies. He might have felt an attack coming on, had time to pull off and park, and just hasn't been found yet."

"Um," said Rhys. "Well, we'd better put out the A.P.B. I'll have Communications get it on the air, this won't wait till the day watch gets briefed."

And she had a terrible nightmare, in the middle of the night. She thought that she came home from work, just in the ordinary way, and came in the back door and walked down the hall to the living room, and they were sitting there waiting for her. But when she went closer, it wasn't Alex and Steve at all, but just two big stuffed dolls in the wheelchair, the armchair, and she was engulfed with the most deadly fear she had ever known— Where were they, where had they gone? Frantically she rushed from room to room, searching the house—Alex's bedroom downstairs, the dining room, kitchen, lavatory—upstairs, Steve's room, the spare bedroom, closets— They were nowhere, they were gone—

She had to get help to find them, and it came over her like a warm wave of light that she had to call Isobel, because Isobel would know where Neil was and Neil would always help her, Neil would find them for her—

She ran to the head of the stairs and down, her mind desperately and only on the telephone—and they were all waiting for her in the entrance hall, and they were all laughing at her hideously, gleeful and mocking because she was so frightened— Isobel in her wedding dress, and Neil, Mr. and Mrs. Fordyce, Sergeant Hagen, Marcia Hunt, Geraldine Fulmer, Harriet Catlin, Sergeant Julie Murdoch who taught the phys. ed. class at the Academy, little Dr. Garcia from the Spanish class, and Dr. Borchard, she'd never known what he looked like but he was there too, and Laura Varallo, Sergeant Dominick, her first watch com-

mander, and away back in the shadows behind them a queer
robed figure that even might be old Omar the tentmaker. . . .
Laughing at her, pointing fingers and howling . . . She tried
to call to them, Help me, help me find them . . . but they were
all retreating from her now, the hall opening to a vast chamber
beyond the front door, and they were sliding farther and farther
away, all still laughing and mocking and jeering at her, until
they disappeared in the dark and she was left alone with nothing, nothing, nothing, only a speck in a dark place alone—
Delia woke with a start, covered in perspiration, her heart
pounding, and couldn't get back to sleep for a long time.

On Sunday morning O'Connor didn't come in, of course—he'd
be out with that dog of his. They all discussed the queer disap-
pearance of Gregory Cunningham—he ought to have been found
by now, whatever had happened to him. Brian Cunningham was
calling in by the time the day watch came on, and there was
nothing to tell him. They still had a couple of burglaries to follow up, a couple of heists.
"There aren't many places a man can disappear in a city," said
Katz. "It's funny."
"Funny is not the word," said Varallo. "The A.P.B. should
turn up the car eventually. We can trace his route, we've got the
address he was heading for—chase a squad up to cover it. He
could still be parked somewhere dead of a coronary."
"Could he have had a brainstorm and thought he was on his
way back to Palm Springs?"
"Unlikely, though you never know."
Delia finally got the report on Gloria Carson written. She
checked the hospital and a doctor told her that Bruce Watkins
was suffering extreme withdrawal symptoms; he was evidently
an old-fashioned user, hooked strictly on the heroin. Remembering what those women at the apartment had said, and they
would all be coming in to make statements today, she checked
with the Hollywood precinct to ask if he'd been picked up on
anything last week. A Sergeant Rambeau went to find out, and
came back to say that Watkins had been dropped on last Tuesday, making a narco sale to juveniles; he'd been arraigned on
Friday and made bail by Friday afternoon. Delia explained, and

he said disgustedly, "What a hell of a thing. It beats all how sometimes the nice girls fall for such bastards."

Delia agreed, and put the phone down. Everybody had gone out somewhere. She sat back and lit a cigarette and began to proofread the report.

"Oh, Miss Riordan, I didn't know if you'd be in on Sunday."

She looked up. "Yes, it's just another day to us."

"I suppose so," said Mrs. Frances Potter. "I'm going home tomorrow—Fred's driving down today to get me. But I wanted to stop by and thank you for being so nice. I was so upset over Marion's death, I guess I just couldn't believe it was true, her going so sudden, and had to imagine there was something wrong about it. But—" she let out a sigh— "I guess it must have been just the way you figured out. Poor Marion, so alone, not a chick or a child of her own—but she was always a brave woman, and it would be just like her to do that, never mentioning her troubles to get us fussing about her. Well—it won't be the same world without her, is all I can say. The first one of us to go, the three of us friends for nearly sixty years—"

(*Whether the Cup with sweet or bitter run, The Wine of Life keeps oozing drop by drop, the Leaves of Life keep falling one by one.*)

"I just hope that young woman appreciates her good fortune," said Mrs. Potter.

"What young woman do you mean?"

"Why, the one used to do housework for Marion, I forget her last name, Rena something. Marion was going to leave her the apartment, you know."

"No, I didn't know," said Delia. "She was? That seems—well, rather a large legacy for—"

"Well, you might think so." At tacit invitation Mrs. Potter sat down in the chair beside the desk. "But on the other hand, you can see how Marion was thinking. Oh, she told us both all about it. You see, the only relative either she or George had was George's niece Yvonne back in Chicago, they were going to leave everything to her. After George died, Marion made another will leaving it all to her, which was only right and proper. But about six months ago Yvonne was killed in an accident—only about forty-one, she was, a terrible thing, and she'd never married, so that left Marion without any relatives at all, her own or in-laws. She said it put her in a little quandary. She didn't have much, you see, but there was the apartment—main property she had to leave someone. It brings in a nice steady income, those places rent for two-fifty a month now, and even with the taxes up— Well, she thought of this and she thought of that, and as she said, she might leave it to be sold and each of us to get half, but there wasn't much point in that. We were all the same age and getting on. And we're both *all right*, you see—in fact a lot better off than Marion was. And we've got families. Fred and I have the ranch paid for, it's worth about a hundred times what that apartment is. And the children all doing fine, they'd always see I was all right. And Sylvia's son is into land development over there, he's really made the money, Sylvia says. And all our children well provided for. And there wasn't anyone else. So she thought it over—Marion was always so practical—and she said, well, the nice steady income from the apartment had kept her and George comfortable, and it'd certainly be no use to her after she was dead. She'd known this woman for years, you know, and she said she was such a good soul, a hard worker and a nice woman, and she'd had a lot of hard luck in her life, never had it very easy. As long as it didn't matter to us, and of course it didn't, she was going to leave her the apartment house. In fact, she made the will about three months ago. She left her few pieces of good jewelry between Sylvia and me, and she left her sterling flatware to Sylvia and the antique dining room chairs to me, I'd always admired that set. And the rest to this Rena."

"That was generous of her," said Delia slowly. "The place must be worth quite a bit."

"I don't know real-estate values down here any longer. But as she said, when she was finished with it, why not see that somebody had it who'd appreciate it, and Rena was still a young woman. She'd be glad to think that she might have a little easier life." Mrs. Potter got up. "I really just stopped by to thank you, didn't mean to take up your time. It's been a pleasure meeting you, Miss Riordan."

Delia responded automatically. Her cigarette had long burned out in the ashtray; she lit another.

Rena Perry. That place would bring in—what?—even a modest

apartment building, a little gold mine in a way. Taxes and maintenance would cut into it sharply, but—

Rena Perry. No, it looked like a modest legacy in a way, but when you thought about it, with real-estate values so high—

Rena Perry.

She looked up the number, and listened to empty ringing before she remembered that Rena Perry had been going off for a little vacation. Damn, she thought. And then she thought, did she want to talk to Rena? Ask her pointblank, had she known about that will? Because, even if she had—

And she remembered the woman chattering on, in her warm friendly voice, something about her sister Lois, and Lois worked part time for a Dr. Dally "down on Alameda."

She got out the phone book. He was there, Harold J. Dally, D.D.S.

At that point, Poor came in with Mrs. Colquhoun, and Delia put the phone book away and prepared to take the statement down in shorthand. The various statements would keep her busy for a while.

Surprisingly, there were no burglaries and no heists on Sunday night. And Gregory Cunningham still hadn't shown up, or his new VW Rabbit. Which was more surprising.

The pace slackened a little, with no new ones down, but there was still enough to do, still the statements to take, and undoubtedly the DA's office would want a consultation about Weiss, about Erwin. The doctors still weren't saying much about Erwin.

Among other things, they hadn't got the formal statements and confessions from Roberto Esperanza and Carlos Calderon, and at ten o'clock Varallo had his mouth open to suggest that Delia accompany him over to the jail to take those down in Spanish, which would be easier all around, when he noticed that she had picked up her handbag and was on the way out.

"And where are you going?"

"Out," said Delia briskly. "I'll be back sometime."

If anybody had asked her, she couldn't have said in all conscience that she was on any business concerned with the job. It was just a niggling little feeling up the spine; or maybe just simple female curiosity.

She walked into Dr. Dally's office, which was a modest one but well appointed and pleasantly furnished, and looked around. It was a small waiting room, with a counter across one end with a sliding glass panel; that was open.

"Can I help you?" The voice was friendly; the woman appeared there at the other side of the counter, and Delia saw the resemblance at once: the light brown hair, pale blue eyes, general shape of face, tone of voice.

She said, "You're Rena Perry's sister Lois, aren't you? She mentioned you, and where you work. I've been trying to reach her, but I remember now she said she was going on a vacation."

"Oh. Yes, that's right, I'm Lois Farber." She would be a couple of years older than Rena, possibly thirty-six, around there. "Yes, Rena took a few days off, thought she might go up to Big Bear. What was it you wanted to see her about?"

"Oh," said Delia vaguely, "I'm from Mr. Adler's office—the lawyer, you know. Mrs. Austen's lawyer. It's just some red tape about the will."

"Oh!" said Lois Farber. "Gee, I hope it isn't anything that can't wait till Rena gets back."

"Well, maybe you could help me."

She looked uncertain. "Anything I can do. It's about time for my break—and there aren't any appointments until eleven-thirty. Look, I usually go across the street for a cup of coffee, would that be OK?"

"Fine. By the way, my name's Riordan."

It was a garish little place with tiny plastic tables and teetery chairs. They ordered coffee and Lois Farber accepted a cigarette. She was, seen full length, a little too comfortably plump, but she had the same warm voice and forthright manner of her sister. Delia thought, not too much education, or it hadn't taken; not the brainiest woman around, but honest and very probably a good wife and mother.

She added cream to her coffee and said, "So you knew about the will."

Lois Farber nodded. "She told Rena about it. She must have been a real nice woman, Miss Riordan—Rena always liked her.

She told Rena she didn't want any thanks, and she surely hoped it'd be a good long time before Rena inherited from her—they both laughed about that, Rena said—but she just wanted her to know. And Rena told her it'd likely be years and years, as lively as she was—but there, maybe Mrs. Austen had a kind of premonition, because it wasn't three months. Of course she was pretty old. But it's going to make a lot of difference to Rena, I'm glad she's had some good luck finally." Lois sipped her coffee.

"Has she—had a lot of hard luck?" asked Delia.

"Well, you could sure say so. She was the youngest of us, you know, and Mama died when she was only ten—I was twelve. Bill and Ray were both older, and they got away as soon as they were old enough, they wouldn't stand for Dad slave-driving them and all his meanness. Rena and I had all the housework and the vegetable garden and the hens to take care of, and Dad kicking like a bay steer over laying out any money—grudged every cent, but he expected three big meals a day even so, how that man could eat— Well, I had to run away with Henry, Dad had a fit when I told him we wanted to get married—of course he'd be losing all my work, see. And I hated to leave Rena, but Henry said we have to live our own lives, which is so. Heavens above, that was sixteen years back. And Rena was stuck there with all that work till Dad died so sudden—he was only fifty-five but the doctor said he wasn't surprised because he'd been such a glutton for food, it was something enteritis. Only it turned out the farm was mortgaged to the hilt, so there wasn't anything left."

"Oh, I see," said Delia.

"Well, Rena came down here, that was about twelve years back, and she got married after a while and had the baby, only her husband, Jim Perry, he was kind of a lazy bum, didn't make much money, and she fretted that she couldn't go out to work on account of the baby, you see, but—oh, that was just awful!—the house burned down one day and Jim and the baby were both burned to death. It wasn't much of a house, little old frame place they were renting outside town. Rena was out at the market, the pilot light on the stove went out and the gas started the fire. At least Jim had some insurance from the union. But you can see what hard luck Rena's had."

"Yes, I see," said Delia. "Were things better after that?"

"Well, yes and no. She went to work at one of these convalescent homes, and Rena's always been a smart girl, she picked up a lot about nursing even if she never went to school for it, she worked in a couple of those places and did housework for people on the side. Then she got a good job with an old lady who'd been in the rest home where she worked, the old lady was in a wheelchair and she needed somebody to take care of her, do the cooking and cleaning and so on. She couldn't abide the rest home, so her relatives got Rena to take care of her. Rena said it was a real easy job, and she got good money for it. Only wouldn't you know, just a couple of months later the old lady died real sudden. So she went back to the rest home, but they don't pay much, and a little bit later she got another job taking care of an old lady at home, and then that one died too. And after a while Rena decided she could make a lot better money just doing housework for people."

"I see," said Delia.

"You can see she hasn't had an easy life. It's a shame she didn't find a good steady husband after she lost Jim. But this is going to be a real break for her, when this Mrs. Austen thought enough of her to leave her that apartment building. Good rents coming in, maybe now she can take it easy for a while. I'm real glad for her."

Fascinated, Delia said, "Yes, I can see that."

Lois lit another cigarette. "Well, what was the red tape you wanted to ask about?"

Delia couldn't think of a single plausible thing to say.

At one o'clock, just as Varallo had got back from lunch, the desk relayed a call up to him. He picked up the phone absently. "Glendale Police, Varallo."

"Hey, *paisano*. What passes for my mind finally rang the bell, and I remembered."

"Don't tell me. What?"

"Well, I told you the name rang a bell," said Olly Lanza. "Joe Esquibel. I was just making up a margarita a minute ago, and it hit me like lightning. It was Bill Dorman—he's one of our regulars comes in a couple times a week—it was him said the name.

Maybe five, six months ago, he said he'd won a bundle on a horse Joe Esquibel told him about."

"Well, *grazie molto vero*," said Varallo. "Can you tell me where to find Dorman?"

"Oh, sure. He and his brother got a printing shop a couple of blocks up from the bar, on San Fernando."

# NINE

"But I don't understand this at all," said Dr. John Hervé perplexedly. This time Delia had got an answer on the phone. The house on Redwillow Lane was a rambling redwood place with a tall background of eucalyptus trees. A little robinlike woman had let her in and left her alone with Dr. Hervé in a long living room furnished in early American. "I'm very sorry to hear of Mrs. Austen's death," he said, "but I don't understand this at all." He looked again at the filled-out medical form in its manila folder. "It's quite impossible." Dr. Hervé was a tall spare man with a lean intelligent face, scholarly horn-rimmed glasses. "Who," he asked, "is this Cushing? I never heard of the man."

"Well, she went to see him for an examination. As her new doctor," said Delia.

He snatched off his glasses, polished them on his handkerchief, put them back on. "But why? When I was planning to retire, I gave all the patients recommendations to different physicians. It's standard practice. There were five physicians agreed to take on my old patients, and I recall distinctly that Mrs. Austen chose Dr. Seligman because his office was fairly close in. I sent all her medical records to him." He looked at the form again. "Mrs. Austen had been a patient of mine for many years, not that she came to see me often—a very robust woman—but this," he said flatly, "is impossible. For any physician to suggest that a condition like this could develop in six months' time—I had seen her in December. Her heart was as sound as that of a woman half her age. What did the death certificate say?" he asked sharply.

"I don't know, we haven't seen it."

He said doubtfully, "Well, people do die suddenly, for all sorts of reasons, and I hadn't given Mrs. Austen a complete physical in several years, but—I can't understand this at all, it doesn't make sense." He read over the form again and said absently, "I suppose you're sure it *was* Mrs. Austen who died?—of course that doesn't make sense either—"

Delia, thinking of the fictional plots about substituted bodies, had a wild vision of Marion Austen kidnapped and a convenient corpse left in her place—which was nonsense, people who knew her had seen her body. But Dr. Hervé was obviously a man of great common sense and absolutely trustworthy, and Delia sat back and told him the whole story, including what she had heard two hours ago from Lois Farber. He listened quietly, his eyes keenly intelligent. At the end he said decisively, "There are certainly some grounds for investigation here, though I confess I can't see how such symptoms could have been artificially induced—I'd like to talk to this Cushing. Perhaps it's not strictly ethical, but under the peculiar circumstances—"

"You might get more out of him than I did," agreed Delia.

He followed her back to Glendale in a middle-aged Dodge sedan, and they went into the spanking-new medical clinic together. The receptionist was cold, giving the distinct impression that it might be days before an appointment with Dr. Cushing could be arranged, but Dr. Hervé had a lifetime of experience with her ilk, and overrode her easily. That, and Delia's badge, brought them Dr. Andrew Cushing in the cramped tiny office within fifteen minutes.

"I've seen you before—oh, the policewoman," he said, annoying Delia considerably: she had spent some nine years getting to be not a policewoman but a detective. He listened to them and looked very annoyed himself.

"If you're suggesting that I made a completely wrong diagnosis, all I can say is—"

"Not at all necessarily," said Hervé stiffly. "We aren't accusing you of anything, of course. I am just as puzzled as you are over this, we're simply trying to get at the truth. Mrs. Austen was my patient for a good many years and I was conversant with her physical condition, and it most certainly did not jibe with"—he flicked the report onto the desk—"with what you've recorded here."

"Well, all I can tell you is that that was her condition when I saw her," said Cushing belligerently. "I may have only been in practice three years, doctor, but I think I'm a reasonably competent physician, after all."

"If you are suggesting," said Hervé angrily, "that a condition like this could develop within six months' time, I'll take issue with that, doctor. I had seen Mrs. Austen in December, and she—"

"I never suggested any such damned thing," said Cushing in a loud voice. "How could I? All I'm saying is, that's the state the woman was in when I saw her. I'd also have said there had been a series of small strokes, she was obviously not mentally competent, not taking in anything I said—the typical brain lesions that result from that—I had to explain about the additional tests I wanted to the young woman who had brought her in—"

"What young woman?" asked Delia and Dr. Hervé together.

"Oh, a daughter or niece, I suppose, I didn't ask. She was the one who made the next appointment—when I saw the old lady wasn't quite all there, I talked to her and—"

"Mrs. Austen," said Hervé sharply, "was one of the sanest women I ever knew, her mind quite sharp. Could it have been possible that she was drugged in some way, you wouldn't have suspected it, of course, but I still would have thought—"

"For God's sake," said Cushing, "do you think I wouldn't have spotted such a thing? Drugged, for God's—she was just a vague, mentally confused old lady, and—"

"If you weren't expecting—I can't make this out at all—"

"Well," said Cushing crossly, "she wasn't under any influence. She was just an old lady with brain damage from small strokes, and this precarious heart condition."

"What about the young woman?" asked Delia.

"Well, what about her? She was just an ordinary young woman —oh, I don't remember what she looked like, about thirty-five or so, no, I don't know that I would recognize her again, I see a lot of people, you know, and I only saw her the once—"

"Well, you only saw Mrs. Austen once too, didn't you?" said Delia.

"Didn't you examine the body?" asked Hervé in surprise.

Cushing said defensively, "Well, no, when I was informed she had died I wasn't at all surprised, the state she was in. I'd seen her four days before, and I didn't think it was necessary—I've got quite a large practice, I'm a busy man. I made out the death certificate—syncope, cardiac failure—and sent it over to the funeral home." Hervé uttered a snort of disapproval. "There wasn't any reason, for God's—"

"Do you think," asked Delia, "that any of your nurses would remember the young woman?"

"How should I know?" It emerged that only the receptionist Ella and his immediate assistant Ursula would have seen her; he summoned them in. They both vaguely remembered the young woman bringing in a new patient, but couldn't describe her, didn't think she had mentioned any name.

"But there is no way," said Hervé perplexedly, "that such symptoms could have been induced, that I can imagine—"

"Do you remember what Mrs. Austen looked like, Dr. Cushing?" asked Delia.

"Oh, she was just an old lady, gray hair, rather nice looking, probably quite pretty when she was young—"

"Oh!" said Delia suddenly. She looked up at the receptionist, who had lingered. "Could you tell me exactly when her appointment was, please?" She went out, came back with the day book.

"Mrs. Austen was scheduled at two o'clock on April the twenty-sixth."

"Well," said Delia. "Excuse me, do you mind if I use your phone?" She had to look up the number. Clyde Burriss answered on the second ring. "Mr. Burriss," she said after identifying herself, "you told me that Mrs. Austen came to see you the Tuesday before she died. That was on the twenty-sixth. Do you remember what time she was there?"

"Why, yes," he said at once. "She got here about two o'clock, brought us a cake like Helen told you. She stayed about an hour. I know it cheered Helen up, she'd been feeling blue that day."

Delia relayed that to the two doctors. "You never saw Mrs. Austen at all, Dr. Cushing."

"Then who the hell was it?" he asked blankly.

Hervé said severely, "It's not up to me to offer any criticism of another physician, Cushing, but I must say in my opinion you were pretty damned slipshod here, not to have looked at the body. You know what we've got here, don't you? Grounds for an exhumation. I would really like to know what did cause Marion Austen's death."

"Sure," said Bill Dorman, looking with interest at Varallo's badge. "Joe Esquibel works at that big wholesale hardware warehouse in the next block. Nice fellow. We run into him sometimes at the Mexican restaurant up from there, drop in for lunch. Yes, I remember him giving me that tip on a horse—I'm not a regular player, neither of us is, but I'd happened to mention we were going out to the track that Sunday."

"Thanks."

"What do the cops want with Joe? He's a very steady, straight guy—"

"Just a witness to something," said Varallo.

Katz was with him; they found the warehouse, and found Joe Esquibel there. He looked like a good type, fairly good-looking, about thirty; he just looked surprised at the badge. Varallo asked him if he remembered being in the Casino Bar a week ago Saturday night.

"Sure, that's right," said Esquibel.

"You were with another man. Who was it?"

"Ed Novitsky, he just went to work here about three weeks back."

"How did you come to be with him? You close pals?"

"Not specially, no, I don't know him very well. What's this all about? Well, there was a rush order came in, that late afternoon, for all the hardware on a big apartment building going up in the valley, and the boss asked Ed and me to do overtime, get the truck all loaded to be ready in the morning. There was about fifty cases of doorknobs and drawer handles, stuff like that, it was a little job. We got finished about nine-thirty, and Ed suggested a drink, and I remembered Bill Dorman had said that place up there was pretty nice."

"So you went in for a drink," said Varallo, "and you got talking with a couple of women."

Esquibel said equably, "So you know so much about my private life, yeah. Ed started to talk to them first. What's this all about?"

"You took one of them out dancing."

"I did. I like to dance, I go up to this place in Montrose fairly often, it's got a good combo. I been dating different girls, but not that night, of course. This woman seemed—" he hesitated— "well, OK, I mean she wasn't a very young chick, but pretty good-looking, and she said she liked to dance. There wasn't anything wrong about it, I don't know why the cops are interested, I took her home safe, so what?"

"Nothing," said Varallo. "We're not interested in that. You left Novitsky sitting there in the bar with the other woman? At about eleven-thirty?"

"Yeah, that's right."

"Where do we find Novitsky? Is he here today?"

"He called in sick. The boss 'll probably have his address." They left him staring after them curiously.

It was an old apartment building on an old street in Eagle Rock, and Novitsky was there. He opened the door to them and said, "What do you want? I've got the hell of a hangover." He stared at the badges. He was older than Esquibel, and they could see that when he wasn't bleary-eyed and unshaven he wouldn't be bad looking, a dark, rather saturnine fellow. Varallo and Katz went in past him, into a drab living room.

"We can guess most of it but you might do some filling in," said Varallo. "You were in the Casino Bar with Joe Esquibel a week ago Saturday night, and you were talking to two women. Joe went off with one of them to do a little innocent dancing. And when the other one left, you followed her out and had a little argument with her and ended up killing her. Is that the way it went?"

He was taken completely by surprise at this frontal attack; he began to shake his head and then stopped. "The time limit is a little tight for it to have been anybody else," said Katz. "The doctor stretched the possible time of death to two-thirty A.M., but by the processes of digestion it was probably a lot earlier, not much before midnight. And she was left in her car three blocks from that bar. What about it, Novitsky?"

He turned and walked across to the window, stood looking out. After a long minute he said dully, "Oh, my God. It was—just an accident. No, I shouldn't say that. Because I shouldn't ever take more than a couple of drinks, it always sets me spoiling for a fight, ready to lose my temper. It was just a stupid little thing, real stupid. I never meant anything like that—I hadn't anything against the woman—but she made me mad." Another long silence; his back was still turned. "Yes, I went out with her. She had a car in the parking lot. I asked her for a ride home, my car was in the garage for a new radiator. And she turned me down kind of sharp, says she didn't carry strangers in her car. Well, hell, she'd been talkin' with me a couple hours, it made me mad. With the drinks I'd had. I—just grabbed her to kind of shake her, and she let out a scream, and I took her by the throat—"

"About as we surmised," said Varallo.

"I'm sorry—I never meant anything like that."

"And you put her in the car and drove it off?" said Katz.

"I was afraid somebody would remember seeing us together. I just left her there—I had to get a cab home—"

"All right, tell us one last thing," said Varallo. "Why did you clean your prints off the steering wheel? Are they on file somewhere?"

He sat down and put his head in his hands. "I'm so tired," he said dully. "I know it, I know it—I shouldn't ever take more than a couple of drinks."

After they'd dropped him off at the jail, they spent a little while in Records; he hadn't any pedigree with Glendale, but LAPD turned him up. He was just out on parole from an involuntary manslaughter charge: eighteen months ago he had killed a girl friend while he was drunk.

"We see too much of human nature in this type of work," said Katz sadly.

Upstairs, they found O'Connor, Delia, Goulding, and two strangers having a conference around O'Connor's desk. As they came in, Goulding was saying energetically, "I'll get on to the coroner's office immediately. This is the damndest rigmarole I ever heard of—" O'Connor waved Varallo and Katz over. Unceremoniously he introduced the doctors and gave them a brief rundown. They listened, fascinated.

"All right," O'Connor went on, "are we taking it for granted that this Rena killed the woman? Somehow? So where the hell did she get hold of the other old lady to show Cushing? How did she know he'd write out a death certificate all easy and tame?"

"But how could she have killed her?" said Varallo.

"Well, it seems a little fortuitous," said Delia tartly, "that Mrs. Austen died so soon after Dr. Cushing saw the ringer—whoever she was. Rena would have picked that up at the rest homes where she worked, an autopsy usual unless a doctor had seen the patient within ten days."

Hervé said grimly, "And she'd have picked up more than that, too, listening to the RNs and LVNs, you know. Gossip about doctors, and to give the devil his due nobody knows us like the nurses. She'd have a damned good guess that when she picked a busy young doctor very cocksure of himself, not long in practice, the chances would be very damned good that he wouldn't bother to look at the body, having seen what he thought was the patient so recently."

"I'm not going to let that pass," said Cushing loudly. "Damn it, would you have bothered? How could I possibly have guessed—"

"She took a risk there, of course, but she got away with it. And she'd have seen it happen in those places, time and again the attending physicians, aware of the conditions of various patients, called about a death and just sending the certificate over without question. Oh, it was a chance, but she got away with it—"

"Almost," said Delia.

"I ask you," said Cushing, goaded and at bay, "would you have gone to look at the body? I'd seen the woman four days before, why the hell should I? How in hell could I have known it wasn't the real Mrs. Austen I saw? Nobody could suspect such a thing, for God's sake!"

"That may be quite true," said Hervé, "but in my experience—well, better safe than sorry."

"But who in hell could the woman have been?" asked Katz reasonably. "And she must be a good way off her rocker if she didn't realize she was being mistaken for somebody else—I suppose you called her by name a few times. How could—"

"She was quite typical," said Cushing, "of the elderly person suffering circulatory brain impairment. Vague, endeavoring to cover up her lack of understanding. If she had taken in the name, it's at least possible that she had temporarily forgotten her name wasn't Austen—"

"With that kind of patient—" Hervé started to say.

"But where in hell did she come from?" persisted Katz. "How would this Rena get hold of one like that?"

"I don't suppose this is the time to bring it up," said Delia, "but I am wondering, you know, about Dad—and Jim and the baby—and a couple of other old ladies who died suddenly."

They looked at her. "Yes, you mentioned in passing—good God, do you think—" O'Connor swung around in his chair violently to face her.

"Well, Dad was said to be a glutton, the doctor wasn't surprised when he died of gastroenteritis. And she couldn't take a job because of the baby, but the husband was lazy and didn't make much money. So presently she wasn't encumbered with either of them. And she liked the jobs taking care of the old laides, at home—and people do die suddenly but I wonder about those two."

"Sweet Jesus Christ," said O'Connor, "a mass killer?"

"Well, I just wonder," said Delia.

Cushing was now looking excited and interested at being involved in this, Hervé just grimly concerned. He said to Goulding, "The way the death was described, I might guess at one of the barbiturates. I wonder if we'll get anything at the autopsy at all. You'd expect some traces, even after embalming—"

"How long has she been buried? Twenty-one days—well, it's not that long. We ought to be able to tell something. Yes, the way she's reported to have just slipped off in her sleep, something like that is likely," agreed Goulding. "I'll get on to the coroner's office the first thing in the morning. That's the first priority, to try to find out how she died and take it from there." He patted his bald head. "Damndest thing I ever ran into."

Gregory Cunningham was still missing. Nobody could understand that, and Rhys and Hunter discussed it as they sat waiting for a possible call. It was forty-eight hours now, and no sign of him or his car. They'd had his son calling in practically by the hour. By now the search had been widened, the A.P.B. out to eight counties in case he had had a brainstorm of some kind and just driven off somewhere. It must, said Rhys feelingly, be hell for the family.

As usual at the first of the week, it was a quiet night, and when they did get a call it was just something to make more paperwork. A squad called it in at nine-forty: a body in the street along West Glenoaks near Grandview. They went out to look at it. It was the body of a woman lying nearly against the curb there; she wasn't much mangled, had probably been caught by fender or bumper and thrown to crush her skull on street or curb. It must have happened just before the squad came by; even at this hour, Glenoaks was a main drag with traffic passing, and she'd have been seen in headlights. She was a woman about forty, wearing a cotton dress and sandals, and incongruously still clutched in one hand was a stamped letter, now all dirty from the street. It was, they could see by Rhys's flashlight, addressed to Mrs. O. M. Fraser in Lancaster. They hunted around, but there wasn't a handbag in sight. There was a bunch of keys in the pocket of her dress.

"At a guess," said Rhys, "she stepped out to mail the letter. There's a box across the street. Which means she didn't come far —not likely a woman would walk more than half a block after dark to mail a letter." There were apartments all along this block. It took them half an hour to get her identified: the manager of the building a quarter of a block up from the corner said with horror that that was Miss Pauline Fraser, she worked at the library downtown.

They called the morgue wagon. On this felony hit-run, there wasn't any witness to give them the guilty plate number.

"Well, I suppose you've got a reason for asking," said Mrs. Eloise Hubbard, looking from Delia to O'Connor. "I can't imagine that Rena Perry would be in any trouble with the police."

"As a witness . . ." Delia let that trail off. "You always found her reliable?"

"Good heavens, yes." Mrs. Hubbard was curious, but cooperative.

They had got the names of three convalescent homes where she had worked, from a bewildered Lois Farber, without telling her why they wanted to know. This was the first one they had tried, the Resthaven Center on the outskirts of Burbank. As such places went, it seemed clean and bright and comfortable, and like most of these places it housed mostly the elderly, incompetent either physically or mentally, or both. Mrs. Hubbard was its superintendent, a rather grenadierlike woman in her immaculate uniform and RN's prim cap. She was obviously efficient, unsentimental, and trustworthy.

"How long did she work here?" asked O'Connor.

"Why, about three years. I was sorry when she left, it's always difficult to get good reliable help. She was very good with the old people, sympathetic, and they all liked her."

Delia asked, "Was it here that she was offered the job of going home with one of the patients, to housekeep for her and take care of her?"

Mrs. Hubbard smiled. "Oh, yes, that was the first time she left us. Mrs. Renfrew, yes, she was a cantankerous old lady, but Rena was wonderful with her, knew just how to handle her. But she died just a couple of months later, and Rena came back to us. Oh, no, that was the only time I knew of she took on a private job."

"When did she leave here?"

"Well, I'd have to look it up, I think around two years ago. It's queer you should be asking about Rena just now, because she's just been dropping in again lately."

"Oh?" said Delia. "You mean, to work here again?"

"Oh, no. No. She said she's really been doing very well at domestic work, and I can see, it's so hard to find decent workers, people who can afford it are willing to pay almost anything—a lot more than we can afford to. I was glad to know she's doing so well, I always liked Rena. No, she's been coming in to visit the patients—quite a few of them still here whom she knew, of course." Mrs. Hubbard shook her head. "It's disgraceful, you know, how these old people get neglected. Even the ones with families, so often people just don't bother to come to see them, and it makes such a difference to them. We have a church group that comes in, a few individual volunteers who are very faithful about coming with little treats for them, but all too few. Rena knew that, of course. She said, the first time she came back, that

now she had a little more time to herself and a bit more to
spend, she felt she'd like to share with the poor old people."

"She brought candy and so on?" O'Connor was a little out of
his depth.

"Oh, little treats, yes, but you know what counts with them
mostly is just someone to talk to, someone to listen to them.
We're all so busy doing just the necessary things, we don't have
time for that, and they do appreciate it. And so many of them
never get out anywhere at all—of course some of them aren't
physically able to, but those that can— One of the church groups
around here gives a little picnic every summer for the ones who
can get out, they do look forward to that. And Mrs. Levenson
and Miss Lejeune—two of the most faithful volunteers—take
some of them out, just for little rides in a car, anything is such a
treat to them, you see. Rena said she could find time to do that
too. Of course, we wouldn't let just any patient go out with just
anyone who offered, but those three are very capable, would
know just what to do in any little emergency."

"And had she?" asked Delia.

"Had she what? Oh, yes, she took Mrs. Sanders out for a little
outing once, I think."

"And when did she start coming back here to give the patients
little treats?" asked O'Connor.

Mrs. Hubbard thought. "I believe it was about March. She
didn't actually tell me anything, but I gathered that she'd, well,
had a little windfall. So she wasn't having to work so hard. I
wondered if perhaps she was going to be married again." Mrs.
Hubbard looked from one to the other of them. "I wish I knew
why you were so interested in Rena."

"I wonder," said Delia politely, "if we could see Mrs.
Sanders."

Mrs. Hubbard stared. "*Mrs. Sanders?* Why, whatever for?"

"If you wouldn't mind—"

"So do we think she borrowed some old lady she knew was in
the precarious health, to show Cushing?" O'Connor relaxed, sliding down behind the steering wheel, and lit a cigarette. "Not
that old lady. She seemed fairly sharp mentally."

"It's the one way she could have done it," said Delia. "And

what an idea it was. Of course she'd know the routine of these places. I'll bet you that Vic and Joe have found out she was visiting the other rest homes too. Thoughtful sympathetic Rena, coming to visit former charges and give them little treats—the nice ride in the park. March, you notice. Just after Mrs. Austen made that will and told her about it."

"But, for God's sake, when she brought the old lady back, she'd tell everybody how Rena took her to see a doctor."

"And would anybody take any notice? The old lady Dr. Cushing described? A little muddled and incompetent. Everybody would say, wasn't that nice, dear, and pay no attention at all. I expect some of the old people get queerer ideas than that. It was," said Delia, "a very cute little idea. Tricky, but cute. She took a chance on the doctor, she took a chance on the old lady, but not really a long chance. I'll bet we'll find that she'd taken several patients out for rides from all three of these places—it might have looked just a little odd if she'd only taken one of them out once. And another thing, the nurses wouldn't hesitate to talk to her about a patient's condition. In any of these places, there'd be a number of patients in—the precarious state of health, that any doctor would spot instantly. That's why they're here."

"True." O'Connor leaned back thoughtfully, and the seat creaked under his bulk. "She was on the premises that morning," he said ruminatively. "I wonder just how she did do it. Morphine or something like that would do just fine, but how did she get it into Mrs. Austen? That one old couple there wouldn't be taking much notice, and we know the other couple works, possibly some of the other tenants. Mrs. Fowler might have been at home—"

"It wouldn't have made any difference," said Delia, thinking. "We were still having the heat wave. She could have easily come over from the Robertsons', say around eleven o'clock, and said what about a nice glass of iced tea. But where would she get morphine or some other barbiturate? She wasn't working at any of these places, and anyway they're very careful about accounting for any of that."

O'Connor let out a cloud of smoke. "Ways to buy it under the counter if you know where to ask, and there's so much of any of the drugs floating around these days, any seller takes it for granted you want it to get a high, not to commit murder."

"All the random lies she told me—about the divorce—I really do wonder about those other deaths. But we can fill in some more," said Delia. He moved restlessly, turning to look at her, reaching for another cigarette, and a very queer and irrelevant thought just ran quickly across her mind. This burly tough cop was an exact opposite to that lean sardonic scholar Neil Fordyce, but at close quarters the same sort of immense vitality emanated from both of them. "Look," she said hastily. "The dizzy spells. There never were any, of course. But she had to have an excuse to come back, to be the one to find the body, because—"

"Yeah," said O'Connor, "and wasn't she lucky there too. She had to be the one to find the body, because she had to direct people to the right doctor, too busy and cocksure Dr. Cushing, who—hopefully—wouldn't bother to check the body. Having seen the ringer four days before. Oh, it was a cute little operation. And she was lucky—when she got there, there was Mrs. Fowler on the doorstep, already anxious about Austen. So all three of them found the body together—and she steered them toward Burriss, sure he wouldn't come over, sure he'd think of the law-yer—and if he didn't, she could always suggest it. She had to pass on the doctor's name to some authority, and as it happened it all went like clockwork, going just as she planned it."

Delia laughed suddenly. "There was just one thing she didn't take into consideration," she said. "The tapes."

"What tapes?"

"The three old ladies who sat chatting to each other on tapes, and told each other every single little thing. She probably knew that Mrs. Austen made the tapes, but I suppose if it ever entered her head to think about it, she assumed that she talked five or ten minutes, I'm fine, the weather is hot, hope everything's going well for you, good-bye. She hadn't any idea that they used ninety-minute tapes and talked about every little thing that hap-pened to them. Because—my goodness, didn't Mrs. Potter tell me that—you can't sit and talk into a tape recorder with someone around, to distract you. If she ever heard about what Dr. Hervé said to Mrs. Austen last December, it can't have occurred to her that anybody else knew."

"Yes," said O'Connor, "and now we get this far—because there's a sort of beautiful simplicity to that little plot, the rudimentary cunning that reminds me of the typical professional criminal—I'd be inclined to bet she did take off those other people. The gastroenteritis—rat poison. The pilot light on the stove— I bet Jim was drunk or drugged. The two old ladies, who knows? And now look at the bad news—will we ever prove it?"

"Well, look at all we've—"

"You know the rules of evidence. All this is just deduction and suspicion. Sure, plain as print, but there's no evidence. Or very little. We'll get Austen's medical record from that other doctor. We'll try to find out just which old lady she borrowed to show Dr. Cushing—and would he be able to identify her for sure? Could any of his office nurses? Could they say definitely it was Perry who brought her in?"

"But—"

"Motive says nothing, you know as well as I do. Technically speaking, half the population's got motives for murder—such as being potential legatees. You can't take it for granted they're going to do anything about it. Which is the reason, which I shouldn't have to explain to you, you passed the detectives' exam the hell of a lot more recent than I did, that in bringing a homicide to court the DA isn't going to mention motive except incidentally, it isn't legally required. You've got to have the solid evidence to put X on the scene, connect him with the weapon—the lab evidence and the witnesses and the positive identifications. This woman evidently puts up a good front, looks sincere and honest."

"That she does," said Delia.

"Well, we can read this, but legally speaking it's all up in the air. Of course, the doctors may give us something concrete. Goulding thinks he can get the exhumation order by Thursday."

"I wonder," said Delia broodingly, "just how she did die."

"Autopsy or no, they may never find out."

"I wonder what Vic and Joe are getting at those other rest homes," said Delia.

As it happened, Varallo and Katz were not out asking questions at convalescent homes. They had been just about to leave the office, after Delia and O'Connor, when the desk relayed a call from Hollenbeck Division, LAPD. A squad car wandering around Griffith Park on its regular tour had just come across Gregory Cunningham's brand-new VW Rabbit up there. "Well, finally," said Varallo. "Is he in it?"

"No, it's apparently just sitting there. Up by the zoo. Gomez'll be waiting to point it out to you."

"The zoo?" said Katz. "What the hell would it be doing up there?"

Cunningham was slightly more urgent than any sinister theories about Rena Perry, so they went up there in Katz's car. It was a nice day, warm but pleasant, but it was a weekday so there wouldn't be many people in the park. Other cities, of course, had normal parks, largish squares of lawns and fountains; Hollywood had fifteen thousand acres of wilderness area sprawling up the hills between the city and the San Fernando Valley. There was the Greek Theater up there, the big planetarium at the top of the hill, two golf courses, miles of bridle trails, picnic areas, and the Los Angeles Zoo.

The entrance was off Griffith Park Drive, and there was a black-and-white squad waiting for them. Varallo leaned out the window. "Gomez? Varallo—Katz. Where is it?"

"In a kind of funny place," said the LAPD man. "You go up around the administration building, it's just past a big aviary, and there's all the staff parking. It's sitting there just down from the monkey houses."

"Be damned!" said Katz, and took his foot off the brake.

"The staff parking lot. Who works at a zoo? Animal keepers. I suppose the grounds are kept up by Parks and Recreation people, there'll be administrators—"

"And a few uniformed attendants to direct people to the seals and elephants." Katz was driving slowly up the winding path past the restaurant and the driving range. They came around a curve with part of the golf course off to the right and found the administration building ahead. Katz pulled the car off on the shoulder and they went on, on foot.

There was space for about forty cars behind the building, and the Rabbit, looking pristine new, was indeed just sitting there. It was the Cunningham plate number all right, JTL-909.

They looked around. In the middle distance off to the left

were some of the zoo enclosures—not cages here, the idea was to simulate natural environments—and a sign with an arrow beyond the parking lot said MONKEYS. They walked down that way. A weekday, and school not out yet; there were very few people here.

A uniformed attendant was leaning against a bench down from the big pit where the monkeys were. Varallo showed him the badge. "There's a new VW Rabbit up in the staff parking lot," he said. "Would you know who owns it?"

The attendant looked surprised. "Why, yeah," he said. "It's Frank Gaddis's, he just got it a couple of days ago. It's a nice job, isn't it?"

"Is he around? Where does he work here?"

"Frank? He's over at the children's zoo, where they got the animals you can pat. Why? What's Frank done? Well, it's past the monkeys and just down from the tigers."

They found it, a little enclosure where goats and sheep and a Shetland pony, some little pigs, and a couple of calves were wandering around. A man in the zoo's blue uniform was sitting on a bench outside it, feeding popcorn to the pigeons waddling about his feet.

"Mr. Gaddis?"

"Yeah, that's me." He looked at the badges.

"We're interested in your car, Mr. Gaddis. The new Rabbit. Where did you get it?"

He was a thin gangling young man with a nervous Adam's apple and a shock of dark hair. He didn't say anything. "The Rabbit," said Varallo patiently. "We understand you just got it recently. Where?"

Gaddis scattered the last of his popcorn and watched the pigeons. After a while he asked, "How'd you know where to find it?"

"We didn't," said Katz. "There's been a bulletin out on it, all the squads looking. Because a man was missing in it."

"I know," said Gaddis sadly. Varallo exchanged a glance with Katz. "I didn't know the police could find it—like that. But, seeing you did, I guess I got to tell you what happened."

"Yes, I think you'd better," said Varallo.

"And I don't know what you're goin' to think about it, but I never hurt anybody in my life," said Gaddis. "I never wanted to. This job don't pay an awful lot, but I like it because I like the animals, and the little kids coming. I never did anything to that man. But I suppose you'll say I did."

"Suppose you tell us about it," said Katz.

"I live over in Glendale," he said dully, staring at the pigeons. "I was going—last Saturday night—I was going up to a Mexican restaurant in Montrose, for dinner. And I stopped to get some gas, it was a self-serve station on Verdugo. It was just gettin' dark. This guy with the Rabbit was there, fillin' up the tank."

"Yes?" encouraged Varallo as he stopped.

"Well, I been wanting to get something gets better mileage—I got this old Chrysler, it really eats the gas and it needs a lotta work too, but I can't afford payments. I heard about this new VW, it was a nice car, and I talked to the guy about it, I just made a little joke, asked if he wanted to trade. But he spoke up real sharp and sarcastic, like he thought I was stupid or something. It made me kind of mad but I didn't say anything. I only wanted to look at the car, it was a real nice job, I wondered what the price tag was—I just put my hand in to feel the upholstery, and he yanked me away real rough, said what the hell was I doing, and I sort of shoved him back to get away from him, and he tripped on the curb where the pumps were, and fell down. I guess he hit his head. When he didn't get up, I looked at him, and he—he was dead. I didn't believe it, but he was. And it was just an accident, but I got scared, I thought if—you know, I called cops and told about it, you'd think I killed him on purpose. I didn't even know him—I hadn't any reason to do that. It was an accident."

"So what did you do?" asked Katz. "Why didn't you just walk away?"

Gaddis said miserably, "It was such a nice car. A real sweet job. I just thought— Well, I drove the Chrysler on a side street and parked. It was pretty dark there in the station, back from the main drag. When I got back there, nobody had found him yet. So I—I—put him in the car—and I drove up here—the gates don't get locked till eight o'clock, you know, and I know the park pretty well, worked here five years. But I just got under the wire at that—Tom Weingard was just starting down the hill to lock the gates, he was right behind me when I was drivin' down the hill."

"Why did you come up here?"

"Well, him—the guy. I had to do something with him."

They looked at each other. "And what did you do?"

Gaddis said dully, "I rolled him down a slope into some bushes, up past the Mineral Springs picnic grounds."

"And you've been driving the Rabbit ever since." Not surprising it hadn't been seen until now, quietly parked here Sunday, yesterday, and today. "What did you plan to do about registering it, transferring the title?" It was, of course, a foolish question.

"I guess," said Gaddis, "I just hadn't thought about that."

# TEN

Late on Wednesday afternoon they forgathered in the office to compare notes—O'Connor, Varallo, Delia, and Katz. "So what have we got?" asked O'Connor, rhetorically when they'd been kicking it around for a while. He leaned back in the desk chair with his jacket off, the shoulder holster bulging, his jaw blue-stained at that hour. "We know now that she'd been going to all three of those convalescent homes since March, on the average of once a week. The sympathetic volunteer, charity worker, talk to the old people and bring little presents. She wouldn't have been lost in a crowd, but there are a few people like that do go to these places—and she had to make it look plausible, over a period of time, because she could hardly march in on one occasion, take one old lady out for a ride in the park, and never go back. And it makes her look so good to the nurses—and she's known at all those places as a reliable former employee. We know she'd taken four of these women for the little outings, on four occasions—but we haven't, damn it, got any definite dates. The one we think was the ringer for Mrs. Austen, this Mona Strachey, all we know is that she was the latest one, and nobody at that place can pin it down to April twenty-sixth."

"No," said Varallo, "and we never will." He was tired. It had been one hell of a job, up in Griffith Park yesterday, to locate Gregory Cunningham's body and get it up the steep hill covered with underbrush; in the end Parks and Recreation men had had to bring in a Jeep. He'd had to go and break the news to the family. And very probably Frank Gaddis would be charged with involuntary manslaughter and get off with a year inside, which might be only justice if he was telling the truth but it didn't make things easier for the Cunninghams. There had been a big pro burglary job last night at a jewelry store in the Galleria, a very slick job, and the lab men would still be nosing around there another day, probably, but a couple of leads were suggested by the general MO. All the other men were out on that, and he had come in on his day off to help out on this.

He had been the one to locate Mona Strachey, at the Brooks Convalescent Home down on Central—in a little flashback, he recalled the polite little vacant-eyed, gray-haired woman, looking very old and frail, smiling vaguely at him and saying, "I don't know you, do I? Excuse me if I should, my memory isn't very good—" They'd have Cushing look at her, but could he make a positive identification? Could the nurses?

Delia said, "Covering up her tracks, making it all look plausible. Which really wasn't necessary because the minute anyone suspected what she had done, it would all fall to pieces—" Varallo thought disinterestedly that Delia looked tired too, washed out and rather pale.

"You're forgetting what I reminded you about—evidence," said O'Connor irritably. "It cuts both ways. Naturally I haven't talked to the DA yet, pending the autopsy, but if we ever take her into court on this, she could show that she'd been charitably dancing attendance on a number of the poor old people, just out of sympathy, perish the thought of any ulterior motive. And I doubt if Cushing will make a positive identification of the old lady, but even if he does a jury could be led to think he was mistaken."

Katz said, "I'd like to know about those other sudden deaths."

"One thing at a time, damn it," said O'Connor. "This Austen thing is abstruse enough."

"Yes, that just confuses the issue," said Varallo. They now had the names of the two women she had gone to live with as nurse-housekeeper: Mrs. Roberta Renfrew, Mrs. Norma Tacy; but that was a side issue.

Katz had seen the people at the Dryden Street apartment. Mrs. Fowler had been home all that day, but she had been in the spare bedroom sewing most of the time, hadn't noticed Rena arrive, but she knew she'd be there, on a Friday. She hadn't seen her entering the Austen apartment, but she had seen her leave at 3 P.M. when she went out to get the mail. She said Rena Perry had come out the front door, and called back, "Good-bye, see you later!" And that, of course, said almost for sure that the woman had been dead then. But it was a handful of nothing, unless the doctors came up with something definite. The Costellos said she had been in their apartment all the time from eight-thirty until about ten; the Robertsons, naturally, hadn't been home. Nobody else at the apartment building had noticed her at all.

Delia said suddenly, "I hope Mrs. Austen didn't know. That she meant—any harm." They looked at her, mildly surprised, and she added, "She seems to have been a good person—and she really sincerely liked Rena Perry. And when you think—just for the money, to make up that cold-blooded plot—"

"The love of money is the root of all evil," said O'Connor shortly. "Nobody should be surprised at that."

She gave a little shudder, said apologetically, "Something walking on my grave."

Varallo said, "Well, it's the end of shift. I'm going home. If you want my opinion, this is going to be another case where we're morally sure what happened but there'll never be enough evidence to bring a charge. So there'll be no way to prevent that will going through, and she can sit back and enjoy the ill-gotten gains. What good would it be to tell the lawyer?" He got up and stretched.

"Yes, I know, damn it," said O'Connor.

"One of those damned things," said Katz, and shrugged.

The doctors now had brought Barney Erwin out of whatever kind of fit he'd been in, and were giving him psychiatric tests; it would depend on those results what charge the DA's office would decide to bring on him. Ken Erwin had come back temporarily from San Francisco; he told them that was one reason he'd been moving up there, he'd been feeling it wasn't good for Barney to be so dependent on him, if he was on his own maybe he'd do better, and it was a little nuisance how he'd fallen so hard for Rosalie. They got the feeling that Ken Erwin was a very hard-nosed young man, sincerely sorry for what had happened, but he wouldn't spend much time grieving for Rosalie or Barney.

Weiss was due to be arraigned tomorrow. Bruce Watkins was still in the hospital undergoing treatment for drug addiction;

probably he would be arraigned on Monday. They hadn't had an autopsy report yet on Gloria Carson.

Dr. Cushing had a look at Mrs. Mona Strachey on Thursday morning and said doubtfully, "Yes, I think that's the woman I examined." She smiled at him delightfully and said, "Do I know you? You look familiar, you're a very handsome young man, you know—my dear brother Arthur had hair the same color as yours." There wasn't much in that. The nurses were even less positive; they hadn't seen her for more than a few minutes. Could any of them identify Rena Perry?

They had had to explain to the superintendent of the rest home why they were asking to borrow Mrs. Strachey, if not all the details, and she had been horrified. "But Rena is such a nice, capable, reliable girl!"

Thursday, with Delia off, they started looking for the possible burglary suspects. At two o'clock O'Connor had a call from Central Division LAPD. The boys down there had just broken open a big fencing ring, and a good many jobs from anywhere around might link up to it. If Glendale had any wholesale victims who could identify the loot, they had stacks of stuff down in Burglary at Parker Center.

Varallo went to see the bereaved jeweler, and of course he had a list of what was missing; they set up a date for tomorrow morning to go and look.

And just at the end of the shift on Thursday, a customer going into a cleaners' shop out on Broadway found the woman proprietor bludgeoned to death on the floor behind the counter. She had been ironing a pair of men's slacks, and it looked as if the iron had been the weapon. They left the lab men dusting surfaces in there and taking photographs; tomorrow they'd have to talk to all the other people in that little complex of shops about possible suspicious characters, find out about the woman's private life in case that entered in. She had been a fat sixty-year-old widow with one married daughter, so it probably didn't, but of course you never knew.

Dr. Goulding had thought he might get the exhumation order on Thursday; if he had, they would probably get to the autopsy today.

Delia located the address she'd been given for Mrs. Adelaide Teadale a little before ten o'clock. It was an expensive house in North Hollywood beyond Burbank, and Mrs. Teadale was a rather typical busy clubwoman, middle-aged, expensively groomed.

O'Connor had said that possibly the more they found out about Rena the better, and Mrs. Teadale had been the only relative of Mrs. Roberta Renfrew who had employed Rena so briefly as nurse-housekeeper. She looked at Delia blankly when the name was mentioned, and then, her memory jogged, laughed musically and said, "Oh, yes, the woman with Auntie. Did she give me as a reference, you mean? Well, she was a very nice, capable woman, Auntie liked her, I could certainly recommend her highly. It's so hard to find a good practical nurse for a semi-invalid, the rather difficult old people, and Auntie hated that convalescent place, wanted to be in her own home. I'm afraid she was a cranky old lady, but this woman was really very good with her. Of course she was only with her for about six weeks, we hadn't really expected Auntie to go so soon, but of course her heart was very bad and it was a blessing in a way. We hadn't thought she was quite incompetent mentally, but after she died— the woman had found her gone just before I came to see her that day—we found she'd hidden little piles of cash all over the house, quite substantial sums, behind pictures and so on. Old people do take queer notions sometimes, and they can be difficult—" she laughed again rather emptily— "I must say, I hope I don't get into such a state, to be a nuisance to my family. But I can certainly recommend this woman, Mrs.—oh yes, Perry."

Delia thanked her, and went on to find Mrs. Norma Tacy's daughter, Enid Shipsey. That was a little drive; she lived in Santa Ana down in Orange County. She turned out to be a guileless-looking woman with myopic eyes behind strong lenses, and she told Delia that that had been a very difficult time, and she had been very grateful to Mrs. Perry for, as it were, coming to her rescue. Her husband had never been a well man, ulcers he had and terribly high blood pressure, she had to give him a lot of care and when her mother fell and broke her hip, and kept begging to go home from the really quite nice convalescent place, well, it had been a trying time. Real worrying. And then this Mrs. Perry at the convalescent home was willing to take on the job of looking after her. Really a very taxing job, as well she knew, caring for an invalid night and day, of course she'd been well paid, her mother had had a good annuity, but it had been a godsend. A very nice woman. It was so hard when people got old and queer and difficult to manage, and really Mother hadn't been herself even before she fell and broke her hip. So very secretive and miserly, and after she died it appeared that she'd sold a lot of her valuables, that must have been before her accident, all the sterling and her best pieces of jewelry, and of course there hadn't been any need. But sometimes old people took queer fancies, thought they were destitute, and of course Mother always had been careful—not exactly mean but careful. Oh, yes, she'd had some good diamond pieces, rings and pins.

"Did you ever suspect that this Mrs. Perry might have—"

"Oh, no, indeed," said Enid Shipsey, surprised. "I won't say it wasn't a little facer for me, because I'd rather been counting on getting something for that—of course the house was the main property. But you see, on account of my husband, and Mother living clear up in Burbank, I don't drive and my husband wasn't fit to the last couple of years—he died in January—well, I hadn't been in Mother's house in five years before that. And Mrs. Perry assured me there wasn't any sterling silver, or much jewelry in her little box, when she went home with Mother. She seemed to be quite a nice woman, very efficient. Of course she wasn't there long, Mother died just a couple of months later—rather unexpectedly, really, but of course she had had one stroke and she was seventy-six."

Driving back on the freeway that was largely free of traffic at that hour, Delia thought, you could reconstruct all that with a little imagination. Rena coming on the nice little hoards of cash, and appropriating them, and perhaps one day Mrs. Renfrew discovering that, so she had to be shut up. Rena's reputation was, in a way, her livelihood. And Mrs. Tacy apprehending her absconding with the sterling, the nice jewelry, and having to be shut up. They had both been old and frail, had chronic physical troubles, but she wondered if the doctors had bothered to look at those bodies. Perhaps with some doctors, at least—whether because they were young, or unempathic, or on the contrary very sympathetic—when an old person died, they were inclined to accept it as a release from the chronic troubles.

The necessity for concentrating on driving for that distance had tired her. It was two o'clock when she pulled into the parking lot of the station and suddenly remembered that she hadn't had any lunch. She sat there for a minute trying to decide whether to go down to the place on Wilson. Or just skip it. She wondered whether O'Connor was going to want a written report on all this; she felt very disinclined to go upstairs and face her typewriter. And as she sat there, the realization came over her with something like dismay that what was wrong with her was that she was bored. She was abysmally and damnably bored with this job that was just drudgery and dirt. Which was ridiculous, and something just short of sacrilege; she pulled herself together sharply and sat up straight. This case was a really interesting and offbeat one, different from any case she could remember working on, even before she made rank—

Her mind went back over the years, over the legion of crimes and criminals she had ever had anything to do with, and it was a sad and squalid parade of memories, a depressing list— As Varallo said, they were all so stupid. Too lazy to work for a living like normal people, grabbing for whatever they wanted—unable to reason from one step to the next, easily caught up to by rudimentary logic—giving in to the stray passions of the moment, drifting as ephemeral as wind, without control or reason or understanding. Sad, silly little people. And the occasional ones like Rena Perry, arranging their greedy little plots, not much more intelligent really—only more ruthless, able to think ahead just a little farther.

Thinking of Rena Perry, her warm voice and honest, friendly appearance, she realized, looking back to that little encounter, that the warmth and friendliness had never extended to the pale protuberant blue eyes.

She told herself, bringing the discipline to bear, that she needed some lunch. She started the car, drove down to the place on Wilson, and ordered a sandwich she really didn't want much.

Varallo, O'Connor, and Delia were the sole occupants of the
office at five o'clock on Friday afternoon when the two doctors
came in. They were surprised to see them. They hadn't expected
to hear anything about the autopsy for some time: especially one
like this, the various tests they'd be running, would be a long-
drawn-out business.

"Don't tell me you've found out something already," said
O'Connor.

Goulding sat down in the chair beside his desk and brought
out one of his noxious black cigars. Dr. Hervé just sat down
heavily and stared out the front window.

"Yes," said Goulding absently, "the tests on the organs, stomach
contents, and all that rigmarole—the results won't be in until next
week. But whether anything shows up there or not, it was just
a little simpler than that, Charles. Like the idiot boy and the lost
horse, you know—I thought how I'd have done it, and so we had
a look first at the mouth and throat. The body's quite well pre-
served, by the way. We took the stomach and intestinal tract, and
we'll run tests for barbiturates and so on to be sure, find anything that's there, but now we know what the primary cause of
death was. She was smothered. Present at the back of the mouth
and in the trachea, scraps of cloth and feathers—goose down, I
think, of course we'll get it analyzed."

"Feathers!" said O'Connor.

"The bed pillow," said Goulding, nodding. "Very simple crime,
Charles. The easiest thing to use, you can see that. This woman
said Mrs. Austen was lying down taking a nap when she left.
She could very well have slipped her something, an hour or two
before, to make her sleepy. In any case, it's likely that Mrs.
Austen did lie down on the bed of her own volition. That's only
a guess, but there can't have been any overt marks of violence,
or the mortician might have noticed. Pending the analyses, I'm
betting that the Perry woman got a little dose of barbiturate into
her to send her off to sleep. Then she just held the pillow over
her face. But obviously Mrs. Austen wasn't completely uncon-
scious, or there wouldn't have been these traces to find. She woke
up enough to struggle—"

Delia made a strangled little sound; he didn't glance at her.

"She bit through the material of the pillow case, and inhaled some goose down and the scraps of cloth she'd bitten off. It wouldn't have taken more than a couple of minutes, and this woman had done practical nursing, was probably much stronger physically. And at an advantage, above her."

Hervé said heavily, "And then, of course, seeing the damage done to the pillow case, she'd simply have changed it and carried the other one away with her to be destroyed. We'll never see that. The mortician wouldn't have noticed anything, she must have looked as if she'd died quite peacefully."

"She'd have clutched at the woman's arms, struggling, but if Perry had on long sleeves," said Goulding, "there wouldn't have been any marks on her."

"That was probably," said Delia, "how she killed the other two. They were a good deal frailer than Mrs. Austen, they couldn't have fought back much." She told the doctors about that, and they agreed somberly that it was a likely supposition.

O'Connor flung himself back in the desk chair, which creaked protestingly; as usual he had taken off his jacket and the shoulder holster bulged threateningly. "For the love of Christ," he said roughly. "So that is that, and you know what it means." Sitting still, he seemed to swell with the impotent anger building in him. "And I'll put it to the DA, but he'll laugh at me."

"Very probably," said Goulding. "Of course it's quite impossible to estimate the time of death—all we can say is, some time that day. There's nothing at all to say that Perry was the one to hold the pillow over her face. It's an inference, but there's no evidence. She will swear that Mrs. Austen was alive and well when she left at three o'clock. Four hours later Mrs. Austen was dead, and nobody ever looked at the body to estimate just when she'd died."

"Oh, for the love of God!" said O'Connor disgustedly. "I see it, I see it! We've got Cushing's rather doubtful identification of Mona Strachey—what the superintendents of the rest homes can tell us—Austen's medical record, Hervé's testimony about her physical condition, and that's six months old— We know Perry knew about the will, which ties up with the dates she began to haunt the rest homes, and if you find traces of barbiturate in the organs that's just that much more. But—"

"No," said Goulding, "probably not enough." He sniffed his cigar in a troubled way.

"I wonder if she's home from vacation yet," said Varallo. "If we bring her in and lean on her—"

"Oh, no, my boy," said O'Connor. "We'd never break that one down—I know that kind. The rudimentary cunning, yes, but also as stubborn as hell, and very damned hardheaded. She wouldn't try to make up any alibis or evasions—she'd just go on denying it till hell froze over, she never did such a thing and we can't prove she did, we've just got some nasty ideas about her, everybody knows cops have low dirty minds. And we can see what the DA says, but I think I know already."

Goulding looked at his cigar meditatively. "You can haul her in and at least try to put the fear of God in her, Charles. But you know, whether you do or not, she'll do it again. Sometime. Somehow. For a little reason or a big one. For advantage to herself— or safety for herself. They always do. And it just could be that the next time she'll be a little careless. When she's got away with it fairly easily before—"

"You do not console me," said O'Connor.

"Well, let me know what the DA says."

The DA wanted to think it over, but agreed that there really wasn't enough evidence; probably they'd have to let it go.

The jeweler from the Galleria had identified his missing stock from the loot LAPD had recovered from the fences, but the lab gave them no evidence on the burglars. LAPD was still sorting out the fencing operation, and something might show there eventually.

Goulding finally sent up an autopsy report on Gloria Carson; she had died of a depressed skull fracture. The proprietor of the cleaners' shop, a Miss Wilma Haydock, had definitely been bludgeoned with the iron, her blood and hair on it; there were a couple of her prints on it too, and some smudges. However, on Monday Katz turned up a customer who had been there at four-thirty, an hour before she was found dead, and he said that she was alive then and that there'd been a young black fellow in the place at the time.

So Varallo and Katz made the rounds of the little shopping

complex along that block—there was a record shop, a bicycle shop, an insurance office, a fabric shop, a watch repair shop, and a little variety store—all small independent places; and the owners told them about Jason Ott. They all hired him to do basic cleaning up and odd jobs, on a regular basis—to clean floors and lavatories, wash windows.

"He's kind of a slipshod worker," said the woman at the record shop to Varallo. "But he does things after a fashion and we've only got to pay him minimum wage."

"He's a no-account black rascal," said Doug Osborne at the insurance office. "Yes, he was here that day, it wasn't his regular day to come, but he was around asking for an advance on his salary. I told him to go to hell. Pay him in advance, you wouldn't see him for a month. I suspect he's hooked on the galloping ivories, and that's where it goes."

So then they made the rounds again asking if he'd approached anyone else—it was surprising what the ordinary citizens would forget to mention unless they were asked directly—and the woman at the fabric shop next to the cleaners' said he had tried to get some money out of her too. "I had to be quite firm with him, he kept asking. He was rather ugly about it when I turned him down."

So they arranged a line-up, and the customer pointed him out as the young black fellow who had been in the shop at four-thirty. They brought Jason Ott into an interrogation room and began talking to him, and finally got it across to him that the doctor said Miss Haydock had died before five o'clock, and that put him on the scene just about when she must have been killed.

He thought it over; he was a moon-faced, brown-skinned fellow just turned seventeen. After a while he said, "Well, she made me mad. I never meant to kill her, but she made me mad."

"How?" asked Varallo.

"Well, I needed some bread. I lost nearly twenty bucks to Hoagy the night before, I dint have no rent money. I asked ever'body and they wouldn't give me none. An' when I asked her—Mis' Haydock—she said she had bills to pay too an' I was a fool for gamblin'. She sounded like a ole schoolteacher or somethin'—an' I got mad."

It was quite often depressing, what a simple job it was. Of

course he was still, technically speaking, a juvenile, and would probably just be put on probation until he was twenty-one.

They now had another burglary to work, reported this morning.

Varallo let Katz take Ott over to jail, came into the office and told O'Connor about him. "I'll toss Joe for who does the final report."

"And I just got Rena to answer her phone. She's back from vacation. Suppose you go and ask her politely if she'll answer some questions." O'Connor's mouth looked grim.

She made her usual good appearance; the sensible clothes, neither smart nor dowdy, marked her as a simple, respectable woman. Her comfortable slight plumpness, the warm contralto voice, the friendly manner, all added up to a picture that a jury would probably like.

And she didn't exhibit any alarm or fear as O'Connor, lounging back in his chair with the .357 magnum prominently visible, carefully outlined to her just what they had figured out about Mrs. Marion Austen's death. She just shook her head occasionally as if marveling at such ingenuity. At the end, she looked around the office, at Katz, Varallo, Delia, and said, "That's all a wicked set of lies, and I don't know where you get your ideas from, I must say. I never did such a thing and you can never prove I did. If Mrs. Austen thought enough of me to want to leave me her property, I'm just very, very grateful to her. I thought a lot of Mrs. Austen too, and I never expected her to die for years, or wished for it, goodness knows. It's a wicked thing to accuse an honest hard-working woman of such a thing, and it's not true and you can't prove it."

The phone rang on Varallo's desk and Sergeant Duff said, "Cushing's here."

Varallo went down to get him, and positioned him at the head of the stairs where he could get a good look at Rena sitting there facing O'Connor and the door. He didn't know or care whether Rena noticed Cushing. After a minute Cushing backed out to him on the landing. "Well?" asked Varallo.

Cushing said helplessly, "Yes—no—I really can't say, Varallo. I only saw the woman once, very briefly. I think it could be the same woman, but I can't say positively."

"So, thanks for coming in."

"I'm sorry, but I can't honestly identify her."

"Yes, it's all right, doctor. We're not asking you to commit perjury." He went back into the office, strolled behind Rena's chair, and gave O'Connor the thumbs-down sign. O'Connor's expression didn't change.

"I don't know how you got such ideas about me. Why, I can call all sorts of people to speak to my good character, and—"

"Yes, we've heard some of them," said O'Connor casually. "And you're quite right—we can't prove the murder on you. This time. But you know you did it, and we know you did it, and you had better believe, by God, that we won't forget you, Mrs. Perry."

"I could sue you—"

"But I don't think you will." He gave her his sharklike grin, very mirthless, very cold. "You can walk out of here now—you know we can't hold you."

She got up in a flash. "I should think not! It's outrageous to think of such a thing." She made for the door rapidly, but as she turned she couldn't quite disguise the vestige of a tiny triumphant smile.

"Oh, the DA won't touch her with a ten-foot pole," said O'Connor. "It is one Goddamned shame, but there it is."

At one o'clock on Tuesday Delia came out to the parking lot on her way to a belated lunch. As she came up to the car, she saw that there was someone sitting in it, and suddenly her heart lurched.

He opened the door for her, sliding across to the passenger's seat to make room. "I found your car by hunting registrations, all very illegal—I hoped you'd come out alone." She got in behind the wheel. He looked older, even leaner, but he'd never change much. "I've got a plane to catch to Lima in four hours," he said, "but I wanted to see you. After what Isobel said—and it's been two years—well, I just wanted to see you." He took her shoulders, turned her to face him.

"Neil—"

"Ah, Delia. Just a little bit of my girl left now. Yes, you've just turned twenty-eight, haven't you? Been a while since I gave you a birthday present." His eyes were searching, in the bright sun pouring in, and she wanted to raise a hand to shield her face, not from the sun. "Yes," he said, "the mouth a little tighter, and the eyes a little harder, and all the pretty hair still cut short. In a few years, there won't be anything left—but a female cop. But I want to tell you, darling, that I've realized the truth of it now: It was all you, wasn't it? I thought it was mostly that domineering stupid old bastard egging you on, against all your natural inclinations—but I can see now it was all your own idea from the beginning."

"Yes," said Delia steadily, "that's the way it was. For Alex, but my own idea."

"Yes, darling. It's all right. We all have to go our own way—I'll just always be sorry you had to go this way, not mine. I wanted to see you—a last time—before I left."

Delia said, "Yes, I'm glad to see you, Neil—" And she wanted to ask about Isobel, the baby, how the work was going, but her throat closed up tight.

"I've got to get back and finish packing," he said. He looked down at her one more moment, bent and kissed her quickly, and got out of the car. "Good luck always, Delia." He turned and walked across the lot, to a car parked on the street; he didn't look back once.

Laura noticed the car pull up at the front curb, and thought idly that it looked like Delia's. But nobody got out of it, and after a while she went halfway down the front walk—and then all the way.

Delia was bent over the wheel shaking convulsively; she was incoherent, out of control, and Laura just managed to get her out, shaking all over, and into the house before she broke down to great gasping sobs that shook her whole body. She lay prone on the couch and Laura thought she would never stop crying. Helplessly she stayed with her, patting her, making meaningless soothing sounds, until after a long while the tears stopped and Delia lay quiet, and Laura said, "If it would help to talk about it, darling—whatever it is—you know I'm safe—and if you don't

want to, just stay quiet and in a minute I'll get you an aspirin—"
Delia turned slowly onto her right cheek. Her voice was thick
and slurred. "All my own doing," she said. "Oh, yes, of course it
was—not Alex, not Alex—I've just seen that—you know, I don't
think he'd have cared what I did, of course he's proud of me but
it wasn't his idea—got it in my stupid head what I had to do for
him—" Suddenly she sat up, and completely unaware of her wild
hair and gaping blouse, her eyes strangely rapt and wild, she
said, "Oh, God, but it's funny—it's so funny! We always say
they're so stupid, so stupid, the sordid little criminals—but I was
stupider than any of them! So very damned stupid, all that time,
waste all that time—even old Omar," she said queerly, "knew
better than that—*Alas, that Spring should vanish with the Rose*—I
thought it was the most important thing I had to do, something I
had to do or die—and it doesn't mean anything at all—and oh
God, it's doggerel, isn't it, but it's true, oh God, it's true—*Moving
Finger— moves on nor all your Piety or Wit can call it back to
cancel half a line—Nor all your tears—nor all your tears—*"
"Delia—"
"And Neil, and Neil, and Neil—oh God, you don't know how I
wanted, back there the first time, he asked and asked—and I
thought, just sex instinct and I wasn't going to let it get the better of me—and he's such a damned puritan he wouldn't, unless
I'd marry him— But he's got other important things in life,
you've all got other important things, that's just what I—what I
saw just now, don't you see? Don't you see? You and Vic and the
children—and O'Connor and his Katy and the baby—and Joe's
married with children, and John Poor—Jeff's going to be married
—you've all got something important, and it's those things are important, more important than any little job you do to earn a living— It's just me who's got nothing, nothing, nothing—except the
job, the stupid boring dirty little job, and it doesn't mean anything at all—"
"I'm going to leave you half a minute to get you some aspirin
and a cup of coffee." She was shaking again and Laura put the
afghan from the couch around her.
"*One Thing is certain, and the rest is lies—the Flower that
once has blown forever dies—*"

"Are you all right?"

"I'm all right. Sorry to be such a fool—inflict all that on you."

"It doesn't matter. But you can change, you know. You can always change things, if you really want to. There's no law—"

"No," said Delia with a long shuddering sigh. "It's too late now, don't you see? He doesn't want me now. And it would break Alex's heart. Of course Alex would hate any strong character—tried to take me away—but it wasn't anything to do with—anything else. And it doesn't matter now. This seems to be the life I've made for myself—for better or worse. I'm all right, Laura—don't worry. Isn't there the old saying—we all make mistakes. I'm a big girl now, I'll be—all right."

The burglary investigation was grinding down to a halt, with no result. There had been a new heist overnight, no leads on it at all. O'Connor was down at the DA's office discussing the charge on Weiss. It had been a slow, boring day—Varallo yawned and thought, thank God tomorrow was his day off. And he had better take advantage of it to feed his roses.

Forbes had just taken off early, and everybody else was either out talking to suspects or, probably, on their way home. Varallo went downstairs, lifting a hand at the sergeant on the desk, and out into the late afternoon. The sun was a little hazy, on its way down; they'd have the usual overcast, coolish June, and then the summer heat would strike with a vengeance.

He detoured on the way home to pick up a couple of bags of rose food. When he came in the back door, Laura called to him from the nursery, "Fix yourself a drink, and me too, while I get Johnny settled down. Dinner's going to be late." Ginevra came nattering happily at him and he swung her up in his arms.

When Laura came down to the living room he handed her the glass with its pleasantly tinkling ice cubes, but she set it down on the coffee table and put her arms around him tight. Varallo laughed, put down his brandy and soda, and kissed her soundly. "What's this in aid of, at this hour?"

"Oh, Vic," she said fiercely, "it's just that we're so lucky—sometimes I think we don't know how lucky we are."

He laughed and kissed her again, let her go, sat down with his drink. She took up her glass and went to stand at the window,

K51

looking out at the roses. "Vic," she said presently, "that father of Delia's—he's awfully old, isn't he, he probably won't live much longer."

Varallo said in indolent surprise, "Why? Well, who knows?" He rattled ice cubes in his glass and yawned. "Thank God I've got tomorrow off—I can forget the job for a few hours."